The Alliance of Worldbuilders

I0618568

A World of Their Own

A Collection of Short Stories

All proceeds from this collection will be donated to the World Literacy Foundation. The Alliance of Worldbuilders believe that everyone should be given the opportunity to learn to read. It is a right, not a privilege.

Illustrations by Sophie E Tallis & Hazel Butler
Cover Image by Evelinn Enoksen.
Cover Concept by Lindsey Parsons
Cover Design by Hazel Butler
Cover Layout by Valerie Willis
Book interior design & typesetting by Valerie Willis & Sammy HK Smith

Paperback

ISBN-13: 978-1-909845-81-7

Kristell Inklings, an imprint of Grimbold Books
4 Woodhall Drive
Banbury
Oxon, OX16 9TY
United Kingdom

DEDICATION

This anthology is dedicated to our dear friend and fallen comrade, Lindsey J Parsons.

Lindsey, who affectionately called herself Sergeant Gummie Dragon, joined the HarperCollins writing site, Authonomy, in January 2011, and quickly found our strange little group of fantasy geeks and writers – The Alliance of Worldbuilders.

She soon became the beating dragon heart of our Alliance. She was a fantastic friend to all of us, those she met in person and those who live a thousand miles away or more. Oceans were no barrier for Lindsey. Her warmth, kindness, generosity of spirit and encouragement were an inspiration to everyone.

Lindsey was so many things to so many people, that was her magic. To all of us in the Alliance, we knew her as a dragon-loving, snow-loving, horse-riding, cowboy boot wearing, fantasy enthusiast and a hugely talented author, artist and medal winning archer. She touched all our lives and we are profoundly richer for having known her.

Lindsey Jane Parsons died suddenly of a brain aneurism in January 2014. She achieved so many astonishing things in a life that was tragically cut short, but her legacy and friendship will live on.

We shall miss her every day in a thousand different ways.

All our love, from your friends in The Alliance of Worldbuilders.

TABLE OF CONTENTS

Introduction 1

The Dragon & the Serpent..3

Matilda..7

    The Visitor 7

    Youth Potion 12

    Rescue Attempt.. 16

    Flight North 21

Where Do Our Ideas Go?... 25

Baby Aga 29

Crew 33

Happiness is a lie 39

Nilameth 45

Deeper Prayers 59

The Thief Gets Away... 63

A San Juan Moment.. 77

Crow's Gold.. 81

Meaningless Kiss.. 87

Dragons of Terra.. 91

Destiny's Game 95

The Portrait 107

Lost Time Memory...109

They Rise And We Smite...141

A Simple Game...157

Death Always Collects..161

Phoenix Feather 163

The Dreaming Moon..169

Autho Nights Critiques 173

Dwarfs R Us 175

Wyrm 191

The Wishing Tree.. 213

How To Create A Villain or Let Sleeping Candemons Lie....... 221

This One Safe Place 235

Final Entry.. 249

Night of a Thousand Spells.. 253

Finish The Page 259

The Artist.. 263

Troll 267

The Bar 285

Sniffers... 287

Dante's 291

Infection 299

Worldbuilders, Inc... 301

Author Bios 305

Andrea Baker... 307

Sam Dogra 308

E. R. Enoksen ...:... 310

Lucas Hargis 311

Will Macmillan Jones 312

Kay Kauffman.. 313

Emily McKeon 315

David JM Muir 316

TRM.. 318

Lindsey J Parsons.. 319

Jeremy Rodden 321

J C Rutledge.. 322

A. F. E. Smith 323

Sophie E Tallis... 325

Valerie Willis 327

INTRODUCTION

At the beginning of any journey, travellers do well to contemplate where they start from, so that they know when they have arrived. And the Worldbuilders are indeed on a mighty journey.

This is not a showcase of talent, but a labour of love for a fallen Worldbuilder who was an active part in the creation of the Alliance.

First there was Authonomy.com and its little universe with all its foibles, all its successes and all its defects; an interesting place all told, and one well worth exploring. Within that community of nascent writers, a number of threads pulled together. Fantasy and science-fiction writers congregated in a community within a community on a number of discussion threads. Kate Jack was one of the early luminaries, and as her thread came to its end I decided to rekindle the flame and see what would happen.

I had the daft idea of entitling my thread "The Alliance of Worldbuilders" back in September 2010, expecting it to die off before long. However, it would appear that somehow the name struck a chord. Hundreds flocked to the banner, and the chatter swelled the thread to the "hottest" thread on Authonomy.com. Once we'd blown the servers, we were asked to start another thread. And guess what? That became the second "hottest" thread in its own right. The Worldbuilders are now onto a third thread leading into a Facebook Page and Official Website:

www.facebook.com/TheAllianceOfWorldbuilders

And by the time you read this, they will probably have moved on again.

From journey to conquest! But with all seriousness, it just goes to show what a bit of good will can build. The Alliance is now a merry band of friends, helping each other on their journey to publication with mutual support, constructive criticism, editing and professional guidance. Several amongst us are published already. Many more will soon be. The Alliance looks set to grow in strength and depth. Check out the individual biogs for each of the participants in this Anthology for more details of where to find them.

You'd better get ready world, for the Worldbuilders are on a roll. Take a read of this collection, have a taste of the talent on offer. The Worldbuilders have arrived.

TRM

THE DRAGON & THE SERPENT
BY A F E SMITH

For Lindsey

Once upon a time, not so long ago, an adventurer trudged through a field of long grass. It had been a challenging journey, full of obstacles he had barely conceived of existing when he set out, and he was weary beyond words; nevertheless, he took time to breathe in the fragrance of the flowers and tilt his head back to feel the heat of the sun on his skin. For if there was one thing he had learned on his travels, it was the importance of small details.

And so, finally, he came to the last test.

At the far end of the meadow stood a grove of silver trees; and when the adventurer stepped beneath the shade of their branches, his light-dazzled eyes gradually perceived that he was not alone. In the centre of the grove lay a sleek and sinuous amethyst dragon, steam rising from her nostrils, iridescent wings folded along her spine. And around her neck like the rarest of adornments coiled a little emerald snake with ruby eyes.

"Welcome, traveller," they greeted him as one.

The adventurer stopped still, his heart filled with sudden doubt.

"Who are you?" he whispered.

They didn't reply; but as he gazed upon them, dragon and serpent together, it came to him that he knew. A shiver ran through him, but he stood straighter and addressed each of them in turn.

"Ah, lady Dragon, I have chased your likeness through many a long night. You are the most elusive of all creatures, and yet, on those rare occasions you deign to be caught, your wings can carry a man to greater heights than he ever dreamed possible.

"And you, master Serpent, I have sought you all my life. Once or twice I have succeeded in tasting the fruit you offer to those who are willing to take it, and always it has left me wanting more."

He bowed to each in turn, and as he did so, he named them. "Inspiration. Knowledge. Without the two of you, I could never be what I aspire to be."

The great amethyst dragon arched her graceful neck; the little shimmering snake regarded him unblinking. "Then I suppose you want us to let you through the portal?"

Now they came to the crux of the matter. The adventurer squared his shoulders and spoke with pride. "I ask for nothing. I stand before you a most devoted servant, no more. But if you deem me worthy to pass –"

The dragon shifted on the bare earth, and over her shoulder for the first time the adventurer saw it. The golden gate. The mysterious portal. It shone beneath the shadow of the trees as if it held the sun at its heart. He started forward, but still the dragon blocked his path.

"Not yet, traveller," she murmured. "First you must show us you deserve this prize. For many seek to tread the path you are on, yet only a few reach the end."

"And still fewer recognise Knowledge and Inspiration when confronted with them," the serpent added. "But even your prowess there is not enough."

The dragon lowered her head until the adventurer was staring directly into the infinity of her multifaceted eyes.

"To pass through the portal," she said, "you must answer a single question."

Hope leapt bright and strong within him. "Ask it."

"Why should we let you pass?" the serpent hissed.

"Why should we let you pass?" the dragon breathed.

The adventurer bowed his head, and for a time there was silence in the sacred grove. How to answer? How best to demonstrate his dedication, his passion, his sheer longing for what lay beyond? His mind turned in dizzy circles as he sought a way to prove himself – and then he looked up, and smiled. "Because I am here."

He waited, palms sweating, to see if he had given an acceptable answer. Then:

"Yesssss …" The snake's tongue flickered. "You have toiled after knowledge."

"And inspiration smiles on you," the dragon added. "But most of all …"

"Most of all …"

"You have never given up."

"And that, beyond anything else, is what matters."

The serpent coiled tighter around the dragon, who rose to her feet and stepped aside.

"Go, now, traveller," they said together. "Go, now, builder of worlds."

The portal blazed. The adventurer walked forward. Just before he crossed the threshold, he stopped and turned.

"Thank you," he whispered. Then he took another step and was gone, into the place of his heart's desire.

As to what he found there … well, that is another story.

MATILDA
BY LINDSEY J PARSONS

The Visitor

A sharp pain shot up her arm, causing her hand to jerk sideways and knock over a small green bottle. Holding her breath, she watched as it rolled away along the shelf in a wide, lazy arc, coming to rest against the wall at the back.

Massaging her shoulder, Tilly started to breathe again, a sigh of relief escaping with her first breath. The pain had been sharp, radiating through her whole body. I'm getting too old, she thought, reaching up and taking hold of the bulbous-shaped bottle she had been attempting to retrieve from the shelf. Glancing at the small green bottle, sighed again. I will need to get a stool to stand on to reach that now.

"Are you all right? Do you need a hand?" a man's voice asked from the other room.

"No, I have what you need – but like I was explaining, this will only hold off the symptoms while you are taking it. It isn't a cure and I haven't a lot left either." Tilly pushed aside an old dusty curtain that was hanging over the doorway and stepped through to the other room.

The man was sitting on an old wooden chair pulled up to a well-scrubbed oak table. He was tall and strong, with broad shoulders, and had the look of a soldier about him. His clothes were those of a traveller, with a thick woollen cape over a brown leather coat. But his shoulders were hunched over, with his elbows resting on the table and his right hand pressed against the side of his head.

"As I was saying, the discomfort you are feeling is coming from a lump that is growing inside your skull," Tilly said as she pulled up another chair to sit opposite him.

"Discomfort? More like blinding agony," the man grumbled, looking unhappy.

"If you had come to me sooner I may have been of more use to you, but it has grown past the abilities of my potions." Tilly shook her head and pushed the bulbous bottle across the table. "I fear your only hope now would be a magus or maybe an elf, both of which are in short supply these days. You have travelled north from Camlain, did you not think to seek Hadrid's counsel?"

The traveller shook his head and winced. "I have served in Hadrid's army – in his personal guard, no less – since I was a boy. You would think he would have been happy to help, would you not? Well, no, he will not sully his hand or his powers on the likes of me." There was bitterness in the traveller's voice and his free hand was balled in a fist. "I've left his employ for good and will probably be run though if they ever catch up with me. I've heard it told there is a young and powerful magus in the north, come from over the sea. They say he's named for freedom. I am on my way to find him."

"Freedom? I'd heard all those with the Shrilan name had been executed or murdered in the magi wars in the vast lands."

"Aye, but according to a traveller from the east I met by chance, this one managed to escape with his baby sister and has fled here to evade those who wish to wipe out his bloodline."

There was a loud creak from somewhere in the cottage and the traveller's horse, which was tied up outside, snorted and started to paw the ground. The traveller's eyes darted around the room, checking out every shadow, nook and cranny, while his free hand shot to his belt, curling around the hilt of a dagger.

"Don't worry yourself, I haven't got Hadrid's army hiding in my cottage." Tilly smiled at him.

"It's not Hadrid's army I'm worried about." The traveller stood up and pulled four gold sovereigns from his pocket. Placing them on the table, he picked up the bottle. "I've also heard it told that the old witch Matilda keeps a fire demon for a pet."

Tilly laughed. "Oh, to be that powerful. Do you really think it's possible for anyone to keep a demon for a pet?"

"My philosophy is to believe anything is possible. Thank you for the potion – and take care. These are troubled times. A pet demon could be a good thing to have." The traveller made a hasty exit and Tilly heard his horse hurrying away.

Easing herself to her feet, she closed her eyes and steadied herself against the chair. Almost a hundred winters had taken their toll on her slight frame; her joints creaked and protested with every movement.

"You look unwell, old woman." A deep, silky voice spoke from the shadows.

"Less of the old, if you don't mind," Tilly said, shuffling the chair and making out she was pushing it back to the table rather than using it to prop herself up.

"More tales of unrest in the south and a mysterious stranger in the north," the owner of the voice said, stepping out of the shadows. His eyes, taking in Tilly's unsteady stance, were a strange silver colour. His skin – stretched tight over his tall, thin, wiry frame – was pale and powdery, and a pair of steel-gray horns protruded from his untidy black hair. His only clothing was a pair of worn leather trousers. "And what does 'a pet' mean?"

"Like a dog or a cat." Tilly's finger tapped on the back of the chair and her brow knotted as she thought about what the traveller had said about the magus.

"He thinks you keep me like a dog?" The silver eyes narrowed into a frown.

"Damian, these days I fear it is more you that keeps me. I seem incapable of the simplest of tasks. I knocked over a small green bottle on the top shelf, could you fetch it for me?" She sank back down onto the chair and carried on tapping her finger on the table. She was so deep in thought that it made her jump when Damian placed the bottle on the table in front of her. He crossed the room and hopped up to sit on top of the big range in the inglenook, his bare feet resting on the hot plate. Tilly shuddered. She had seen him sit like that thousands of times and she knew he would never burn – in fact the hotter it was, the more he liked it – but it still disturbed her.

"The news worries you?" Damian nodded towards her tapping fingers.

"I was thinking about this magus. If he is a survivor of the Shrilan family he will have powerful magic. The Shrilan magi were one of the most powerful magi families in all the vast lands."

"If they were so magical, how come they were destroyed?"

Tilly shook her head sadly. "Betrayal, deceit and treachery. Other magi families were jealous of their power. When a magus turns bad he can become pure evil."

"Like Hadrid?"

"Yes, it would appear from the news of the south that Hadrid is using his powers for his own benefit, to suppress and dominate. Let's hope this new magus lives up to his name and uses his power and wisdom for the good of others." Tilly stared at the bottle in front of her. "Could you go and see what you can find out about him?"

Damian jumped down off the range. "I will go, but I will not travel too far. You may need me to reach for more bottles." Grinning, he turned and left through the door the traveller had used. Tilly could see him through a window, standing with his back to her. Folded

against his back were two large, black, bat-like wings, which he now opened and stretched wide. Then, with an easy beat, he thrust himself up into the sky and was gone.

Youth Potion

Tilly sat staring at the little green bottle, memories flooding back. It was the hardest potion she'd ever created and it had been waiting on her shelf for fifty winters. Laying her hands flat on the table, she took a deep breath. A potion that gave back youth for one whole cycle of the sun – it was powerful, complicated magic. The downside was that once the effects wore off, the taker would end up many winters older than before. Tilly had saved it to use once her time was over: one last youthful day before her life ended. She now felt sure this time was fast approaching and she was almost ready. Her only problem was Damian.

The ingredients had been difficult enough to find in the first place and Tilly had searched for many winters to find the right kind of fungi. Finally she had come across a cave that ran deep into the mountains. In the darkest recess, a small amount of Mortus Fungi clung to the cold rock. As she gathered what she needed, she had become aware of someone else in that cramped place: a being of some kind squeezed tight into a crack in the rock face. With a lot of gentle persuasion she had coaxed it out, only to be horrified at what she'd found.

The being had been human-shaped but skeleton thin, with bat-like wings and skin bleached of colour. Tilly guessed what he was – a powerful evil spirit, a demon of some kind – but it took time for her to figure out what was wrong with him. He had somehow gained a conscience, which had subsequently destroyed the very essence of who he had been, leaving him trapped in an earth-bound form, destined to be forever tortured by memories of what he'd done. Tilly had taken him in, cared for him and named him Damian. Unable to break the curse that had caused this, she had cast spells of her own to try and counter the damage. Having no family, she came to look upon him as a son; he became her family. What was worrying her now was what would happen to him without her protection and guidance.

There was a muffled knock at the door, so quiet Tilly only just heard it. Closing her eyes, she eased herself to her feet.

"I'm just coming," she said, forcing her legs to wake up and work.

Opening the door, she gazed out at the forest clearing around her cottage, but there was no one there. Shaking her head, she turned to close the door but stopped when she heard a faint moan. Curled on her doorstep was a small, green figure. It moaned again as its head lolled sideways; large amber eyes stared up at Tilly, full of fear and pain.

"Rowan!" Tilly's hand shot to her heart as she looked down at the figure. "Whatever has happened?"

It took a tremendous effort for Tilly to bend down and scoop Rowan up into her arms. He weighed very little, but it used up every ounce of the modicum of strength she had to get him to her bed. As quickly as she could, she found a restorative potion and, pressing the bottle to his lips, encouraged Rowan to take a sip.

After a few moments the small green face relaxed, but the eyes still looked haunted. Tilly checked him over for injuries, giving him a few more moments to recover. She was horrified at what she found. His arms were covered in bruises and a large angry welt stretched across his back from his right shoulder to his left hip. Another angry bruise on his left side suggested he might have a couple of broken ribs.

"Who would do this to a harmless goblin?" she asked herself out loud.

Rowan turned his head. His wispy silver hair was plastered to his head with dirt and his thin face looked gaunt, making his big pointed ears seem extra large. "Please help." His voice was little more than a whisper. "Please help goblins."

Reaching out, he grabbed Tilly's arm with long, bony fingers. "Soldiers come, they take everyone, even Daisy," he said, turning his face away. "They have Daisy. Rowan escapes, manages to get away." Then, turning back, he pulled her closer. "Please help get goblins back, get Daisy back … please." The grip on Tilly's arm loosened as his eyes rolled back in his head and his hand dropped away.

Tilly stared at the unconscious goblin. He had said soldiers. The only soldiers around came from Camlain: Hadrid's army. What did Hadrid want with a group of goblins? The only thing she could think of was for slave labour. He was building a bigger, more impressive castle – perhaps he needed a work force?

Anger welled up inside as Tilly thought about it. Hadrid had no right to take anyone against their will and goblins had just as much right as anyone else to live a free life. She needed to act fast; there would be no chance of freeing the goblins once they arrived at the castle.

Grabbing a bag from on top of a wardrobe and heading back into the kitchen, she started making a mental note of what she would need. As she placed the bag on the table, another sharp pain ripped through her body. Sprawling forward, she crashed on to the tabletop, her hands scrabbling at the surface, trying to gain purchase but failing. Slipping and sliding, her fingers found and fastened onto the small green bottle as her body twisted, falling backwards. She felt rather than heard the loud crack as her hip slammed onto the flagstone floor and white-hot, blinding pain burned through her. The world spun around her, nausea mixing with pain, blackness threatening to engulf her.

Tilly lay trembling, fear clouding her thoughts, pain filling her senses. She didn't dare move; even the act of breathing hurt. Slowly, as her mind began to clear again, she tried to work out her best option. She couldn't move without causing more pain – she felt sure her hip had broken in the fall – so crawling or dragging herself up was out. Waiting for Damian to get back was the only option, but even so he couldn't mend her hip; she was going to be crippled. Tears welled in her eyes, spilling over, running down the side of her face and soaking into her long gray hair.

Her fingers tightened around the small green bottle and she raised her hand so she could see it. Blinking the tears away, she made her decision. Removing the stopper, she tipped the contents of the bottle into her mouth and swallowed. The potion had a sharp metallic taste that burned her throat as it went down. The burning spread through her whole body until it felt like she was on fire, getting so intense Tilly began to beg for death to take her, before finally she passed out.

Rescue Attempt

At first Tilly thought she had gone blind – as she opened her eyes there was nothing but blackness, until they grew accustomed to the night. She was lying where she had fallen, looking up at her kitchen ceiling.

Checking out each limb in turn, she held her breath, waiting for the sickening pain to return. But apart from a small amount of stiffness, everything seemed to work. She pulled herself up, and the ease with which she managed to get to her feet shocked her. Then, remembering Rowan, she headed straight for her bedroom, grinning at the nimble way her body was moving.

Rowan was just where she'd left him, but now he looked a lot more relaxed and his breathing was steady and peaceful. Gently opening his mouth, she dripped a couple more drops of the restorative potion on to his tongue. He'll be almost as good as new when he wakes up, she thought, returning to the kitchen.

The bag was still on the table where she'd dropped it, so picking it up she again started to decide what to take. A large ham and two loaves of bread, a candle that if left burning behind you hid your path from anyone following, and a handful of pine cones that rendered anyone close by unconscious if placed in a fire. She changed in a hurry, putting on a pair of dark leather trousers and a black sheepskin coat. Finally, before leaving she fastened a belt around her middle; it held a small scabbard containing a short dagger with a large ruby embedded in the end of the hilt.

With her bag on her back and her wand in her right hand, Tilly stepped out of her cottage, scanning the darkness for any threats. The moon was still in the early stages of its nightly journey, which pleased Tilly – she couldn't be sure how long she'd been unconscious.

She struck a path straight for the goblin settlement Rowan called home. As she jogged along, her legs strong with youthful fitness, she cursed herself for not leaving a note for Damian. By morning Rowan should have woken. He will fill Damian in on what has happened, and Damian will guess where I am and follow, she thought.

Goblins made their homes in the branches of trees, high up away from predators such as wolves. The one predator this couldn't avoid, though, was man. As Tilly reached the settlement she gasped in horror. The ground around the tall oak trees where the goblins lived was littered with the remains of their homes. Each tree house had been dragged free and brought crashing to the ground. Walking through the devastation, she noticed a large arrow tipped with vicious-looking barbs embedded in a piece of wood that had once been flooring. Attached to the arrow was a long piece of rope that had been used to pull the house down once the arrow had hit its mark. The air smelled of soot and woodsmoke where numerous little fires had shattered on hitting the ground. Tears flooded down Tilly's cheeks as she noticed that twisted in the remains were ten or twelve little green bodies. Taking a deep breath, she turned away. There was nothing she could do for them now.

It was easy to track the soldiers with their prisoners; a wide path had been forged through the undergrowth by their passing. Tilly took off at a steady run, hoping their progress had been slow, as she needed to catch up with them before daylight. This wasn't how she'd planned to spend the time the potion would give her – she'd had all sorts of different ideas. Sometimes the Fates have other plans for you, she thought, trying to keep her mind on the job at hand.

As the eastern sky started to glow, Tilly came across their encampment. At first it was the dwindling campfire through the trees she could see; then she nearly tripped over a mass of little green bodies all huddled together in nervous sleep. Skirting around the goblins, she edged closer to the campfire and spied the soldier who should have been on watch duty. He sat leaning against a tree between the sleeping goblins and the rest of the camp. He was dozing with his head sagging forward and dribble running down his chin. The rest of the soldiers were lying as near as they could get to the fire.

Careful not to make any noise, Tilly crept closer. When she reached the edge of the shadows she took the pine cones from her bag. Holding them out in her left hand, she pointed her wand at them and started mumbling an incantation. The cones rose slowly and hovered in front of her face. She moved her wand to point at the fire and they drifted away towards it as if blown by a light breeze. Once they were hovering over it, Tilly stopped mumbling and lowered her wand and they dropped into its heart. The flames flashed bright blue and emitted a dense blue smoke which spread out, engulfing the sleeping soldiers.

With a satisfied smile, she turned back to the goblins. It was then she felt a drain on her energy, only slight but enough that she noticed it happen. Using magic is going to affect the youth potion, she thought, biting her lip.

The goblins were easy to rouse, but they were all shackled and chained together. Tilly raised her wand and pointed it at the padlock on the shackles of a goblin she knew called Acorn, but then glancing around at the others she saw around forty sets of eyes gazing back at her. The drain from unlocking forty or more sets of shackles with magic was going to undo the effect of the youth potion completely.

Someone must have a key, she thought and, gesturing to the goblins to wait, she turned back to the campfire. Holding her breath, she stepped into the remains of the blue smoke and started to search the first soldier. Unsuccessful, she moved on to the next, but by the time she'd searched three she had to step away as she couldn't hold her breath any longer. Most of the blue smoke had dispersed by now and she could see the soldiers easier, so she took a moment to study them. They were all dressed in mail covered with red tunics that bore a gold crown on the front. Not very comfy to sleep in, she thought, smiling. Most of them were also wrapped in red cloaks and blankets, making it impossible to work out who was in command. She chose the three that lay closest to the fire, assuming they would be the highest ranking and more likely to hold the keys.

This time Tilly had success when she searched the second of the three she had chosen. Hurrying back to the goblins, she noticed the sun had appeared on the horizon and the birds were well into their morning chorus.

There were eight keys on a big metal ring, so after unlocking Acorn's shackles she unhooked the keys and passed them around the waiting goblins. They didn't need telling what to do or that they needed to be quick.

"What do you think you're doing?" The soldier on watch duty had woken up; since he'd been further away from the fire than the others, the blue smoke hadn't reached him. He marched straight for Tilly, ignoring the goblins squirming around his feet trying to undo their shackles. Tilly reached for her dagger but wasn't quick enough. He was burly and tall, with dark dirty hair poking out from under his half-round helmet. He towered over Tilly as he grabbed the front of her coat, lifting her bodily into the air and slamming her against a nearby tree. The weight of her body hanging in her coat pulled her arms up and made it impossible for her to get her hands down low enough to reach her dagger. The soldier brought his face so close to hers that their noses almost touched.

"What do you think you're up to, then?" His breath was stale and his brown eyes drilled into hers with a look of confident triumph. "Thought you'd steal our merchandise, did you?"

"They are not your property. They are sentient beings who have just as much right to live free as you or I." Tilly stared back defiantly.

The soldier threw his head back and laughed, but his eyes went wide with shock and his laugh turned to a blood ridden gurgle. He dropped Tilly and staggered before crashing backwards to the ground. As he fell, she saw Acorn scrabbling to jump free from his back.

The soldier lay still, a deep gash across his throat, his blood oozing onto the forest floor. Acorn clambered to his feet and held out Tilly's dagger for her to take back. She nodded a thank you and wiped the blood off on the soldier's tunic before replacing it in her belt.

"We must hurry," she whispered, watching the last of the goblins free themselves. There were adults of every age and a number of children too; it was going to be difficult to move very fast or quietly. She was relieved to see Daisy, Rowan's soul partner, amongst them. Checking everyone was ready, Tilly set off at a quick march back along the trail to the goblin village.

"Will it not be this way the soldiers look for us?" Acorn asked, trotting beside her.

"Yes. I have a plan, though." Tilly smiled down at him.

Flight North

Tilly glanced at the sky: the sun was drifting towards the western horizon. Biting her lip, she frowned, returning her gaze to the path through the forest.

Before the sun had reached its midpoint she had sent the goblins off eastward on a new trail, and once they were out of sight she had lit her candle and placed it on their new path. Waiting behind, she had kept watch to make sure the soldiers continued on the path back to the goblin settlement.

They had come rushing past not long after the goblins had disappeared, and Tilly had followed them to make sure none of them got suspicious and turned back. When it was obvious the soldiers weren't going to turn around, she had taken a path of her own, conscious of how far the sun had travelled. The effects of the youth potion were already starting to weaken and she still had a fair distance to travel before reaching her cottage. After a while, she had got the feeling someone was following and had hidden at the side of the path to find out.

She gripped her wand tighter, feeling the stiffness returning to her fingers – she really needed to keep moving. Just as she decided it had been her imagination, two soldiers came jogging past, following her trail.

Tilly's heart raced as she crept backwards away from the path. Holding her breath, she turned to take a different route and crashed straight into the chest of a soldier who had crept up behind her. He grabbed her arms, pinning them to her sides, and lifted her from the ground.

"Put me down," she said, trying to keep her voice steady.

The soldier just laughed and shouted, "I've found someone."

Tilly panicked and, pointing her wand upwards, hissed an incantation. There was a loud crack and the soldier flew backwards, crashing to the ground. Tilly turned to run, but his comrades had arrived and were blocking her path. The drain on her strength from the spell made her gasp and her body stiffened as old age returned.

"You old bi…" Tilly didn't hear the rest of the insult. She turned to see who was speaking and the back of a gauntleted hand caught her across the face, sending her spinning to the ground.

"Let's see how you like it!" She was dragged roughly to her feet again and the soldier she had blasted grabbed her, flinging her like a rag doll across the path. She crashed sideways into a tree and fell to the floor, pain exploding up and down her spine. The soldier marched over and reached down to grab her again, but just before his fingers touched her, the air ripped apart with a tremendous roar and he flew backwards away from her.

Tilly's sight was blurred with pain, but she could make out Damian. He had one of the others by the throat. With an easy squeeze, he crushed the life out of the soldier and threw him away. With another roar he took off after the rest of them, who were running for their lives.

Moments later, he was back to kneel beside Tilly, scooping her up gently in his arms. "Do not worry, old woman, I will get you back to your cottage."

Tilly shook her head. "No, take me north. Take me to the magus." Her voice was raspy and quiet. Damian nodded, spread his wings, and with a blast of air they took off.

Tilly's whole body was racked with pain. She screwed her eyes shut and pressed her face against Damian's chest. His skin was very warm and smelt of spice and fire. She was so proud of how he'd turned out, of who he had become. She was going to miss him. He would never follow her to the afterlife – he was never going to die, never going to be mortal. She wished she'd had more time to plan a future for him, to be sure he was going to be all right.

The journey was long but Tilly, drifting in and out of consciousness, didn't notice most of it. It had taken Damian a while to find the half-built castle where the magus was making himself a home.

A welcoming committee soon gathered as Damian landed in front of a set of large oak doors. Tilly couldn't make most of the people out – pain was blurring her vision – but she could hear the angry mumbling and Damian had come to a standstill.

The mumbling suddenly died and Tilly could make out a figure walking towards them through a parting in the crowd. Damian spoke first, not waiting for the man to stop.

"Are you the magus?" Tilly could feel the urgency and tension in his voice.

"I am Etienne Shrilan and yes, I am a magus." He stood tall, taking in the sight before him, showing no sign of the fear Damian usually provoked in people. Tilly was transfixed by his eyes. They were the most piercing blue she had ever seen; they seemed to pour energy and understanding into her just by looking at her. She sighed and relaxed. She had been right to come here after all.

"She is hurt, will you cure her?" Damian shifted impatiently. "Please."

Etienne hesitated for a moment. Then, turning back to the oak doors, he said, "Bring her this way."

There was a repeat of the mumbling and a voice from the crowd said, "But sir, you're surely not going to invite it into the castle?"

"I am sure if he meant us any harm he would have picked a better disguise," Etienne said, laughing.

He led them up some stairs to a large, plain room with an enormous four-poster bed. Damian placed Tilly on the bed and then moved back to allow Etienne to get closer. She looked up at the magus. He was young, with shoulder-length blond hair and handsome features. The air around him shimmered with energy as he placed a hand on her shoulder, and warmth radiated from the spot where he touched her. Tilly shook her head and closed her eyes. The pain had faded into a bone-deep ache and an immense tiredness had swept over her.

"You cannot save me." Her voice was barely more than a whisper. "I took a youth potion and it has aged me further than a human body is able to survive. I had Damian bring me here so I may ask something of you. He needs somewhere to live – would you take him in? Will you promise to give him a home?"

"It is not true! You must save her," Damian said, stepping forward, anger and frustration in every word.

"She is older than anybody I have ever seen. I am afraid there is nothing I can do." Etienne paused, his hand still on Tilly's shoulder, and she got the strangest feeling that he was walking around inside her head. After a few moments he said, "Yes, I will take him in."

Tilly relaxed, feeling too tired to breathe – too tired even to think. She looked up at Damian. He was the closest she had to family. It took more strength than she had to pull her dagger from her belt, but she managed it. Pressing it to her lips, she whispered a last incantation.

"Take it, keep it," she said to Damian. He shook his head but she whispered, "You must."

The spell had sucked the last of the life from her body. She closed her eyes as a kind of blackness washed over her. It had been a very long and, in most parts, a good life. She had done what she needed to and now it was time to rest.

And so Matilda, the old witch of the woods, headed off into the afterlife.

WHERE DO OUR IDEAS GO?
BY JEREMY RODDEN

Art by Cami Woodruff

One of Juan Hernandez's favorite activities was sitting at his kitchen table while drinking his morning coffee and watching his four-year-old son Carlos draw pictures. Carlos had a fascinating imagination for such a young child and would often try to copy the cartoon characters he would see on television. Lately, Carlos had even begun making up his own creations.

Juan took a sip of his coffee and watched his son's idea come to life on the paper. The creature had the bill of a duck but long ears that didn't fit. After Carlos drew the webbed feet, he penciled a long, curved tail. Juan felt his eyebrows meet in the middle of his forehead as he tried to sort out what his son was creating. Carlos was clearly oblivious to his father's ponderings as he went to work drawing a large sombrero and a vest on the duck-type invention.

"What are you drawing, son?"

Without looking up, Carlos answered, "It's a kangaroo-duck, papi." The boy put down his pencil and reached for a yellow crayon, supplying the kangaroo-duck with color on the hat and vest. In a strange sort of way, the animal reminded Juan of The Man In The Yellow Hat from the Curious George books

His son's intensity and focus on the drawing were more amazing than the drawing itself. Trying to get a four-year-old to sit still for more than a few minutes at a time was a challenge, but Carlos would sit and draw for hours.

Juan wondered where these ideas came from.

What he should have been wondering was where they go.

A kangaroo-duck popped into existence in a grassy field. The hybrid animal quickly assessed his surroundings. On the horizon, he saw a whole bunch of buildings and a sun shining brightly above them. The sun had a face on it. To many people, this would seem strange. The kangaroo-duck, though, had only existed for a short period of time so had no basis for comparing strange versus normal.

His eyes paused when he saw a bewildered-looking young boy standing in the field across from him. The boy was dressed in a bright green shirt and bright purple pants. His thick-rimmed black glasses were a little off-kilter and the boy's red hair was a mess.

"Hello?" asked the confused-looking boy.

The kangaroo-duck cocked his head and stared at the boy. He searched his mind for an appropriate response but only a few words jumped out from his bill. "Hola con queso!" he squawked at the boy.

An unnatural desire to be in the city on the horizon gripped the kangaroo-duck at that moment, and he sped away from the brightly attired boy. As the animal hopped toward the strange-looking city at the end of the field, the kangaroo-duck suddenly vanished. His last thoughts were, Donde está Toonopolis. Then he ceased to exist.

Juan Hernandez looked at the ball of paper on the floor. He had just watched his son get bored with the drawing of the kangaroo-duck, crumple the artwork into a ball, and toss it aside. Carlos was already working on a new drawing of a familiar cartoon character that Juan saw on the television regularly.

Juan placed his coffee cup on the table and bent down to retrieve his son's discarded art. Opening up the wrinkled sheet, he pondered the kangaroo-duck. "I guess it's a good thing these drawings don't have feelings, huh?"

"Of course they don't, papi, it's just a drawing."

"I suppose you're right," Juan replied. "But I like this one. Can I keep it?"

Carlos nodded and reached for his yellow crayon again. He began coloring in the square underwater creature on the page. Juan folded the picture of the kangaroo-duck and looked forward to adding it to the growing stack of original Carlos Hernandez drawings that Juan kept in his bedroom.

Juan didn't even realize that he was the only reason these creatures continued to exist in the cartoon city of Toonopolis. Maybe someday he'll find out.

BABY AGA
BY K A SMITH

"Ask the neighbours. I don't have time to go to the shops, I have to finish this for tomorrow."

"But Dad, it's raining!"

"Use an umbrella. Do you want to eat or not?"

"Stupid stove!" Slamming the door behind her, Beth peered through the rain-wet gloom. Most of the windows were dark since the houses had been zoned for redevelopment and everybody who could afford to had moved out. One house was lit, squatting alone between heaps of rubble; it looked even more rickety than the odd paling that fenced it round, as if it might collapse at any moment.

The door opened at her knock. The old lady behind it looked even more tottery than the house. "Come in, dear. Get your bonesh out of the rain." The toothless mouth gummed the words into soggy mush.

"Um."

"I don't get many vishitorsh." She held the door wide. A flicker of firelight beckoned.

There was an odour on the still air in the hallway; Beth wrinkled her nose. "I don't mean to be cheeky, but do you have any matches?"

"They'll be in the pantry, it'sh thish way." She led Beth down the hallway, opened a door. The kitchen was gloomy; the only light came from the chinks in an old-fashioned stove that looked like the great-granddaddy of the clunky little wood-burner at home. To one side was another door, which the old lady opened. "Here, you look. My eyes aren't so good."

Beth peered into the dark space behind the door. A shove in her back, and she was tumbling down a flight of wooden steps. She hit her head on something hard; stars danced before her eyes, then everything went dark.

Cold stone grazed her cheek as she moved. Beth eased herself up and sat, shivering. Her fingertips brushed the floor, met a wall of rough brickwork and stopped.

"Hello?" Thin echoes died into silence. She sniffed. "Dad's gonna kill me."

A faint pad, pad, pad broke the stillness. She felt something tickle her leg and she twitched. Something moved against her hand; it was warm, furry. Breathless, she held herself still and silent. There was a noise like distant traffic. Purring? A weight settled in her lap. Is that a cat? It feels as big as a Doberman. She brought her hand up, slow, and lowered it onto damp fur. The purring grew louder. She stroked, gently, then even more carefully, feeling the tangles and lumps in the fur. "Poor pussy. Does nobody look after you? Sorry I have no milk for you."

"Mrrrowrrrrrrrrrr."

"Lie still, then; I'll try to get some of these tangles out." She eased her fingers around one of the smaller clumps and worked it loose, careful not to tug. The cat dug its claws in a couple of times, but didn't scratch. She started on the next one.

Between the darkness, the repetitive task of grooming the matted fur, and the almost hypnotic thrum of the purring, Beth thought she must have fallen asleep; the cat spoke. "Come, she's busy now, attending to their horses."

"Horses?"

The cat uncurled and stepped from her lap. "Hold my tail."

Beth found the cat's tail and took a tentative hold.

"Follow me." Beth scrambled to her feet, and the cat walked slowly into the darkness; the cat was so large Beth could hold his tail without stooping. She nudged something with her foot as she walked – it made a hollow noise. Then something else, which clacked.

"Hush."

"Sorry," Beth whispered in apology.

"Up here. You'll have to climb, but be careful, don't make a sound." The cat turned towards Beth – she could tell, even in the pitch dark, because she could see two eyes that glowed with their own light. "Let go of my tail. I'll go first, you follow."

The eyes disappeared, then Beth could see them again, looking down at her. She felt in front of her. There was what seemed to be a log-pile, or stick-pile, as they were all too thin to be logs. She got down on hands and knees and inched her way towards the glowing eyes, careful not to disturb anything.

"There's a trapdoor above you. Push hard, it will open."

Beth eased herself upwards so that her back was against the boards and pushed with all her body. Slowly the trapdoor rose. A chink of light grew wider, revealing the old lady's kitchen. The cat leapt through the gap, stood on its hind legs and held the door steady while Beth crawled out. As she did so, she could see what she had been standing on wasn't sticks at all. She was glad her stomach was empty.

"Take this, leave by the front door, and don't look back until you get home."

Beth took the lantern and fled.

"So. What's your excuse this time, cupboard lover? Feed you, did she?"

"She would have, had she any food." Cat sat on the mat before the fire, lifted his hind leg and licked.

"Really?"

"She shared her warmth, and she combed out my tangles so nicely." Cat rose and rubbed against a spindly leg. "She was too good for you, Grandmother. What did she want?"

"Matches."

"Ah! Matches? I don't have to give you no stinking matches … The gift of fire."

"Of course, what did you expect? It was not cheaply won." Grandmother took out her black iron teeth and put them back on the mantelpiece. "There will be another. There always is; I can wait."

"Where have you been? I was starting to worry."

"Sorry, Daddy. Everyone has electric now. But I got this." Beth held up the lantern; a steady flame burnt inside.

"That's a little macabre, isn't it? It almost looks like a real skull."

CREW
BY LUCAS HARGIS

Scape clenched the cuff of his sleeve and crashed his elbow through the glass. He grinned back at us from within his hoodie and dropped his backpack through the window. The cans clanked as they hit. With a quick dive, Scape slipped into the opening.

Rox balanced on the handrail next, kicking the remaining jagged glass with her boot. She hoisted herself up and squatted on the windowsill. I glanced down the street. Deserted. I pointed the beam of my flashlight on her jeans, willing it to push her through.

"Hurry the hell up, Rox."

She wiggled her ass at me, flipped me the bird over her shoulder, then disappeared into the dark.

I mounted the window, took one last look around, then dropped inside. The broken glass crunched under our feet as we searched the room with our lights. Old plaster walls left to chip and crack. Mosaic tiles set in the marble floor in the shape of a swan – a symbol of the company that had let the building sit empty for forty years.

"Hope there aren't any damn hobos in here," Rox said.

Scape sniffed the air. "No way. Doesn't smell like piss or smoke. Just old metal and grease."

"Nobody's tagged the entry," I said, "I bet this place is *virgin*."

Rox unzipped her backpack, whipped out a can, and shook it. "Not anymore." She tagged her sinewy *MINX* on the plaster. Letters stretched out to form a tail, the body, and its snout.

"Quit dicking," Scape said, "We've got work to do."

We followed him up the stairs, taking two at a time, zipping, using the rails at the landings to whip around and keep climbing. We raced up the twisted flights, laughing and wooting until we ran out of steps. Rox kicked open the door, and we passed through.

The whole top floor was one massive room. An expanse of floor-to-ceiling windows covered the far wall. I imagined the space filled with clangs and sweat and steel. All that was gone now. All that remained was a few busted worktables and some odd debris scattered around the perimeter.

We checked out the space, avoiding the stagnant puddles from the leaky roof, and all three of us saw its beauty at the same time. A blank wall stretched from the doorway to the far corner.

"It's perfect," Scape said.

They handed me their flashlights, and I arranged them on the scarred wood floor. I rummaged through the junk and found three hunks of wood to chock the lights. Angled just right, their beams converged on the plaster. Dry. A grungy white. The perfect ground for our mural.

Rox groaned as she yanked on an old worktable. "Help me drag it over," she ordered Scape, "This bitch is heavy."

I tilted one of the lights up a little. "Better moving that than standing on each other's backs again."

We stood in the beams, three sharp shadows scattered into dozens across the wall. Scape slid the bandana from his neck up over his nose, then scrolled his finger over the glass of his iPod. That was the sign. He was ready.

"Where we heading?" I asked him.

"I'm feeling nature tonight," he answered.

The rattling marbles in the cans added their own layer to the flowing, orchestral music streaming into the space. Scape saturated the plaster with large, sweeping arcs. He created instant hints of the curves of hills. He feathered the edges into blocks of yellow and green. Trees sprouted with a few masterful strokes.

Rox and I added our rattling cans to the symphony. We needed to warm up. I walked to an end wall, scaling the rubble to tag my *COUNT* in the triangle of light by the windows. *FIN* was for the murals only. The three of us agreed. We'd keep our aliases separate – just in case.

The sweet smell of aerosol and pigment filtered through my bandana. A mist of red hung in the air, transformed to purple by the streetlights below. I added the pair of fangs dropping beneath the letters as Scape called out to us.

"You two are up. Which playlist, Rox?"

"Screamo Love!" Rox answered, thrusting her hips, teeth bared, bobbing her head.

I glared at her as I stepped into the light. "Really, Rox? With this sweeping landscape?"

"I got this. He's gonna be tall and sleek. Tight pants. Dark. Silver eyes."

I rolled my own eyes. "When are your characters not *dark*? Can you please not turn him into one of your fucked-up creatures? That damn Circus Demon scared the shit outta me."

"I painted him in chains, didn't I? Just worry about walling the edges in, *Border Boy*. We don't need another screw-up like last week."

"My damn black ran out. It was too thin in one spot. One damn, tiny spot!"

Rox ignored me. She was already lost in thrashing to the dense beat and the whine of some androgynous boy wailing like a girl. She laid down the base of a figure, to the right of center. I sorted through my cans and set aside all the black. Plenty of it. First I sprayed the solid line of the border all the way around. Precise. Purposeful. Rox and I shared the top of the table. When I was ready to slide it over, Scape was there to help move it. As always, we worked seamlessly, like cogs in a machine.

I added swirls and arcs embellishing the border. Scape quietly joined in, shading and smoothing the tones in the mural. Clouds of rainbow aerosol filled the air. My tongue tingled with the sharp taste. We worked over one another's sections, dancing, adding details and highlights.

Rox jumped off the table, and her shadow rummaged in its backpack. "Shit. I need a tight nozzle. I lost mine some fucking where."

"There's one in my pocket," I said with a smile, "If you want it, you gotta get it."

She sauntered to me and grabbed my hair. She faked heavy, ecstatic breaths in my ear as she slid her hand into my pocket and fished the nozzle out. "Ohhhh, ohhhhh, unnnhhhh. Oh yeah! Oh yeaaaahhh!"

Scape peeked at us from beneath his hood. "You two are sick."

Rox skipped to him. "You know you like it, baby." She grabbed Scape, kissed him on the cheek, then sealed it with a playful slap.

Back to work, we navigated one another, fluidly filling in the details high and low. Scape stepped back to view the whole, then dove in for some tweaking. Rox hopped down and turned off the iPod. We moved behind the flashlights, checking out our work.

"Damn, Scape. Look at the rhythm of those strokes," I said.

"Our best one yet," he said.

Rox agreed. "We get better each time."

Scape broke the silence of our admiration. "You guys ready?"

We approached the mural and tagged our 'real' names: *SCAPE, ROX, FIN*. Scape connected the triangular pattern with three straight lines. Only one more step.

"Should we do it?" I asked.

"Hold on," Rox said. "Let me give him one last look." I whistled the Jeopardy theme song to annoy her. She flipped me off, and Scape followed through with a light punch on my arm.

"Shit! I forgot his lips. There's too much shadow on his face."

"Oh, you definitely want dark, sleek boy to have a luscious pair of lips," I teased. I expected a *Fuck you, Fin,* but Rox was on task.

With a few expert strokes, she added highlights on the right half of his face: the bridge of his nose, a sharp cheekbone, the hint of a strong chin, two quick bursts for lips. Rox stepped back. Pleased. Her guy looked lean and proud. But not arrogant. Like aristocracy.

"What's his name?" Scape asked.

Rox answered in a whisper, "Craven."

Simultaneously, we all three placed our palms inside the triangle. Color rippled out from the center of the mural, bounced off the thick, black border, and echoed back. Wind gusted from the wall, driving the aerosol fumes across the room to hover by the windows.

Craven shivered and rounded out into three dimensions. He blinked, rolled his neck, sending the sound of cracking vertebrae through the old factory. He looked down at the three of us, his creators, and parted his lips to speak.

His face contorted. Slowly, his feet left the painted grass, and he rose into the spraypaint sky.

"Wait … wait!" he screamed. Bewildered and scared, Craven floated to the top of the mural, bracing his hands against the upper border.

"Oh, fuck!" Rox jumped up and scrambled to the row of cans on the worktable.

"We forgot to paint a shadow to anchor the dude …" Scape said.

"… again," I finished.

Rox smiled at us. "Well, don't just sit there, numbnuts. Help me pull him down."

HAPPINESS IS A LIE …
BY SOPHIE E TALLIS

"Happiness is a lie," he mumbled, gazing at the grey-flecked linoleum of the floor, scratched and scuffed after countless years of shuffling feet and shifting chairs. This place was depression itself, but it was exactly what he had sought, what he had fought so hard to be in.

The boy sat impassively. Suddenly he had no idea why he was here, why he had wanted so much to see his grandfather. He scanned the room; it was exactly how he had envisioned it. Walls painted the colour of sick, just like school. Windows heavily barred behind safety glass and mesh grilles, tables fixed to the floor, everything starkly functional. Yes, this was precisely how Daniel had pictured prison: an austere Victorian edifice, designed to instil awe and strip the individual of who they were.

"Why are you here?" The old man was staring at him. "Your father know you're here?"

Daniel shook his head.

The old man smiled knowingly. "I thought so, couldn't see James approving … not that I think he gives me any thought, or to anyone else for that matter."

"Why did you do it?" The question burst out, blunter than he had meant it to. Daniel shifted in his chair, feeling his cheeks burning beneath the adversarial glare meeting him from across the table.

His grandfather had always been a leviathan of strength, a physical presence that only came from a lifetime of physical labour. Despite the white hair, time hadn't diminished him; he was still a rock you could dash yourself upon. Broad-shouldered from years of working on the docks, Bristol and Gloucester, from tug boats and trawlers to the huge cargo tankers of Avonmouth. He had done it all. He knew every inch of the River Severn, its treacherous sandbanks, shifting currents, mud flats and silted channels. One of the highest tidal ranges in the world, home of the mighty Severn Bore – yes, he knew it well. His 'lucky lady 7', he called it.

Daniel looked at the bear of a man. He was so different from his corporate father, all grey suits and soft belly, hands that had never seen a callus, that had never held anything weightier than the weekly shopping bags.

"You were there in court, weren't you?" the old man asked.

Daniel nodded.

"So, what else d'you want to know?"

"Why …?" Daniel hesitated. "It doesn't make sense. You looked after Granny for years. If you'd had enough, why not divorce her or put her in a home?"

"You don't believe what I said in court?"

Daniel shook his head again. "I don't."

"Your father seemed to believe it quick enough."

"He … he doesn't care, that's why."

"And you do?

"I do."

"Then you tell me, why d'you think I did it?"

"Because … because you loved her. She was in pain and you wanted to help her. You didn't murder her. I don't know why you said that. It's a lie."

"Is it?"

"You loved her!" Daniel protested. "I remember when she first got ill, you'd brush her hair. You did everything for her. You could have left, but you stayed. You took me on a butterfly walk, and there she was, you carried her through the woods and we had a picnic. You wiped the cake crumbs from her cheek … you loved her, I know you did!"

The old man sighed. His eyes flickered with memories. Sunny, sandy days when he was young, eating fish and chips in the rain on Clevedon Pier; the thrill of making love for the first time; the feeling of heart-bursting love when they'd married and Meredith had whispered to him as they stood under the old yew tree for photos, "I'm pregnant."

Meredith, a woman of little height, but such passion and vitality. Her beautiful hair, the colour of spun amber, used to envelop him. They had worked, played and loved as hard as any. The years had flown by at an alarming rate. Life had been sweet, filled with simple happiness.

But all that had changed twelve years ago, almost to the day.

Their beloved daughter, Charlotte, had been murdered by her ex-partner – killed by a coward with a history of violence. Charlotte had left him and been tormented for months after. Phone calls, letters, broken windows. The old man had pleaded with her to stay with them, to leave her flat and come home. They had tried everything to protect her, but she had wanted to reclaim her life. She had returned to her flat and been brutally stabbed less than an hour later, her head almost severed in the frenzied attack.

The murderer had claimed 'diminished responsibility' and, with a clever legal team, got only seven years. He was out in less than five.

Meredith had a stroke three days after Charlotte's murder; something just died in her. The grief was unbearable, all their happiness shattered forever.

Daniel hadn't known his Aunt Charlotte very well. His father, an arrogant shit who he didn't get on with, looked down his nose at his working-class roots and so Daniel had only ever visited his paternal grandparents or aunt with his mum.

"Why did you plead guilty to murder?" Daniel asked.

"What else would you call it?"

"Euthanasia."

"Many people think it's the same." The old man sighed.

"But you didn't do what you did out of hate, you did it out of love."

"You don't know what I did … not everything I did. I'm happy to be here, Daniel, leave it at that."

"Why?"

"Because some things are better left alone … I did what I had to, to set things right."

"I don't understand."

The old man smiled at him, so much like himself at that age. He looked around; the guards were out of earshot.

"I committed a murder, Daniel, that is why I am here."

"But it wasn't murder … you could appeal."

He shook his head. "It was murder. Cold-blooded, very bloody as it happens, and I was pleased for it. I can never bring her back, but at last I have avenged her. Every stroke was worth it. He felt the same fear she must have and I hope he felt more pain. These hands have wielded more than just oil drums and cargo over the years – they have wielded an axe." He flexed his hands.

Daniel looked lost.

"Happiness is knowing that you've done your best. I loved Meredith to the end and I know that she loved me. Happiness is knowing that justice has been done, that the loss has not been for nothing, that I have saved others …" He paused and took a deep, satisfying breath. "Happiness is avenging my little girl. I murdered her murderer. All these years, while I've been looking after

Meredith, I've been looking for him. I found him and, when I did, I knew what I had to do." He looked down at his hands with pride. "I ended his life with these hands. I took his head and took pleasure in it. He's rotting in a barrel at the bottom of the Severn. That was the last thing Meredith asked me to do before she asked me to take her pain away."

A smile crept across his face. "That's the irony. I've been jailed for the murder I didn't commit, not for the one I did."

Illustration by Sophie E Tallis

NILAMETH
BY ANDREA BAKER

Vi, Sansi and Gelaf, the Triumvirate of the Savant, sat along the far edge of the table. Their striking emerald-green eyes, belying their significant age, flitted between the images being cast from the antiquated table standing before them. Each vision of the busy worlds would stay for a brief moment, only to be replaced when their eyes moved away. The sole static item on the table was the aged blue diamond, nestled within a carving in the centre. The encasing metal claw had dulled over the years leaving only the upper surface visible to the naked eye. It dominated the scene as gently pulsating colours skimmed across its face.

Facing the Triumvirate on the opposite side of the table was a tall, angular Master Cheari Seraph, his semi-opaque golden colour shimmering against the changing light. Wordlessly, communication appeared to flow through the small group, charging the atmosphere. In response to each decision the Master turned to his left or right, selecting from the ethereal silver Seraph that stood against the sides of the room, indicating the one chosen to carry out the required task. None of the waiting creatures appeared to question the seemingly random selection, or the orders being given.

Around the Master's head circled several sparkling, lucent orbs. He would give a brief indication as an individual Seraph was selected, and a single orb would make its way towards the chosen one. It would pause, hovering overhead, and then gently descend towards the creature. A transformation would begin when the Seraph turned away, as the orb started to absorb into their bodies. Gradually each one began taking on a human form. Arms formed from the more angular limbs possessed by the Seraph, and legs appeared where previously had been a silver gown and barely visible feet. As the Seraph passed the Master they would pause, bowing their heads and allowing him to place a hand on them. He would also lower his head and mutter an indistinct phrase, almost as an incantation. A surge of swirling, iridescent light flowed from his hand through the heads of the Seraph and into their still-changing shapes, glowing stronger and stronger, until finally the transformation became complete. As they raised their heads, identical cobalt eyes briefly acknowledged him before they turned away.

None dared to look across the table towards the superior Triumvirate as they adjusted to their new identities. Their heads bowed slightly as they made their way towards the huge, weather-beaten, solid oak doors, as though absorbing the wealth of information and knowledge that had just been passed on. Occasionally a tear fell as unbidden memories came to the fore of their new, previously human, minds. Some bore obvious scars that told the tale of what had happened to the humans they now resembled. Car accidents, illness or some other misfortune – their appearance briefly told the story of the loss of those lives, but by the time they passed through the doors, all visible remnants of the tragic events had disappeared.

On the opposite side of the room, another pair of doors – twin to the ones passed through by the transformed Seraph – flew open, and two arrogant Cheari marched in. They were a much lighter gold in colour than the Master and his lack of acknowledgment toward them indicated their position in the hierarchy. Despite this, the remaining Seraph cowered against the walls, and those leaving the room seemed to speed up their step as though anxious to get away. Standing proud and strong between the Cheari was a young man. Despite his human form, Ben was almost as tall as the two creatures that flanked him. There was a defiant, angry glint dominating his cobalt eyes that almost succeeded in masking the occasional glimmer of panic. The random strand of red that was mixed in with his brown hair flashed with the light as the orbs hovered towards him, trying to examine the stranger now in the room.

Despite the noise, the Triumvirate showed no sign of even noticing their presence. The two Cheari grew impatient, shuffling their feet slightly, waiting to be acknowledged. The Triumvirate's eyes flitted along with the rapid images, barely seeming to notice any change. The Master finally glanced up briefly from his routine, and acknowledged the presence of the Cheari by nodding once. Reaching forward he touched, for an instant, the aged carved diamond in the centre of the table before him. Everything in the room froze; from the normally fleeting images to the floating orbs, the entire world within that room seemed to be suspended. As the Master turned towards the Cheari, he gently folded his hands together, the only outward sign that he was anticipating the coming events.

"What is the meaning of this interruption?" The sound resonated around the room, although it was not apparent who had spoken. Ben jumped at the sudden sound and glanced quickly at the two guards that flanked him. They showed no outward sign of being disturbed by the question, but neither did they give him a clue where it had come from.

Deciding that attack was the best form of defence right now, he stepped forward. "Why have I been brought here like this?" he asked, trying not to betray the turmoil of his feelings as he spoke.

"You dare to address us without invitation! We are the Triumvirate of the Savant, and we are your Masters," the voice responded.

Ben turned towards them, trying to mask his surprise. "I dare because I have been brought here against my will, summoned for a crime that has not been committed, and treated as a prisoner." As he finished he glared pointedly at his two captors, who continued to stare ahead, avoiding eye contact.

"They will leave us now." The Master's quieter, smooth voice permeated the silence. It still carried authority despite the lower volume, and the Cheari beside Ben stood to attention as he spoke. "I said leave. You were asked to summon him to answer for his

47

behaviour, not deliver him as a prisoner. This is not yet an arraignment. You should have treated him as your equal." The Master glanced briefly at each of the Cheari. Their heads dropped at the admonishment. Reluctantly they turned and left the room, all sign of the initial haughtiness of their movements now completely gone.

"Come here, child." The Master spoke again, indicating that Ben should join him at the table. Still a little perturbed, but less angry than before, Ben stepped forward, unsure of whether to address the Master or the Triumvirate.

"He has broken the rules of Guardianship," the voice said more quietly. Ben turned towards the Triumvirate. Now he was closer, he was shocked at their appearance. Their faces were drawn with age and their skin was taut, stretched so tightly across the bones that it appeared opalescent. Those vivid emerald eyes belied this, however, and now all six were staring right at him. He could feel them boring into him, looking into his soul as though analysing the content. Suddenly, Vi blinked and then he spoke, his voice quiet.

"It is apparent that you had no knowledge of this girl, Leah, when you met her – is that correct?" He watched Ben carefully as he spoke.

"That is correct. It was a chance encounter. I did not know who she was, or even that my mentor Jon had a new charge at that point." Ben returned the stare, open and honest, waiting for a response, knowing they could see in his mind that what he said was true.

Gelaf grunted a signal of some kind to the others. Vi spoke again. "That seems apparent from our reading. Should we therefore be having this discussion with your mentor?"

Ben shook his head quickly, instinctively responding even though he knew they would read his mind anyway. "Jon was not at fault either. He had only received his latest instruction from the Master that very day, and there was no reason for me to suspect that anything was wrong. I only found out the truth after the accident, and by then … well, the connection between us had been made."

There was no response from around the table, but Ben was sure he caught a brief flicker of acknowledgment in Gelaf's eyes. The Master interrupted.

"It is most unusual, yes, but it is perfectly natural for Ben to be called to another of his own kind. This girl, Leah, is of Cheari heritage herself, and you yourselves have acknowledged her importance in the schema. Once such a lifetime connection is made it is impossible for him to break it – you created us to pair for eternity. These circumstances are very different, I believe, from any that have gone before?"

"That is not the point," boomed the voice. This time Ben realised what was happening. He glanced at the Triumvirate. Again they had not moved, but he now realised that this was how they usually spoke: together, with one voice. "A Guardian cannot make a lifetime connection with a charge!"

Ben flinched at the statement, but was determined to make his point.

"I am very aware of the rules of Guardianship. But as you yourselves have pointed out, I was unaware of the situation at the time we met. I found myself called to her, and before I knew it, the connection had been made. I don't understand – if she is a Cheari, why is she a charge rather than a Seraph?" As the question left his lips Ben saw the Master flinch, and glanced quickly towards him.

"This Cheari is young, wise ones; he has only just begun his Guardianship training. He meant no offence with the question. Perhaps a short lesson on the history would be of some use, if you would grant us the time?" Although spoken quietly, the authority in the Master's words rang through, and Ben felt confused. It was obvious that these ancient men were the most senior, and yet the Master, standing beside him and the head of the Cheari clan, carried almost equal authority – as though his respect were granted to the Triumvirate out of admiration, rather than superiority.

"Let it be," commanded the voice. Ben heard a gasp of exasperation from one of the Triumvirate, but couldn't make out which.

A swirl of light shot from within the diamond, showering colour across the room. In awe at the sight before them, the Seraph began to edge their way forward, until they had formed a semicircle behind the Master. Entranced though they were by what they saw, they kept a respectful distance from his side.

All eyes focused on the light as it swirled and settled, displaying a scene before them. A beautiful young woman dressed in a simple, white, Roman-style gown walked into a garden. Fluffy clouds scurried across the sky, flowers bloomed pink and red along the path, and a large tree covered in white blossom provided filtered shade.

The woman hummed gently to herself as she walked, her robe swaying gently in the breeze, a peaceful smile on her face. As Ben watched the scene unfold, he caught a slight movement across the table; as he looked, he saw that Sansi – the third being, and the only one that had yet to speak – had turned his head and had a look of utter fury on his face. Ben refocused on the scene being portrayed in front of him, and the singing woman, but his mind kept going back to the expression on Sansi's face. He watched as the woman continued her journey, the soft sound of her song permeating the room. As she turned on the path, he was surprised to see that she was pregnant. The drape of the robes had hidden her swollen stomach from the front, but now there was no mistake. Ben glanced back over at Sansi – was that why he was so furious? But what could be so wrong about a pregnant woman?

He didn't have long to wait for his answer. As he watched, the cotton-wool clouds started to darken, and before long the sky had turned a deep purplish grey. The Seraph behind him jumped as a loud clap of thunder erupted and lightning forked across the sky. Despite the fact they were watching an image, he could feel the apprehension growing amongst them. The young woman abandoned her stroll in an effort to get out of the rain. Wrapping her arms around her swollen stomach, she turned and hurried back along the path, worry creasing her face.

Suddenly, as the thunder roared again, a horrible screech filled the air. The young woman glanced quickly over her shoulder. Her face froze with fear and she started to run, stumbling as she went, her hands instinctively covering her unborn child. Ben felt the Master brush his arm and glanced up at him quickly. Wordlessly, the Master gestured towards the Triumvirate. Sansi had stood up and walked towards the rear of the room. With his back to the scene, he held his hands over his ears as though trying to block out the sound. His posture was rigid, echoing the fury Ben had noticed earlier, but it was impossible to say whether that same expression was on his face.

Another screech disturbed his thoughts, and Ben dragged his eyes back to the scene they were meant to be watching. As his brain absorbed the new vision, his eyes became riveted to the spot, all thoughts of Sansi driven from his mind by what he saw. Appearing to come directly from the swirling purple storm was the most horrendous creature Ben had ever seen. Long, dirty, ragged clothes hung from the sinewy body, revealing cloven feet below. Angular arms and hands clawed at the air as the creature flew in towards the ground, the haggard, skeletal face contorted from making the terrible sound. Bright ochre glaring eyes focused in on the young woman, and pointed, discoloured and jagged teeth protruded from its jaw as it uttered another screech.

The room around him fell silent as the Seraph, like Ben, watched transfixed with horror, fearing the worst for the young woman as they looked on helplessly. Without conscious thought, a name came into Ben's head, and he knew at once that this creature was one of legend. It was Nilameth.

The screeching creature landed, expelling a harsh, guttural cackle as she did so. Desperately the young woman continued to run back up the path. With a hiss, Nilameth took a huge leap and landed just in front of the fleeing woman. Screeching loudly, she raised her arm and long, sharp, claw-like nails sprang from her hand, ready for the attack. The young woman fell to her knees.

"Please, please don't hurt my baby," she begged.

An ugly grin grew across Nilameth's face, accompanied by another loud screech. Slowly and deliberately, she stepped forwards to ensure that she was within striking distance. The young woman cowered at her feet, hunching forward with her back arched, trying desperately to protect the child with her body. As her assailant took a final step forward, the young woman averted her face and stiffened, bracing for the attack that was to come.

As the claw began to move, a hand shot from behind and grabbed it, twisting the creature's body away from its prey. A shriek of surprise escaped from the ugly mouth.

"Leave this child alone!" exclaimed a voice. Not the huge, booming voice of the room they were in, but somehow it was familiar. Ben found himself glancing around the table again, but the voice had not come from within the room.

Nilameth screeched and raised her other claw for attack, only to again find herself trapped. Ben started with surprise as the protector came into view. Although it was obviously many hundreds of years earlier, the protector was Sansi himself. Standing tall and strong, dressed in the same cloak as now hung tattered around his shoulders, he wrestled with Nilameth, trying to subdue her fight.

Nilameth spat at her assailant, contorting and twisting her body in a vain attempt to escape.

"You will not harm that child, do you understand? It is of the Savant bloodline, and you gave an oath not to harm them!" Sansi instructed.

Nilameth cackled, then threw back her head and uttered the most horrendous, ear-piercing cry that Ben had ever heard. The storm clouds circled above; through them came two harbingers, creatures from Nilameth's army. With hairless bodies and sharp, pointed teeth, they had the same claw-like hands as Nilameth herself. They had long, angular legs, however, shaped for running and jumping long distances. As they landed, Nilameth started to laugh. She twisted and turned in Sansi's grip, keeping him occupied with controlling her whilst her cohorts grabbed the young woman. One held her while the other brought his balled hand down against the side of her face. She fell limp against her captor.

Once they had the woman secure in their grasp, Nilameth snarled back at Sansi and spoke for the first time. A rasping, guttural sound that set Ben's nerves on edge came from her throat. Laughing in Sansi's face, she responded.

"This woman is not a Savant – she is of human descent. The child is therefore not protected by the oath. You should have been more careful in what you forced me to swear, Sansi – only whole Savant are protected, and when you connected with this human, the protection was lost. These chosen ones, the children that carry Savant blood and inherit your gifts, are mine if I want them, and I will use these gifts to conquer the worlds! I promise you, I will capture and absorb the powers of each and every one of them until I can destroy your Triumvirate once and for all."

With that, she finally broke away from his grasp and jumped to her supporters. Away they flew, carrying the young woman with them. Sansi stood watching them, unable to take his eyes off the disappearing figures, but powerless to help or protect his own as they went.

Appalled by what he had just witnessed, Ben dragged his eyes away from the scene, searching out Sansi now in the semi-darkness of the room. He was still standing with his back to the scene, but now his shoulders had slumped forward, and Ben could read the despair. He shook his head slowly, filled with remorse that he had been, in some small way, responsible for making Sansi have to relive this horrible event.

He started to turn towards the Master, wanting to ask a question, but as he glanced up the Master raised his finger to his lips and nodded back towards the table. As he shifted his gaze, the magnificent lights that had carried the scene before them swirled and died back within the diamond. More confused than ever, Ben continued to watch in silence. Once the colours had died away completely, the loud, resonating voice spoke again.

"Now you understand why it is not possible for Cheari blood to be mixed. You must forsake this girl, leave the Guardian to protect her, and continue your studies!" it boomed.

Ben shook his head slowly. "No, I'm sorry, I still don't understand. I am Cheari, I know that, but if Leah is of Cheari blood then neither of us are descendent from the Savant, so what I have seen still does not explain it to me."

An angry hiss came from Sansi at the back of the room. He finally turned and returned to his seat at the table. A single, lingering glance passed between the Triumvirate before he spoke.

"Must we explain everything to you, child? Do you know nothing of our history?" he demanded. Sansi's voice was a slightly higher pitch than the others', however, and more melodious in its delivery, even when he was riled like this.

"I'm sorry," Ben stuttered. "I obviously don't know as much as I thought, please explain. I'm not trying to be difficult, honestly, I just need to understand." He almost begged as he spoke.

The Master shook his head. "Sires, it is not essential that the Seraph know this level of our history before they begin Guardianship training. It is something that some of them will never need to know, given that it is only relevant to the Cheari line. Perhaps you would allow me to provide the final answers this child is looking for to him alone?" he asked. "It seems the most appropriate way to deal with it."

After what seemed like a moment's hesitation, the deep, resonant voice boomed again. "Let it be done!" it commanded. "But time must be allowed to resume while you are gone."

The Master looked up in surprise; then he nodded. "You must freeze time for the chosen ones, if need be, until I return and can allocate Guardians for them," he instructed. Ben was amazed to see the Triumvirate nod briefly, as though agreeing to the Master's command.

More confused than ever, he followed the Master through the large doors on the opposite side of the room to where he had entered. Stunned by the bright, pure white room on the other side, he stumbled slightly as his eyes reacted to the intense light. Glancing around quickly, he could see that they were alone. The only other things around them were large pieces of dark furniture, made to look even more ancient in the brightness, although Ben guessed they were the same age as the table in the main hall he had just left – they certainly looked to be made from the same material.

The Master seated himself on the chair closest to him, and indicated that Ben should do the same. Feeling that he had no other choice, Ben sat, turning his chair slightly to face the Master as he did so, anxious to finally discover the explanation.

"Ben, you have become a victim of events that occurred long before you were born into the Cheari. I appreciate how difficult this is for you, and wish there had been a way to prevent it, but unfortunately we now have to deal with the aftermath."

Ben was suddenly scared. What did the Master mean by that? Was he about to be severely punished simply for falling for Leah? He felt himself tense, preparing to run as the Master reached out his arm, unsure whether the Master would now punish him. Just as he had witnessed in the great hall, the Master laid his hand on top of Ben's head. He felt his eyes close as a feeling of great warmth and peace filled his mind. Although he could not see it, he was suddenly stripped again of his human shell and communicating with the Master as a fellow Cheari, the embodiment of grace and tranquility. For an instant he wondered what would happen to his human shell, but the question was immediately answered.

"You will return to this body once our discussions have ended. It is just far better that we converse as ourselves."

Ben felt himself smile; it felt good to be freed from the mechanical human forms of communication. Turning his attention fully to the Master, he waited for an explanation. To his surprise, the Master revealed another screen within the table that had gone unnoticed beside them. He'd expected a conversation, not another light show.

He turned his eyes towards the Master, sending the unspoken query forward. This time there was no answer. The Master turned and faced him.

"I know you were a little confused as to my relationship with the Triumvirate of the Savant earlier," he said. Ben was surprised; he hadn't realised that the Master could read his thoughts even when he was in his human body. The Master smiled and nodded. "We can still communicate normally, even when in our Guardian form – it just takes a little practice," he responded.

"You understand the difference between the Cheari and the other Seraph?" the Master asked. Not waiting for an answer, he continued, "Do you understand that the Cheari are the master race here – that we have a destiny beyond ordinary Guardianship?"

Ben nodded slowly. "I knew we were different, and that you, as leader of the Cheari, are effectively the leader of the entire Seraph – is that correct?"

The Master nodded once. "The reason that we are special, that we lead the Seraph, is quite simple – we ourselves are not pure-blood Seraph."

Ben looked up again in surprise. "So why are they so against my being with Leah, if none of us are pure? I don't understand the difference."

"Don't be impatient, Ben. You must understand first, before I can explain about Leah," the Master responded.

Ben shifted in his seat – this still didn't make too much sense. He understood the relevance of what had happened to the young woman; after all, she was human. But if the Cheari themselves were not pure, how could there be a problem?

"Quiet!" Ben jumped as the word forced its way through his thoughts. "We are here to help you understand, which I can't do if you keep clouding your mind, and I need to return to my duties before any of the chosen ones find themselves exposed again!" Humbled by the tirade, Ben cleared his mind.

"You saw what happened to Sansi's partner? Human blood mixed with the blood of the Savant leads to the creation of the chosen ones: humans with extraordinary powers and a destiny that is essential to the schema of existence. These powers are supposed to only belong to the Savant. Our Triumvirate – Vi, Sansi and Gelaf – are the ones who have been granted the power to protect the three worlds Earth, Earos and Eaneth. Do you remember from your initiation the relevance of these Triumvirate worlds?" the Master demanded.

Ben nodded slowly. They were the Triumvirate of Earth, where Earth was the central planet. The other two, Earos and Eaneth, were the parallels, allowed to continue in an almost identical path to ensure the stability of this particular part of the universe.

"Good – at least something has happened as it should. After what happened to Sansi, the Savant decided that they needed an elite mix, a species that would protect the chosen ones."

Ben frowned; he still didn't understand the concept of the chosen ones, not if Nilameth could attack and control them.

The Master sighed. "For centuries, it was believed that the truce agreed with Nilameth and her harbingers would protect everyone with Savant blood. Like us, they make an eternal connection. Whilst the Savant themselves are, of course, immortal, in the early days they mated with humans, who of course are not. Over the course of several centuries, many children were born from these unions. It quickly became impossible to keep track of all of the descendants, and what you saw earlier was the culmination of Nilameth's strategy. One by one she had been absorbing their powers, inherited from the Savant line, until she was strong enough to take on Sansi himself. As you saw, he was powerless to help, consumed with the cries of his unborn child."

Ben couldn't stop the shudder as he thought about what Sansi must have experienced at that time. The Master smiled grimly. "I see I don't need to explain that part?"

Ben nodded.

"For two hundred years, Nilameth ruled the Three Worlds, and it was an extremely dark time. Plague, massacre and hardship spread throughout the worlds. Unable to compete against her, the Triumvirate instead focused on creating a defence, a means of protecting the chosen ones and regaining control of the powers that run these worlds. The Cheari line was created as a mix of Savant and Seraph – we ourselves are immortal, but in order to carry out our work, the Seraph now have to live as humans within the world, guarding the chosen ones until they come of age."

Ben looked up; this still didn't explain about Leah.

"There are still many human chosen ones, and each Seraph Guardian protects them until they have lived out their mortal lives and become a Seraph – gaining immortality in return for following the Triumvirate and protecting future generations. Over the last five hundred years we have gradually reclaimed control of Earth and Eaneth, but at the moment Earos is still under Nilameth's control."

"OK, I understand all of that, but it still doesn't explain about Leah – if she is one of us, then there shouldn't be a problem," Ben demanded.

"There is a huge problem," the Master responded. "Leah is descended directly from Sansi himself. You both have a crucial part to play in the schema that will bring all the planets back under our control. We cannot risk your union distracting either of you from your destiny!"

Ben looked at him, even more confused. If Leah was descended from Sansi then her destiny made sense, but he was a simple Cheari Seraph, no different from any of the others.

The Master slowly shook his head and smiled. "I cannot tell you your destiny, child. It would influence, and perhaps change, the outcome of certain events. You must go now and return to your mentor. All will be revealed in time."

The Master placed his hand on Ben's head once more. Ben felt his eyes and limbs return as he drifted off into a deep sleep.

He awoke to the sound of his bedroom door opening. He smiled at the older woman as she entered the room, and then shook his head slowly. What was it he had dreamed that night? It had seemed so important at the time, but now he couldn't remember any of it. Stretching slowly, he climbed out of bed and started to get ready for his day. Whatever it was, if it was important, it would come back to him.

DEEPER PRAYERS
BY EMILY MCKEON

The bright light pierced through the darkness.

"C'mon. Time to get up."

"Go 'way." The girl pulled the sheets over her head in a vain attempt to block out the light.

"Wake up, sunshine. We're going to be late." The man left the room. The young girl groaned and reached behind her to turn off the lights. With the annoyance out of the way, she settled comfortably back into bed. As she closed her eyes once again, the sound of a radio erupted throughout the house.

"Why can't he leave me alone?" she muttered, clutching her pillow to her head.

"You gotta get up now." The man had returned to the doorway. When the girl didn't move, he clicked the lights back on.

"Go AWAY!" The intended shout came out muffled from under the covers and pillow.

"Do you want to walk in late?"

"No. I don't want to go at all."

"Well, that's too bad because we're both going."

"Why can't you go alone today?'

"Because."

"Because what?" The girl had removed the covers and sat up.

"Look, I'm not going to argue with you over this. Get up now. You have ten minutes to get ready, so you better hurry up."

The girl settled back under the covers. "I'm not going."

"Fine. Have it your way." The man left the room, slamming the door behind him. The girl turned to face the wall and curled her body up, happy to have won this argument. She could hear the man tromping around downstairs, slamming things around, turning the radio up and stomping whenever he walked. The girl sighed and stared at the wall. In a few minutes he would leave and she could sleep peacefully again.

Suddenly the door flew open and in rushed two full-grown golden retrievers.

"Attack!" The man egged the dogs on, encouraging them to jump on the bed. The dogs, ever hyper, playful and eager to please, did as they were commanded. In their excitement they stepped on the girl.

"Ow! Get them off of me."

"Get up."

"No."

"Get her. That's it. Kiss her. C'mon, wake her up."

The girl pushed the dogs off her chest and sat up. "I want you out of here. Now."

"And I want you to get up."

"Listen. I was up half the night working. I'm in no mood to get up right now. If you don't leave me alone you are going to be very, very sorry."

Missing the dangerous edge in the girl's voice, the man stayed in the room. "Hey, I waited for you to get home. I've been up for over an hour, meaning I got less sleep than you did. You have no excuse."

"I have no excuse?" The girl got out of bed and approached the man. "You think I have no excuse? I was working all night to support you. *You*, you jerk! You could have gone to sleep if you wanted to, or taken a nap. For all I know, you slept until I pulled into the garage and then pretended to have been waiting for me."

"Well, I didn't." The man fought to keep his calm. He knew if he lost his composure he would lose the fight as well.

"It's your own fault if you're tired. You didn't have to stay awake. I did." The girl was face to face with him. He took a step back and bumped into the wall.

"Wait a second. I slept just as much as you did. What does it matter if it was because I chose to stay awake or not? It's the same amount of sleep no matter how you look at it."

"No, it's not," she hissed, her warm breath hitting him in the face. "Were you on your feet for eight hours? Did you have to deal with dirty, drunk old men trying to grab at you? No, I don't think so."

"You should be glad. No sober man would even think of touching you."

The slap resounded through the room. In shock, the man raised his hand to his burning cheek.

"I want you to leave." The girl was sobbing.

"Fine." The man grabbed his coat from the back of a chair. "We'll discuss this when I return from church."

"Why bother going? You're going to rot in hell anyway."

The man smirked, amused at the girl's comment. "Oh, I don't think so. If I were you, however, I would consider praying really hard. You and I are going to have a long talk when I get back."

"You might want to ask God to help you while you're there, because you might not have a place to come back to."

"We'll see about that."

"Fine."

"Fine." The man stormed out of the house.

Going to the window, the girl watched as he sped off in anger and frustration. When she could no longer see him, she went to the bed and collapsed in a heap, her body wracked by sobs. Once she could regain her composure she knew she had a phone call to make. For now it could wait. Getting rid of him was something she had always wanted to do, but at the same time dreaded. Now it was only a matter of time until he was gone. For good.

THE THIEF GETS AWAY
BY TRM

Dinah hugged herself as tight as she could as she walked down the street. She rubbed her arms and shoulders for warmth under her thin, scratchy cape. Her breath turned to wispy clouds under her sore nose. Feeling a sudden bite to the air, she looked up. The sky had turned from a lumpy sheet of grey to an angry, swirling darkness. The wind picked up too, dancing fiercely down the lane, and brought with it a clatter of hail amidst icy rain.

With a shriek, she whipped up her hood and ran for cover. The old stone arch of a stable's gate yawned to one side, and she was first to take refuge there. Others joined her in a rush, huffing and stamping and shaking water off their cloaks. They all ran on a few moments later. Dinah soon stood alone, trying to untangle blobs of hail from the straggly ends of her hair. No one came to shoo her away. As she had nowhere to go, she stayed put for a while and tried to get dry. She wiped her chapped skin with a fold of her cape, but that was soaked too and speckled with ice, which only made her face worse. She stamped her sodden shoes on the only patch of dry ground she could find, but could not beat any blood into her aching feet. Cold, hungry and miserable, she huddled in her draughty shelter, waiting for the rain to sweep over the tall slate roofs of the market town and away to the fields in the south.

There were people in the stable as well as horses. Soft voices and laughter drifted over to her, together with the occasional snort and stamp. She could feel the heat of the animals in their stalls even from where she stood, and she longed to sneak in and hide in a warm corner. Oh, to find some dry straw to curl up in – maybe even a discarded blanket! She knew that would be asking too much of Lady Luck, so she leaned against the gatepost with her back to the stable hands and glared at the weather.

She also kept a keen eye on the people hurrying up and down the street, waiting for an opportunity, but the swirling wind and the stinging rain made everyone clutch their cloaks tightly around their bodies or run as quickly as they could across the wind-whipped puddles rippling over the cobbles. She felt her day would be wasted by the cruel sky. Tears made her cheeks sting again. She knew all too well that if she failed, she would not be the only one to go to sleep hungry that night.

She felt a comforting tug on a lock of her hair, under her hood. A tiny, delicate voice tinkled by her ear. "Don't worry," it said, with words lighter than the caress of a summer breeze. "The rain will pass in a short while, I promise."

Another voice came from the other side of Dinah's head. "Here, let me try a little trick," it said. It was lower than the first and a little gravelly, but still no louder than the insolent buzz of an insect.

Dinah replied in a voiceless whisper, barely moving her lips. "Just what *are* you doing, you silly thing?" However miserable she felt, those two always made her smile, somehow.

A moment later, one of the stable hands appeared at her shoulder, making Dinah jump. Gruff and grizzled, the craggy-faced man smiled, halting her flight. He held out a little bowl of steaming soup and a hunk of crumbly bread. Dinah just stared at them, so the man thrust both forward.

"Take them," he rumbled. She tucked the bread in the crook of an arm and cupped both hands around the wooden bowl.

"Th-thank you, s-sir," she stuttered, still amazed.

"Had me a bairn," the man mumbled, fiddling with his pipe. "She'd be your age by now." He gave her a smile with a quivering lip and his eyes misted. He turned back towards his workmates without another word, billowing blue smoke as he shuffled along.

Despite her hunger, Dinah stared into the soup. "You *beast*," she whispered as she blew on the watery broth. "You *knew*."

The buzzing voice replied, its tone almost a shrug. "A bowl of food is worth an old memory."

"Don't know about that," she hissed through her teeth, but Dinah sipped the soup nevertheless.

"Told him. Didn't listen," chimed the other, haughtily.

"Oh, hush!" Dinah drained the bowl and shoved the dregs into her mouth with the bread. A couple of bites and the bread was gone but for a few crumbs, which she placed on one shoulder, and a scrap of crust that went on the other. Warmth spread out from her belly, but she was still cold in her damp clothes and still hungry. She wished the bowl was full again, and held it in her hands for as long as there was any warmth lingering in the wood. Then she placed it on the floor and returned to stamping her feet and rubbing her arms against the nagging cold.

After a while, she leaned out of her shelter to look at the sky, as the downpour seemed to be easing off. Soon it stopped and the good townsfolk began to dawdle once more, with their cloaks thrown back over their shoulders to show off their rich doublets and their pretty kirtles. Their belts and purses were once more within reach.

Dinah glanced over her shoulder, but none of the stable hands were looking her way. Wishing her thanks on the kind man with the pipe, she slipped out onto the street.

There seemed to be some commotion at the end of the street, where it joined with the main thoroughfare. People were stopping to gawp at something. She joined the throng. Unsure where first to cast her nimble fingers' net, she let herself be swept into the sea of people. There, she knew she was almost invisible: a skinny slip of a girl, in clothing tatty enough to make the wealthy disregard her, but not so tatty as to arouse their suspicions.

The delicate voice urged her on. "Now, Dinah! That one, there!"

"Go on!" the other voice added. "He'll never notice. Promise!"

She edged closer to her quarry, slipping past this elegant merchant, then past that good lady, as discreet as her own shadow, ever closer to a carelessly tied purse bouncing on an unguarded hip. Dinah flexed her fingers under a fold of her cape. But just as she was about to snatch, she was startled by truly horrible voices barking over the heads of the crowd.

"Stand aside!" they rasped. "Make way for Master!"

The words sounded as if they were hacked from croaks and snarls. Dinah felt a sickening jolt of fear. The tiny companions by her ears fell into anguished silence.

Those hideous voices clawed at the air again: "*Back! Move, now!*" They were slashing their way through the throng, coming nearer and nearer. Men and women pushed and shoved in their haste to get away from whatever made that horrendous sound, almost leaping out of the way.

Dinah was jostled to one side then the other, still invisible to these careless folk as they scattered. She found herself spinning around, suddenly alone in the middle of the street, and ending up nose to snout with the swart, leathery face of a monster.

"*Get BACK!*" it roared, baring yellowed fangs. "*NOW!*"

Dinah staggered away from the stench of its breath and the pit-like glare of its small, widely parted eyes, but then froze in terror like a rabbit confronted by a fox. The squat creature curled a clawed hand around the hilt of the sword that hung from its filthy buckler, and drew a palm's width of blade from the scabbard.

"*Enough*, Shodzlug!"

A tall man clasped a hand on the monster's shoulder, and the sword slid back into its sheath. Dinah stared up at him, her mouth open in surprise. He towered above the thing called Shodzlug, resplendent in shining breastplate and billowing sleeves of scarlet-slashed velvet. His elegant hair was uncovered, but his handsome face was marred by a sneer of disdain as he glared at the brat in his way.

Dinah felt strong hands pull her a couple of paces back, but she could not tear her eyes from this strange vision: a man as noble as any she had seen, guarded by this misshapen, thick-set brute. For all the terror it caused, the ugly creature was barely taller than her, but three times as wide. And then she realised that there were many more men behind Shodzlug's master, just as richly arrayed in armour or ceremonial robes. They stood bemused by their unexpected halt. Many more vile beasts like Shodzlug formed a ring around them.

"Curtsy, you silly girl!" hissed the woman who still gripped her arms, curtsying clumsily herself. "Don't you go upsetting the Seneschal, now."

There were chuckles and tut-tutting in the throng. "The little idiot!" someone snorted. "Picking a fight with a Carrlund!" scoffed another.

Dinah's knees buckled of their own accord and that seemed to satisfy the Seneschal, who turned to the bearded gentleman beside him in emerald robes and continued their conversation as if nothing had happened. "But surely, Chancellor, you are not proposing to tear down these dwellings?"

"Ah, my lord, the town would surely benefit from a second marketplace just here," the Chancellor simpered in reply as the strange cortege moved on. "You can see how popular the stalls on this street are …"

Shodzlug stood for a moment, transfixing Dinah with its malevolent stare. Then the Carrlund cocked its head to one side, like a dog, snorted wetly and stomped off in a forceful, bow-legged stride. "*Move now!*" it bellowed at someone else.

Dinah suddenly felt as if she could breathe again, and turned to thank the woman who had pulled her to safety, but there was no one there other than a wall of uncaring faces. The bustling crowd pressed in again behind the procession, like the sea rushing to fill the wake of a ship.

She found she was pushed forwards again, into the path of a few servants following the retinue and carrying an awning to shelter their masters. They were not important enough to warrant their own guard of snarling Carrlund warriors. They shoved her aside without as much as a glance, but she wasn't going to stand for that. Fully recovered from her fright but with her pride still smarting, Dinah let her fingers deftly turn up the hem of a rude lackey's jerkin as he pushed past, and slip a little purse of coins off his points.

The man turned and slapped a hand to his hip, but Dinah was already running as fast as her feet and her elbows allowed. "She robbed me!" the man wailed, in such a tone of hurt and surprise that Dinah had to chuckle.

But then a terrifying order rang out behind her. "*Shodzlug! Take two and fetch!*"

Once again the crowd shied away from her, and Dinah found herself exposed, as if she had turned into a snake. But she was the prey now, not the predator.

She didn't turn to see her pursuers. She pelted down the nearest alley at full stretch. Her sodden shoes slapped through the puddles of slush swamping uneven cobbles. Her thin coat flapped open, letting the cold tear at her belly. The icy air burned her lungs with every gasp. She ran like never before.

Behind, the three Carrlunds barked and snarled, loosened curs baying after a doe. They crashed into walls at every corner and knocked over anything in their way, stumbling and recovering on all fours as easily as they ran on two. They were horribly fast.

Dinah was faster. She turned left, then right, then left again into the narrow alleyways of the Old Town. She ran up steps, under arches, through courtyards. With every new direction she gained a little ground. She could still hear their panting breath not far behind, but they were just out of sight when she cast a glance over her shoulder.

Around one last corner, she tumbled to the ground and dived headlong through a low arch in a wall, merely a skylight for a cellar. She was scraped raw by the tight fit, but she was skinny enough to slide through in a flash. She landed on her hands and rolled with the grace of an acrobat. Her roll brought her instantly to her feet, and she ran into the deep, dark cellar. It was a broad area of low brick arches and columns, filled with stacks of barrels and dusty racks of bottles. Away from the skylight, it got very dark. With outstretched hands, she felt her way towards the far end of the cellar as quietly as possible.

The heavy boots of the three Carrlunds thundered past the skylight, making her leap into the murk behind a shadow-bound column. She stayed frozen for a moment, then wriggled her way between two huge, fat casks, each twice as tall as her even though they were lying on their sides on wooden cradles. She shuffled around in the narrow wedge of space between the casks as they abutted the wall and sat with her back pressed against the cold bricks.

Shivering with fear and exertion as well as the chill of her sleet-drenched clothes, she whispered, "Are they gone?"

A minute hand parted Dinah's curtain of lank hair and pushed aside the damp hood. A feminine figure, no taller than Dinah's hand was long, stepped out onto a trembling shoulder. With the appearance of this graceful form, a faint shimmer of summer from her almost naked body lit up Dinah's terrified face.

"I think so," the tiny creature whispered. She allowed her glow to increase and a suggestion of butterfly wings glittered behind her back.

"Are you *mad?*" hissed the other voice. A slender arm reached out with a gnarled hand and snatched the shining one back into the bower of hair. "You can't sense a Carrlund, you little fool!"

"Oww, that hurt! I can! And anyway, I would hear them if they were near."

"Hush! Oh, hush, you two. Not now ..." Dinah groaned.

Then she clapped a hand to her mouth.

For all it was far away, she had heard the faint snuffle outside the skylight. There was a jingle of ringmail and a scrape of boot on cobbles. Then the snuffling was louder, excited. Snarls and barks echoed around the cellar, and a frenzied scraping told of a Carrlund's efforts to squeeze through the narrow gap.

Dinah crushed her knees to her chest, shaking in terror. Her little voices quavered, trying to be brave: "They can't get in. We're safe in here. We're safe, Dinah."

The scraping at the skylight ceased and was replaced by a fearsome argument in the Carrlunds' appalling language, out in the lane. It sounded like a pack of dogs fighting, complete with barks, howls and squeals of pain.

Then came even more frightening sounds, much worse than anything before. There was an insistent hammering of fist on door, somewhere. An argument flared between human and Carrlund voices, then fell away. Before Dinah could draw breath, more hammering rang out but at a different door, nearer this time. A further angry exchange of snarled threats and shouts of protest echoed in the street. This time, the argument led to heavy feet clumping on wooden floorboards not far away and then straight overhead.

The snuffling and scratching at the skylight resumed, with the occasional rasping call. Dinah choked down a sob – that way out was covered and she knew of no other.

A door creaked open. She had no idea where it was, but it was close. She had never seen it in the darkness. She only knew of the skylight. Of course a cellar would have a door, she moaned inside. All cellars have doors. Heavy feet clomped down steps and scraped against the grit of the cellar's hard-packed floor. The glow of a lantern lightened the gloom of the vaulted space, giving shape to the barrels that concealed her.

A Carrlund snarled nearby, making her stiffen in fear. It answered a call from the skylight with an affirmative yelp and a cackle of hideous laughter. Another Carrlund scampered away to take up position under the skylight, cutting off all flight that way.

The one that had stayed outside now galloped across the wooden floor above to rejoin its brethren. Within moments, it clattered down the stairs and leapt into the cellar, snuffling madly and growling deep in its foul throat. The door slammed shut.

Trapped! Her stomach tightened into a knot, and her eyes stung with tears. She willed herself to melt into the bricks at her back. She held her breath and struggled not to throw up her meagre meal.

"Come out," a voice rasped. It was trying to be gentle, but the sound of it still tore through her flesh. "Come on out, missy. Master, he want talk you. No hurt. Just talk." The wet snuffling came ever closer, with a hunter's unerring skill. "Just talk, missy, but you come out – *now!*"

There was a cackle of snuffling laughter from the darkness at the other end of the cleft between the two casks. "Out now, missy," snarled a different Carrlund voice, drawling its words with cruel anticipation. "Or me comes in."

Dinah looked around frantically. There was nowhere to go! On either side her path was blocked by barrels stacked all the way up to the walls.

The beast was far too wide to squeeze between the casks the way she had. It snuffled at the space beneath them, between the cradles, but then decided there was more space between the girth of the casks and the vaulted ceiling. It scrambled up onto the casks and scratched forwards in the darkness.

"Come to Shodzlug quick, missy," chuckled the first Carrlund. "Ishrak won't gentle you. He nasssssssty."

Dinah flattened herself to the dusty floor, praying against all reason that the monster scrambling above would not be able to reach her.

She heard the cellar door smash open. A man's voice roared, and then another's. There was a clank, a whoosh and a thud, and Ishrak loosed an ear-splitting shriek of pain and rage. He spun on himself in the tight space, showering his prey with broken plaster and brick dust, and jumped free of the casks. Shodzlug smashed his lantern on the floor, bellowing a war cry. The Carrlund under the skylight did the same, and the men at the door answered in kind with a clash of weapons.

Dinah pulled her hood over her face and drove her fists into her ears. That was not enough.

There was an awful rumbling noise, and then the roar of more men's voices from the darkest corner of the cellar. The Carrlunds howled in desperate defiance. There was a scuffle in the darkness, dull thumps of heavy blows and bodies thrown against walls or barrels, a scraping struggle on the floor, grunts, snarls, a horrible ripping noise, a muffled scream, then the awful slicing noise of blades punched into flesh again and again. And again.

Then silence.

A few gasped breaths, a groaning in the darkness; then a man's deep voice boomed, "Get a light, you idiot!" And still no sound from the Carrlunds!

The flickering of a new lantern bloomed in the murk. A different man spoke. "Here, here we are. Ren! Are you hurt?"

A shuddering gasp, a voice strained with pain: "It's not deep, Mel. Lord, that one's strong!"

"Not any more, he ain't," replied Mel. "Oh, man! Not deep, you say? Don't move! I'll call a healer."

"No, there's no time," rumbled the first voice. "You sure no one saw them come in?"

"No one will ever say they did. We're all loyal in this street," Mel exclaimed. "These swine might have vanished, but never in my cellar. Look! See that mark? They are the Seneschal's own, just as I said."

"All well and good," grunted Ren. "Aren't we forgetting someone?"

"Oh yes," chuckled the man with the deep voice. "Where are our manners?" He took the lantern and held it high above the cleft between the casks. Dinah could see he was bearded and really big. "And it is a girl they were after, too. The shame! Here, missy, are you hurt? It's all right. Those three clawbags are dead now. You can come out. We're friends, I promise. Look, that's a purse I can see in your hand, isn't it? Is that why they chased you? That's all right. We pick pockets too, sometimes."

"A *purse!*" Ren half barked a laugh and half gasped in pain. "Has she gone and lifted the *Seneschal* himself? Give her a job, Gadda!"

"Hang on," mumbled Mel. "No one sets loose three Carrlunds just to nab a footpad, not even that bastard!"

"Oh! Mel, don't go looking for what's not there," groaned Gadda. "She's just got guts and quick fingers, this one. And I'm really sure she's good at keeping her mouth shut. Can you forget all that's happened, missy? And forget that you ever came here?"

"What?" gasped Mel. "You'd let her run off? Just like that?"

"Of course. Why not?"

There was something in that innocent question Dinah did not quite like. From where she lay she could not see the glance between Gadda and Mel, but the pause in Mel's reply chilled her.

"All right," said Mel.

Dinah shuffled to her feet. "It's just some flunky's coin," she muttered.

"Sure it is," Gadda replied. "You just be good and find your way out once we're gone, won't you, little one? We've got some tidying up to do, now. Mel, leave that door there open, will you?"

Dinah heaved her way between the casks into the glow of the lantern. There were five men there, all still gasping for air and stinking of sweat and blood. On one side there was great big Gadda, still holding the lantern aloft, and two other gruff men in rugged traveller's garb like him – one holding the other up, who from the blood soaking both legs of his trews had to be Ren. All still held short, bloodied swords. And on the other side stood a plump householder with a crossbow, who looked just right to be Mel, and a trembling servant with a spiked cudgel.

"Thank you," she whispered with a shy nod. "I'm sorry you got hurt, Ren."

"Part of the job," he coughed. "Get you gone, missy. Forget everything, yeah?"

Dinah cast a glance to the far end of the cellar. There was a narrow gap in the furthest wall, a section of brickwork swung out into the vaulted space. The flickering glow of a torch lit up a passage beyond.

"Not a word to anyone, I swear."

She made her way around the group towards the door, but froze at the sight of Shodzlug's twisted shape in a growing puddle of black, reeking blood, and of the two other Carrlunds, sprawled in their own deathly mires a pace or two away.

Mel and his man stepped forwards and grabbed a corpse each by the ankles to pull the bodies away to the secret passage. "Don't you go looking for things to nick on your way out," growled Mel as he passed by. "I've got servants on watch up there."

Gadda grabbed one more ankle, and nodded Dinah towards the door with a broad smile. She put a foot on the first step but then mouthed, "What do I do?"

"Well, I trust them," tinkled a delicate voice beneath the hood. "They trust us, don't they?"

"And I say be careful," hissed the other voice in the tangle of hair. "Be ever so careful with *him*."

Dinah spun around just as the men were squeezing into their hidden passageway. "Please, sir," she called out. "Wait!"

Gadda turned on the threshold, a satisfied smile briefly on his face. "What now, missy?"

She hesitated a moment, unsure of her next step. She did not like that smile. "Uh, have you ... something to eat?"

"I might just," he chuckled. "And dry clothes and a good warm fire, too. Come along if you want some of that. What's your name?"

"It's Dinah, sir."

"And how old might you be, Dinah?"

"Oh. Thirteen. Fourteen. Maybe."

"Well, Dinah. It seems you've got skills we can use. Quick fingers and quicker legs. Outrunning three Carrlunds is no mean feat. Lifting a warded purse from the Seneschal's own retinue is something else again. But hear me well. If you pass this doorway, you will make yourself one of my men and you will take my orders like a man. What says you?"

"Will you give me the help I need?"

"I look after my own. Look, let's strike a deal over food. Mel's boys have some mopping to do and mine some bodies to hide."

"Fair enough." Dinah marched up and stepped into a torch-lit tunnel of brick. Gadda pulled the pane of masonry shut behind him with a boom.

"You girls are completely mad," grumbled a little voice by Dinah's ear.

"Oh, lighten up!" chimed the other. "Where's your sense of adventure?"

A SAN JUAN MOMENT
BY RICHARD A. WENTWORTH

My hometown of Seattle is an outdoor paradise, if you do not mind the rain, for all to share. Up north, about 90 miles, is a place called Friday Harbor; a port town in the San Juan Island group that you can visit. Now, let us say you have rented a boat, or you own your own. You have decided to spend a few days in one of the many coves that are scattered in the area. A few minutes after you have set the anchor, and everything seems to be going fine. It's time to relax and enjoy with a beverage of your choice.

Water gently laps on the hull and solid planks of varnished teak squeak under your feet. You feel safe and secure on the boat. No phones to answer, no one to tell you that you have screwed up. The sun is warm on your back as you sip your drink. The water is a smooth mirrored surface; the gentle rock of the boat sets you at ease.

A slow rolling swell of two feet lifts the boat up every thirty seconds. Not a hard, dropping feeling, but a fluid motion of up and down... up and down... settles into your bones. In time, this feeling will be lost to you; you will not notice it again, until, the first thirty minutes or so when walking on dry land.

The kids have gone ashore on the tree-filled island to gather supplies and visit with some old friends who have travelled with you. Your spouse and you are standing on the deck, enjoying the view. You have anchored in a horseshoe cove that protects the boat from rough seas. The setting is peaceful and serene; the stress of the work week is slipping away. Trees on the island sway in the gentle breeze. A light wind ruffles your hair and a cry from an eagle reaches your ears.

However, there is no television on board. You look up and lo-and-behold, a live eagle is flying overhead.

You wonder how it would feel to be an eagle. You watch as the eagle glides gently along. So free... no worries at all, a smorgasbord of food is available to you and snacks, too, run on the island. Big old fish cruise below the water's surface. You tilt your head back and then extend your arms and watch the eagle soar along. Your body sways as the eagle turns. Your left arm dips down; your right arm comes up. You try to mirror the eagle's image. Your body turns weightless and you are soaring next to the eagle.

Your eyes are now closed. Miles upon miles of azure seas are stretching before you. Fish are in the water and whatever you need on land, a silent strike and it's dinner time. You look down and see some bozo on a small boat with its arms stretched out, head back and eyes closed. Yep! A real loser, you think.

As you start to really relax and enjoy the moment. A big whoosh of air startles you. Your hands come together; you turn to this new sound. And out of the water, cutting like a knife, a tip of one fin is seen. Your first thought is... Shark! However, the fin is black and growing. Now, its one foot out of the water, slicing with power. Two foot and still growing... Four foot of fin now... Nevertheless, the fin is still growing. Until, finally, all six-foot of black, with some odd shapes of white, dorsal fin has grown out of the water.

A big black body is attached to this fin. It glides past in slow motion. Black with white spots. "What the...?" you say to the dark shape. Until, you realize what you are seeing. Killer whale... orca... assassins of the sea... and, they have surrounded your boat. You are in awe, no danger to you or the boat, you realize. Your feet have riveted in place. You stare in amazement as the whale slowly goes past.

The urge to jump in and swim with the whales crosses your mind. But, of course, that is not possible. Yes, it would be nice to swim with them. But they could tear you into a million pieces in a few seconds. What is left of your body would sink to the bottom: crabs, lobsters and shrimps would have their sweet revenge. You are not the orca's choice of food, but an intruder into their world. Yet, the urge is still there.

In a flash, the whales are gone. As you look around you see your spouse.

"This was a great idea," you say. Your spouse has a goofy grin and stares at you with glazed over eyes. A slow nod of the head and the moment is broken. Then; you reach for your drink, looking for more sights to see. A nagging voice in your head reminds you that in a short while you will have to rejoin the rat race again. But the sights quickly drown out that voice, with the gentle rock of the boat you sip at your drink, and relax into a comfortable chair.

A World of Their Own

Illustration by Evelinn Enoksen

CROW'S GOLD
BY E. R. ENOKSEN

The night was so quiet one could hear one's own heartbeat, like the sound of someone's footsteps crunching through snow. On such an evening, a flock of crows perched on the metalsmith's leaky roof. They huddled together against the cold, their bellies filled with leftover gruel generously given by the smith himself. A feast for a bird, yet hardly anything for a man – but the smith had always been kind and shared what little he had.

The city was a vast forest of chimneys and towers, walls of brick and stone and plaster. In its midst stood a grand palace, tall and dominating, shadowing the other miserable looking buildings like a king feeding off its subjects.

The crows pressed themselves against the bricks of the chimney, still warm even with the forge out. The sun slowly rose and cast its rays on the tiled roofs all around: orange and red, brown and mossy green. The city came alive and the streets below turned into a river of people flowing to do their early morning tasks.

The crows took off with a smack of their wings and circled, hunting for a breakfast morsel. People waved and shouted, threw rocks and curses at the black birds. Soon they returned to their perch on the roof, some with a catch, others with nothing.

"I bet you can't snatch that shiny red apple off the cart down there," one crow said to another. The two of them peaked over the drainpipe.

"Oh, but I'm sure I can." The other answered confidently and ruffled its feathers. It fixed the fruit in its sights and swooped down. The vendor was quick to raise his broom and flail it at the bird, but the crow was clever and agile in the air. It stuck its beak into the apple and hopped along the cobbled road. The corpulent vendor struggled to catch up, but the bird was simply too light on its claws. After a while, it returned to the roof victorious and gloated to its feathered companions.

"I bet you can't steal the pie out of that man's hand." The same crow asked, squawking with laughter at the impossible task. They all looked down at the street again, where a man was walking and eating a small meat pie. "Oh, but I'm sure I can." The crow let itself glide from the edge; wind rushing past its body, like a caress. The unsuspecting man called out as his breakfast was stolen from his hand. Again, the crow returned to the roof with its catch, and the others cocked their heads in astonishment.

More people filled the street as a procession made its way through the throng. Four strong men carried a palanquin surrounded by guards, and curious town folk tried desperately to get a glimpse of the one within. They stopped outside the smithy and a wealthy-looking woman stepped out. She glittered with gold and silks and diamonds.

"I bet you can't take the queen's ring," said the crow haughtily, thinking it had found an unachievable mission at last. The people made a crowd around the palanquin; their clapping and hollering and gasps could be heard all the way to the roof.

The queen's ring sparkled alluringly in the sunlight. "Oh, but I'm sure I can," said the crow, though not as convincingly as before. The gold ring had a blue gem the size of an acorn. It glimmered and beckoned its beauty, and the crow knew it had to have it, but this theft needed a little more planning. Therefore, the bird scanned the street and everything in it, noting every detail until a plan formed in its mind.

The butcher across the street stood leaning on his cart, watching intently as the queen made her way to an outhouse in the alley. Laughter floated up from the crowd, along with a few crude remarks such as "Nature calls to all, even the Queen, eh?" There was a barrel full of plums beside the butcher's cart, and the queen's guards were staring vacantly at the gathering of onlookers.

A chance like this would not come again; the crow thought as it flew down to the portly butcher and pecked him on his bald head. Alarmed, he stepped away from the cart so that it tipped the barrel over, strewing plums in the street. The barrel rolled and knocked the queen off her dainty feet; she landed in a gutter, a sprawled heap of silks and lace and jewels. Spotting the opportunity, the crow homed in on the flailing hand with the sparkling ring.

An echoing shriek came as the ring was pulled from her finger, and the guards were alerted to the flutter of black wings. They grabbed after the crow, but the bird was still too quick and clever for the clumsy hands of humans.

As the crow returned to the metalsmith's roof, its companions were stunned to silence by the successful theft. The quiet did not last long, however, as angry shouts drew the attention of the crows back to the street. The queen was ordering her guards to shoot the bird with the ring in its beak.

Bows were strung and arrows were pointed at the flock of birds. As the arrows flew, the crows settled on the chimney, blocked from view by the drainpipe and tiles.

"A hundred gold pieces to the one who brings back my ring," the queen shouted, her shrill voice carrying far. The sounds of desperate scrambling and clawing came from the brick wall, and the crow with the ring felt too curious to hide. It flew up to inspect the scene. The people in the street were milling about in a frenzy, all trying to get up onto the smith's roof.

The crow returned to the chimney. The forge was still not lit, but the smith would be shovelling the coal soon.

"There it is!" One of the guards had managed to climb the wall and was peeking over the rim. "The payment will be mine!" His gaze was firmly fixed on the gold ring as he heaved himself up on the edge. Another hopeful soul was about to reach for the drainpipe, but the guard kicked him and sent him plummeting to the street.

Sweat glistened on the guard's strained face as he scrambled towards the chimney. "Come here little birdie," he said, carefully climbing closer. "Give me the ring, and I won't kill you." But his eyes said something else.

The crow waited until the man was only an inch away; then it dropped the ring down the chimney. The look of utter horror on the guard's face was worth more than any amount of gold.

"No!" The guard shouted and the crow took off and landed on the butcher's roof across the street. After a moment, the smith came out of his house and gave the crowd a befuddling look. In his hand, he held the queen's gold ring, its blue gem glittering in the light.

Illustration by Hazel Butler

MEANINGLESS KISS
BY KAY KAUFFMAN

Grace stared blankly at the antique lanterns suspended from the ceiling of the Weathered Wheel. *They fit the decor perfectly,* she thought as images of ancient miners sprang to mind. She let her eyes wander over the adjacent wall and noticed that the giant wagon wheel was already wrapped in garlands. *Somebody's looking forward to Christmas,* she mused.

Christmas. Now there was a thought. Christmas used to be Grace's favorite holiday, but now it mattered little thanks to too many bad memories. She shook her head to clear her thoughts and turned her attention back to her lunch. But the bowl of chili no longer appealed to her and she pushed it away, sighing as she fumbled through her purse in search of enough money to pay the tab. She left a couple fives on the table and rose to leave, bumping into a man in a black coat.

"Ow!" he exclaimed.

"Oh, I'm sorry," she apologized. "Are you okay?"

"Yeah, I'm fine," he replied, turning. "Grace?"

"Patrick?" Grace's blood ran cold.

He smiled, but it seemed forced. "It's been a while," he said, pulling her into a hug. "If I'd known you were here, I'd have joined you. How've you been?"

"Fine. Just…fine," she replied. "What are you doing here?"

"I just came to visit an old friend," he replied.

Grace knew him well enough to know that his nonchalance was feigned. "I see," she said, wondering why her heart was suddenly hammering away in her chest. "I didn't realize you still had friends in Yellow Lake."

"I sure do," he said. "We go way back and haven't seen each other in ages. Since I had the day off, I thought a surprise visit might be fun."

"Well, then, I don't want to keep you," she said. "I'll see you around. Have fun with your friend."

"Actually," Patrick said as she turned to leave, "I came to see you. I've missed you, Grace."

She turned. "You…what?"

"I've missed you, Grace," he repeated. "I miss you. We never hang out anymore. I miss that."

Her eyes narrowed. "Maybe you should have thought about that the last time we hung out. But I suppose you've forgotten all about that."

"Look, I had nothing to do with that mistletoe…"

"Well you had everything to do with what happened under it." Grace stared at him for a long moment as an awkward silence filled the air. "I have to go," she muttered, heading toward the door. "I'm gonna be late."

"Grace, wait!" Patrick called, running to catch up with her. "Wait!"

"I have nothing to say to you," she said as he caught her arm and spun her around. "And I'm not interested in anything you have to say to me."

"It was just a meaningless kiss – it meant nothing," he insisted.

Something in his eyes told her that he didn't really believe what he was saying, which only made her angrier. She brushed his hand off her arm. "It was not a meaningless kiss, Patrick. A kiss on the cheek? That's a meaningless kiss. What you did was so far removed from the realm of meaninglessness that I don't even know where to begin!"

"Look, I was drunk, and you knew that. Why are you so upset?"

"Because you can't just kiss someone like that and then pretend it never happened! There was meaning in that kiss, Patrick. Everything is different now."

"Grace –"

"And you know what? Drunkenness is no excuse. If you can't –"

Suddenly she was kissing him. Or was he kissing her and she was simply kissing him back? Grace had no idea and she wasn't sure she wanted to.

Patrick pulled her closer, unable to stop himself. He had been longing for this since that night at the Christmas party last year. That was when he first realized how much he loved her, and that he always had.

Grace pulled back, studying him for a long moment. "Patrick, what…what just happened?"

"Grace, I –" His voice cracked as he took her hand. "I love you. I always have."

"But you…you never said anything. Ever. Why now?"

Patrick pulled her close again and she didn't stop him. Resisting him was the last thing she wanted to do, but she wasn't ready to let him know that. Yet.

"Look, I didn't know what I was doing at that party," he began, "but once I started kissing you, I didn't want to stop. I was confused, and then you got so angry…I know I didn't handle it as well as I could have, but not seeing you for a year has made me realize what an idiot I was. I love you, Grace. That's all there is to it."

89

She brushed a tear away as it ran down her cheek. "I felt like such a fool."

He pulled back and brushed another tear from her cheek. "What? Why?"

"Because when you kissed me, I was so excited – I've been in love with you since we were twelve. But then you blew it off as nothing, like I meant nothing. And you did it again just now. I felt like you were making fun of me, then and now, and I can't handle that. Not from you."

As she spoke, Patrick felt a pain in his chest unlike anything he'd ever experienced before; it took his breath away. "Why didn't you tell me?"

She shrugged. "You know me better than anyone in the world – I thought you would understand. I was wrong."

"So this is what it feels like," he murmured.

"What?"

"My heart…I think it's breaking."

"Patrick –"

He put a finger to her lips. "I'm so sorry, Grace. I never meant to hurt you. I just hope that one day, you can forgive me."

"Patrick, I…" She sighed. "I've missed you, too. Nothing's been right without you to talk to." She let him wrap his arms around her again and rested her head on his chest. *I could stay like this forever*, she thought.

Suddenly, she pulled away, leveling an accusing finger at him. "But if you ever –"

"Don't worry." Patrick laughed, squeezing her arms. "Nothing like that will ever happen again, I promise."

Grace snuggled closer. "Good."

DRAGONS OF TERRA
BY J. C. RUTLEDGE

Once upon a time, there were as many dragons roaming the land as there were horses in the stables or cattle in the fields. They flew free as any bird and never bothered anyone.

Each dragon lived for centuries and so a gathering of dragons was a rare thing indeed. But when it did happen, the spectacle was breathtaking.

There were four kinds of dragons, as there are four elements in nature: earth, air, fire and water. Each dragon moved and looked like the piece of creation it emulated.

The earth dragons were gigantic, dark and slow-moving monsters. They slept most of their lives, resting their huge bodies between mountains or in deep seas, forming small islands. When they did move, they caused earthquakes for leagues in every direction. Though they slept more than they were awake, their memories went back to the beginning of time.

The air dragons rarely touched the ground. They were as light and agile in the air as a fish is in the water. Their acrobatics on a sunny day could stir up gales that lasted for weeks. They loved to wander the globe, looking down on the world's activities. They saw all and told all.

The fire dragons leapt and dashed across fields and trees with such speed that they sometimes caused fires. Yet the dragons being gentle creatures, their fire always went around any other living creature, only consuming that which could be recovered. Crops, buildings and forests all came to ashes. This was why the very faithful preached the wisdom of the fire dragons: they knew what was truly important. Life cannot be replaced. Material things can.

The water dragons possessed stunning grace of motion. On land they flowed over all, smooth as a river over polished marble. In the air, they swirled and skittered like raindrops caught in eddies of wind. They alone among all the dragons were social creatures. When they gathered together, the rainstorms lasted longer than the air dragons' gales.

The last gathering of dragons took place a thousand years ago and was called by the eldest of the earth dragons, a creature so old that not even one of the other earth dragons knew her name. She was simply called Terra.

Terra had woken after a two and a half thousand year sleep and looked around. The world had changed. No longer was it a simple place where every creature lived and died according to the unspoken and unwritten laws of nature; rather, it was a chaotic world where one animal ruled supreme over the rest.

When Terra had gone to sleep they had been little more than hairy, chattering creatures, hanging about in trees. Now they dominated, killing without regret or need, ignoring the laws of nature and bending the world around them to their will.

Terra saw all this and wept great tears, large enough to water many, many fields. She then let out a great howl of pain that shook the world. To every corner of the globe the cry echoed. Every dragon heard the call and came: lumbering, swooping, flashing and rippling to Terra's aid.

The old one spoke.

"My Fellows of Sacred Four," she said, turning to acknowledge each group. "My kin of the earth. My sisters of the air. My brothers of the fire. My children of the water. Our home is in crisis."

Terra went on to tell of the horrors she had seen: how the creatures were wreaking havoc over the once peaceful land, sea and sky, and how they had harnessed the power of fire to do their bidding.

The dragons then looked around them and noticed, for the first time, what they had been too busy to see in their centuries of life. They were all saddened and angered by what they saw.

"Burn them!" cried the fire dragons.

"Crush them!" bellowed the earth dragons.

"Drown them!" growled the water dragons.

"Blow them from the world!" wailed the air dragons.

Terra just shook her head in sadness. She knew her race could never bring themselves to harm a living soul. "No. All hope is lost. We will leave this world and find another."

One young water dragon came forward, crouching low out of respect for Terra. He, though young, had the enduring hope of his kind: the eternal faith that anything is possible, given enough time, just as a steady dripping of water on rock can change the shape of that rock forever.

"No," said the young water dragon. "Let us not abandon hope. Let us rest and wait. Let us return to the places we first sprang from and wait. Perhaps someday the world will be ready to accept us back, when peace has returned."

And so all the dragons went their separate ways: the earth welcoming the largest as mountains, air enveloping the lightest as clouds, fire taking the swiftest in its dancing heat and water unifying as it has done since the beginning of time.

The dragons wait to this day. They were born of this earth and though they are not visible, they know what goes on in the world. They wait for a time when the peace of nature will return.

And though no one has seen a dragon in a thousand years, they are still here and you can see them, if you try.

In the majestic arch of a mountain's back, in the graceful shapes of the clouds, in the leaping flames of a fire and in the depths of the sea.

They are waiting.

DESTINY'S GAME
BY VALERIE WILLIS

I think I am losing my mind.

"Angela?" Jessica looked back at me with those large hazel eyes, her red hair bouncing in its ponytail. "You ok? You don't look so well. And you're suddenly so quiet."

"Yeah, I'm – I'm fine." I just couldn't talk to her about it. She would think I was crazy. If I told anyone about it, they would think I was insane. "Sorry, I know I promised to stay here and hang out with you in line, but …"

"It's ok." She smiled as she patted the top of my black, wavy head of hair. "I'm almost to the front now for the concert tickets. You've been here all day as it is. Go home. You are looking paler by the moment, Angie."

"Thanks," I breathed as I ducked under the rope. "I'll call you later."

"Take a nap!"

With a wave, I was gone.

I couldn't believe it was becoming more frequent. It was annoying in my dreams, but lately this was making me question my sanity. He was there. The suave guy in my dreams was in the reflection at the store, in my rearview mirror this morning and just now. No! He is someone I have made up. He was in every dream and maybe my stress was making him show up. That's it. Stress and lack of sleep can make you see things. Dream while I'm awake, *right?*

Frustrated, I pulled a lock of hair out of my mouth. Winter was bad this year, or at least painfully windy in the last month. My car was barely hanging in there, and praying, I begged for it to turn on. Reluctantly it sputtered to life, and I desperately wished the heat would kick in faster. Homeward bound and I needed to get some sleep. Eagerly I clunked it in reverse.

"Ack!" Startled, I saw him in the rearview mirror, smiling at me from the backseat. "What on earth is wrong with me?" Looking into my backseat, I saw nothing.

He was unmistakably handsome. A pretty-boy face, smug smile, dark, mid-length hair and the palest blue eyes I had ever seen. I had seen him so much in dreams I could tell you all about him. He was a bit of an ass, sarcastic but a pristine body of muscle. If he were real, I would hate him and crush over him in one fell swoop.

Exasperated, I continued to focus on my drive home on the icy roads. I hated driving in the snow and ice. I should really think about moving down south some place. Florida, maybe Texas?

The light turned green. I pulled away with the rest of the traffic, but failed to see that a pickup had slipped on the ice at the red light to my immediate right. It was happening so fast. My car was spinning; I could hear metal banging and the screeching of sliding tires. *Someone save me! I'm going to die here!* All I could picture was the lake, and I didn't know which direction I was spinning, or if someone was going to hit … another hit and now I knew I was headed towards the lake. *Oh no! Nonononono!* I could see it out of the driver-side window. The car tilted and was now picking up speed down the slope.

"Not on my watch." Strong hands gripped me, and I felt myself pulled out of the passenger-side door. *What's happening? Wasn't I wearing a seat belt?* The shock was somehow making the events feel surreal to me as I rolled there violently on the slope. Snow flew about, yet there was something warm hugging me tightly. "Snap out of it, Angela!"

"What just happened?" I was afraid to move as I lay on top of my warm mountain. *I must be bleeding out. They say blood is warm to the touch. I've been impaled!* "I'm bleeding out! I'm dying!"

"Ugh!" Slamming face first in the snow was quite the wakeup call. "Get off of me. You're heavy."

That voice – I know it. It can't be ... "You?" I rolled in the snow and faced the squatting figure. "You're not real."

"Oh ... I'm not real, huh?" There was that smug smile and chortle. I hated it. "I should have let you go swimming with your car, then."

"Oh my god!" A hysterical woman came over the hillside. "Are you ok?"

"I, I think so." I sat up in the snow, staring at him, as he stood up rubbing the back of his neck. "Well, I don't know."

"It's either you're ok or you're not. It's not that hard to figure out." Scoffing at me, he started walking up the hill. "Geez."

"I don't think I am feeling well at all." Tears were welling up as the woman knelt next to me, looking over and searching me for injury.

"You're so lucky, young lady!" The plump, red-cheeked elderly woman helped me to my feet, and we walked up the hill behind him. "That was quick thinking of your friend there! Pulling you out in time like that!"

"Wait, what did you say?" Jerking to a stop, I looked her in the eyes. "Say that again?"

"That young man up there –" he waved as she pointed at him – "yanked the both of you out on the passenger side! I would've never thought to do that! You two would have been in the lake for sure!"

Sirens were growing louder as I stumbled my way to the top of the hill. The old woman was talking, but I couldn't hear her. I was busy staring at *him* in disbelief. *He is real? I must be in a coma. That's it. I'm in a coma in the hospital. This is all a dream.* "I'm dreaming."

"Poor thing, she's in shock." The old woman rubbed my back tenderly. "Is she going to be ok?"

"Yeah." He lifted an eyebrow at me and shrugged. "To be honest she's usually like this. Then again, I may have bumped her head on the way out of the car."

"Oh! At least you made it out of the car!"

Blackness swallowed me as I fainted there in the snow. I think I may have slid down the hill a few feet before someone grabbed my ankle. I do remember feeling the cold, icy snow again on my back, though.

"Angela? You may want to wake up, honey." *No, you're not real.*

"What's her name?" *Who is that?*

"Angela Diaz." *That was* him *again. He's* not real. *Don't listen to him.* "She's in a lot of shock. You got anything good over there in that bin? She's going to need something strong. Maybe something that'll leave her feeling … oh, let's just say happier."

"Um, and who are you?" *Happier? Bah!* "What relation are you?"

"I'm her boyfriend, of course." *No! No! You are not! You're an imaginary … thing!* "Michael Kevington. I pulled her out of the car."

"The old lady was telling us about that – quick thinking there." *Michael. What kind of name is* that? "The hospital is just around the corner. She's stable, but hopefully this'll make her feel better. She'll be calmer at least."

"Yeah! There we go." *Ugh, he's laughing, and* touching *my arm!* "Don't worry, Angela baby! You're going to be feeling better in just a minute, doll!"

"Oh, Ms. Diaz!" The paramedic looked at me excitedly as I jerked my arm out of *Michael*'s hand. "You are in an ambulance.

You are headed to the hospital, so we can check you and your boyfriend for further injuries."

"Michael." For some reason I was smiling and my cheeks were getting warm. "I don't like you any more."

"I know, sweetie." Snatching my hand up and patting it, he rolled his eyes at me. "Just rest."

"But you're not –"

He put his fingers to my smiling lips and started shushing me.

"Rest, Angie, you're in shock, honey-bun." His jaw was tight, teeth clenched nervously. I simply started giggling. "What's wrong with you?"

"You said give her the strong stuff." The paramedic frowned as I once more fell back into my black and silent sleep.

"Come on, I need you to wake up." It was *Michael* again. "Things are a little worse than I thought. They're here looking for you – time to leave. Wake up!"

Schmack! My left cheek came alive as it tingled with burning pain. "Ouch!"

"That's a girl. Come on. I have to get you out of here before he figures out where you are!" He was pulling me out of the bed; my IV was tugging at my arm.

"Wait, where am I?"

"Ugh, now's not the time." He jerked the IV from my arm, and I screamed. "Come on, you can scream later."

"You! You tore out my IV!" I was clutching my bleeding left arm as he continued to pull me to my feet, shoving me out of the door. "What the hell!"

"That truck hitting you was no accident after all." I couldn't decide which hurt more: my cheek, my arm or the heel of his hand digging into my backside. "He's figured out where you are. I can't let them get you. I won't let them take you from me."

"What on earth is going on? Who are you, exactly? And who is after me?" I was almost running down the halls through crowds of people who seemed to take no notice of us at all. "I don't know anything! I don't even know why someone would want to kill me. And why does no one notice us?"

"Quick. In here." He pulled a door open and shoved me in. "I need to cover your arm. He'll be able to track us with it bleeding like that."

"You pulled my IV out!" Prying my hand off the blood-smudged arm, he put his own over it. "How is *that* supposed to help? I was already doing that!"

"Just calm down, you have no idea what kind of trouble you're in and no clue what I am." The pain was gone, but my temper was still fuming. "I'll take care of it. I just need a minute to figure out where we are going."

"I must be insane. My imaginary nightmare friend guy is real and causing me issues." Looking about in the dark room, I could see we were standing in an X-ray viewing room. "Are you going to explain to me what's going on at all?"

"Yes. I will." His tone was cold as steel, and his eyes sent shivers across my skin as he caught my own in them. "Listen to me very carefully, Angela. Your soul is a very special one. You are an Archangel who was hurt, near death. In order to heal you, we had to send your soul into a state of rest. You've been healing for a very long time, from mortal to mortal. This was going to be your last round before being reborn a true Archangel again. Unfortunately, Yang caught on to it. You can think of him as sort of something like what you would consider the Antichrist. Right now, in this hospital, his lap dog Deo is looking for you. I have to get you out of here as quickly as I can. Once safe, I can get you someplace more secure."

"Archangel?" He removed his hand from my arm, revealing there was no trace of the IV wound or the blood that had stained the spot. "Who are you?"

"Michael, I already told you." My legs felt like Jell-O as my knees knocked into each other. "Let's get out of this place while we still have a chance."

"Michael, as in ..." I couldn't bring myself to say it as he pulled me along through the hospital. "I'm dreaming, right? This is another one of those bizarre dreams that features you, right? A nightmare, that's right, just a nightmare."

"What a pain." Growling as we neared the exit, he grabbed someone's jacket and covered me in it. "Could you just not mentally shut down on me for once? And for the love of God, don't faint again."

"Hey! Where do you think you're taking that?" A British accent was screaming down the hall behind me. "Yang wants her as a guest for his tea party!"

"Shit." Michael whipped around, gracefully pulling me behind hlm, putting himself in the way of the shouting man. "Deo, back off. You already know you're no match for the likes of me."

"Well, look who it is!" Whistling as he approached was a rather tall man with short burnt-red hair and yellow eyes. "My, my, my! If I had known it was going to be you here I would have invited the others."

"Listen carefully, Angela. When he attacks, run. I will find you but get as far from here as possible. Our fight doesn't do anything to the people and places around us, but with you, it's different. You can get hurt." His pale blue eyes shot me a look of warning that burnt its message well. "Deo, don't tell me you're going to try me again. Last time you went home with your tail tucked between your legs."

"Oh, I will always give you a try." Deo's ears were growing pointier and fangs were showing themselves. "It's always good to measure up how much I have improved against a celebrity like you."

"What is he?" I was stepping back in fear. This *Deo* was transforming into what looked like a real-life werewolf: red fur, yellow eyes and massive. "This can't be happening."

"Run." My legs carried me off against my will at Michael's command.

All I could hear was a huge bang as I burst through the doors. The snow was excruciatingly cold on my bare feet as I continued to increase the distance between me and the hospital. I haphazardly crossed the street, somehow not getting hit, and worked my way down a sidewalk. I had no idea where I was, still baffled from my car accident and with no sense of time. Turning randomly down an alleyway, losing my breath, I finally gave in to my aching lungs. I leaned on my knees as I caught my breath, watching the steam as it rolled out from my mouth. Shivering took over as I slid to the ground, cold and still in a state of shock.

Have I lost my mind? Did I just escape a hospital or a mental institute? 'But when I stared down at the hospital gown under the coat, it became very clear that this was really happening: blood drops stained the fabric, and even my hand was smudged from where I had clenched my arm. All I could hear was Michael's voice repeatedly in my head: *Your soul is a very special one. You are an Archangel.*

"Goodness. You're a mess." My heart could have jumped out of my chest as a soft male voice came from the alleyway entrance. "Michael, what have you done to the poor child?"

"Who – who are you?" He was tall and smiling, his long, stark white hair blowing in the frosty breeze. "How do you know Michael?"

"Oh, forgive me. I am Gabriel. I am here to take you to your new home." I shied away from him as he leaned down, offering me his hand. "Dear child, I am not here to harm you."

"Am I –" I started crying hysterically. I was a complete wreck of confusion and panic. "Am I *dead*?"

"Oh, no! No, you're not. That's not why I'm here!" He shook his hands and head, taking a step back. "I suppose that's when most see me! I am so sorry for that! Oh, how dreadful of me! Moreover, what I was saying must have sounded! Oh, dear me!"

"But you're Gabriel, an Archangel, the reaper?" I swallowed as the cold stung and ached around me when the breeze blew past. "Why do you want me?"

"Oh, boy." He looked up to the sky for a moment before returning his silvery eyes to me. "If it makes you feel any better we can wait for Michael, but let's at least get you into someplace warm first. Is that ok with you, Angela?"

"Ok." I was so cold; I couldn't pass the chance to warm back up. "But how do you know my name?"

"Well, I am the reaper, after all." His jolly laugh only made things more awkward. "Come. There is a tiny diner across the way. I have some warmer clothes for you. He shouldn't be much longer with Deo."

"How do you know so much?" My bare feet were joyous at the feel of the warm tiles. "Were you following us?"

"Not quite. We angels have our ways of knowing and exchanging information when needed. It's almost an instinctual reaction – here." I grabbed the book bag, clinging to it as tears fell down my face. "No rush, dear. I'll be out here with a hot caramel latte. That's what you like, right?"

I only responded with a wail as I cried myself to the bathroom. This was all wrong. I would never be able to live a normal life. My dull life filled with work, school and friends now had no chance of surviving this onslaught of insanity. As I dressed in warmer, drier clothes, I mulled things over. *The man in all my dreams was Michael, Archangel Michael. He pulled me from my car and is now dragging me through a living nightmare. Now, just outside this bathroom door is Gabriel, another Archangel. Who seems excessively happy to be the messenger of death. Worse, he's sitting out there with a drink for me. Am I here doing this? Is this all real?*

I rinsed my hands and face with warm water, staring at my paling skin in the mirror. There was too much here for it to be made up or a figment of my imagination. My cheek was still red from where Michael had slapped me awake. Then there was Deo, a massive werewolf demon, hunting me down, wanting to take me away to his leader. What kind of mess was I in? Taking a deep breath, I managed to gather my last nerve and left the security of the bathroom. Sitting at the booth with Gabriel was now Michael – the only somewhat familiar person in this whole crazy mess.

"There she is!" Michael stood up, offering for me to slide into the booth next to him. "Sit down, warm up. I don't need you fainting. You're doing so well!"

"I hate you." I could have spat on him as I slid on the leather seat and turned my focus to the hot, welcoming beverage waiting on me. "I hate you, and I hate what you've done to me."

"Oh, my." Gabriel's smile faded as concern took its place on his face. "What on earth have you done to her, Michael?"

"Nothing." Scoffing, he looked away. "I've saved her life twice now. So much for appreciation."

"Saved my life! Yes, from the car accident but after that, it's been torture! Slapping me, ripping my IV from my arm and shoving me about like a rag doll! What is there to appreciate in that?" Finally my body was warming up, unfortunately thanks to a newfound sense of anger. "You're ruthless and have no sense of how to keep a situation calm!"

"You were the one that wasn't calm and yelling! And you're still yelling!" Jerking up from the booth, he slammed the diner door open and walked out of view, leaving me fuming and speechless. I huffed and turned to my drink.

"Oh, dear. No wonder you were such a mess." Gabriel sighed, his face softened as another gentle smile came across it. "May I apologize for him?"

"No." I hunched over the latte as if it were a small, cozy fire. "He can apologize if he wants to."

"Dear me, he's not so good at that." He looked up once more; a moment later he continued. "You must understand this whole ordeal has left him heartbroken. Archangels are normally not easily swayed, especially Michael. He loves you very much. Well, er, I think I said too much. Forget it."

"Heartbroken?" I took a sip of the silky caramel latte and stared at the nervous eyes of my diner compadre. "What is the story behind me? If my soul was an Archangel – well, is one – what happened?"

"I really think Michael should tell you." Sighing once more, he looked out into the snowy street. "But considering the trouble we're in, I will share with you a short telling of it. You and Michael were in battle with a horde of demons. Normally this wouldn't be much of a challenge or threat."

"Michael and me?" I couldn't help but shiver. "Fighting?"

"Yes. It was fine up until Yang and some of his cohorts showed. It was a trap or just an opportunity. We still don't know." His jaw muscles twitched. "But he thought he'd lost you forever. You went down when Yang and Karrie came at you and, like skilled assassins, cut you down in the heat of the horde. Michael nearly went too far. A few others and I showed in time. We were able to tell that broken angel that his – that you were still alive and that there was a chance to heal you."

"How long ago was this?" My latte was quickly vanishing as I listened.

"I can't say. We don't keep track of time the same as you do here. Considering it now, though, it has been a very, very long time. I believe the Renaissance was in full bloom when we sent your soul here." I choked on my latte, coughing and sputtering. "Are you ok?"

"Fine." I coughed and gasped as I continued to clear out my drink from my lungs. "I'm fine!"

"Here." I startled as another latte slid over to me and a jacket was placed over my back. "Thought you would want something more than a shirt for when we head out."

"When did you come back in?" Michael was sitting next to me. I hadn't seen, heard or felt him return. "I must be crazy."

"I was worried someone was telling you a fairy tale." Gabriel shrugged at him, smiling softly. "He wasn't there. He has no idea what it was like."

"You can just sneak in on people like that?" I was still fighting back the choking sensation. "I didn't hear or see you or anything."

"It's something we can do." Gabriel looked to his fellow angel. "If you have her for now, Michael, I will leave you two alone." And with his final words, Gabriel instantly vanished.

"No sparkles or anything, just gone." I stared at where he had sat. "Not even a dent from where he was sitting."

"Hurry up. I want to give you a chance to say your goodbyes and finish business here before I take you home." Michael was no longer sarcastic, but stiff and stern. "It is going to take some getting used to."

"Take me home?" It wasn't sounding very good for me. "As in a new home?"

"It technically is your *old* home."

THE PORTRAIT
BY WILL MACMILLAN JONES

The portrait hung in the window of an art gallery in the arcade. Every day, on my commuter's journey to and from the office, I walked through the arcade and its selection of tiny exotic shops. As the arcade was narrow, and roofed with curved glass for natural light, the reflections of the passers-by merged with the reflections of the goods on sale in the various windows. Sometimes I had fun with the curved glass, making silly faces that bounced backwards and forwards across the street from shop window to shop window. Other shoppers would snigger at me, but I sometimes caught them doing the same, and then we would share a smile.

Whenever I reached the art gallery, I would stop and peer at the portrait of a young girl. She was pictured in the first flush of her beauty, a sweet smile on her lips, her head lowered slightly so that she seemed almost to peer upwards through her auburn hair. Her dress swelled and flowed, and when the light twisted, to me, she seemed almost to move.

The label below the frame said simply 'Portrait of a girl', with no artist listed. I did go into the shop to enquire, but the price – well, let's just say it would take me a long time to earn that much money, let alone spend it on a painting by an unknown artist, however captivating. For it was captivating, at least to me. Every time I passed the window, I was drawn to gaze upon her face, and sometimes missed my train home through spending so long before the window. Almost it felt as if we were engaged in some wordless

107

communication; though forever voiceless, she spoke directly to my soul, and stirred emotions I did not know I possessed.

I found after some time that I could not walk back to the station without passing the gallery and lingering before the window. If I tried, I felt uneasy, insecure, and when I finally arrived home I had no appetite and slept indifferently, with disturbing dreams. When next I would see her, I could imagine that her face creased with the hint of a frown. Once I stayed away for two days, and on the third I could have imagined the suspicion of a tear, sparkling like morning dew, in the corner of her eye. What artist could have painted such perfection? I knew not. Then, next time, her tear was gone, and in the shifting, shimmering light reflected from the curved glass of the arcade roof, I caught a glimpse of her smile of welcome in the eternal stillness.

At last I decided I must break this spell, and stayed away from the arcade for a week. A whole week – it felt like a lifetime. Then one night, following a very long day in the office, I was hurrying to catch the last train home. A violent storm raged across the heavens, the rain and wind battering the glass of the arcade, as I followed the damp footsteps of the last hurrying commuter. Would she still be there, in the window? It was inconceivable to me that anyone would have bought her portrait, yet it was beyond belief that no wealthy passer-by would have seen her; that she would not have been purchased by some moneyed connoisseur to hang enigmatically above a richly laden table, forever a guest and yet never to dine.

Rounding the corner within the arcade, I glimpsed a shrouded figure ahead of me. The previous commuter, whose wet footsteps I dogged so relentlessly now. He – I entertained no other thought – shrugged off his wet and dripping overcoat, and paused. My footsteps echoed in that eerie, empty arcade; he moved against the window of the gallery, and seemed to shimmer. Panting, I followed the footprints that led towards the glass – and stopped beside the discarded coat. The footprints led through the glass, and I shook to see the girl gaze adoringly into the eyes of her lover. 'Portrait of a couple' read the label.

LOST TIME MEMORY
BY SAM DOGRA

Leon hunched into his coat as he walked up the frosted hillside. The cold gnawed through his trainers and he shivered, wishing he hadn't left his thermal socks at home. But he needed to do this quickly, before the rest of the household found out he wasn't there.

Clenching his fists, he looked towards the castle. It had overlooked the town for five hundred years, and still people whispered it was haunted. After the incident last year, in which a woman had mysteriously disappeared, nobody visited– though that didn't put Leon off. In fact, it was *because* of its reputation he was heading there.

He reached the main gate. Through the rime-studded bars, the keep loomed, naked without its covering of ivy. As barren and empty as always; just the way Leon needed it.

Vaulting over the scarred metal, he entered the courtyard. It looked so different in winter, the cracked paving glistening with ice. He took a cautious step further when a flutter caught his ear, and he looked skywards. Almost at once he spotted the red flag dangling from the keep's highest window.

Leon frowned. That hadn't been there last summer. Had the Renovators come, despite their bid rejection from the council? He doubted it. They wanted to turn the place into a tourist site. Hanging a flag was hardly something such a powerful company would do. Still, better to be cautious. Getting caught wasn't an option.

A wispy breath left Leon's lips, and he rubbed his hands together. He was actually glad of the council's decision to protect the site. The castle was his safe haven in the summer, and surviving the long school holiday when everyone was home would've been impossible without it.

Nonetheless, in the middle of an icy February, the keep was by no means an ideal place for his...*act*. But his old hideout in the warehouse district had been discovered, and he couldn't go back. If he was caught with the Fae Dust– or worse, if his parents found out he was using...

He clutched the tin in his pocket. He should never have listened to Carl. *He* hadn't touched the stuff, despite being so well-informed about its effects and so eager to watch Leon test the waters. *He* was happily at home, with nothing to hide from his father or his sister, and not forced to crawl about like a criminal. *He* hadn't taken the first step to destroying his hopes, his future. His life.

Yet the alternative was unthinkable. Once before Leon had tried to come off, but the memory of the pain ensured he never tried again. Nobody escaped the claw of the Fae, and he, at only sixteen years, was already trapped in its clutches.

A sharp wind set the flag fluttering again. Leon stared, mesmerised, until the breeze dropped and the flag fell limp. He turned away and scoffed. Who cared about a stupid flag?

Sudden rustling caught his ear, and he spun around. Blood pulsing, he scoured the keep's annex. A train of breath was coming between the ruined walls. Leon tensed, ready to bolt, but then the misted breath moved to reveal a shaggy fox. They exchanged a long glance, before the fox shook itself and slunk away.

Leon scowled. He was dawdling—he needed to find a place to hide for half an hour. Easier said than done, for with all the ice, he'd freeze long before his recovery phase.

He walked straight for his summertime haven: a bleak corridor that ran around the back of the keep, hidden by bushes and shrubs.

As he neared, a twinge surged across his forehead and he winced. The withdrawal was coming. He'd have fifteen minutes or so before the convulsions started. Swallowing, he jogged to the passage, almost skidding on the ice.

When he arrived, his heart sank. Dead branches blocked the entrance, and the corridor was buried in frost. Swearing, Leon returned to the courtyard to look for a better hideaway.

No such luck. Every passageway was too open, too cold. High above the flag mocked him, guarding a single window. Leon frowned. The window was much smaller than the doorways down here. Maybe the winter hadn't penetrated as far in the upper rooms, and he'd be more sheltered there.

He drew his coat closer and stepped to the tower of rubble that lined the keep's wall. The stairways had fallen long ago; this was the only way up. Warming his hands with his breath, Leon began to climb. He had to grit his teeth; it was like scaling a glacier. From brick to brick he went, pausing at intervals to get the blood flowing to his fingers again. All the while the flag beckoned, a fiery beacon in a sea of grey.

Finally, Leon reached the window. The light didn't penetrate far, but inside he couldn't see any hoary glisten. It would have to do. Balancing precariously on the bricks, Leon braced one hand against the wall and used the other to grab the windowsill.

Burning pain singed his fingers, and he yelled. He snatched his hand back, clinging to the flagpole to stop himself falling. The ground was suddenly a lot further away than he'd realised. *Shit*, he thought. He needed to get down.

As he made to release the flag, he hesitated. It was strangely warm, and soothed his numb fingers. An idea came to him. He could use it to keep the cold away and get the time he needed. Maybe it wasn't so stupid to have come up here.

Leon tugged at the velvet. It didn't budge. He brought his other hand from the wall and yanked harder. The flag slid a little, then snapped back to the pole's hilt. Leon jerked forwards. His foot skidded, and he lost his balance.

He fell sideways across the rubble and hit the keep. The bricks shifted and Leon clawed at the wall, stopping himself sliding all the way to the bottom. Breathing hard, he sat there, trembling. Had his body listed in any other direction, he would've smacked headfirst into the ground.

Swallowing, Leon gathered his nerves and slowly descended. It wasn't soon enough when he came to solid ground again. He dusted his hands, looking to the scrape on his elbow. It was bleeding. He pulled a tissue from his pocket and dabbed at it, wincing.

The moment he touched the wound, butterflies stirred in his belly.

"Not yet," Leon muttered. Sweat began to seep into his T-shirt. "Damn it, not yet!"

He staggered across the courtyard. Too late to worry about the cold; he'd have to crawl into a ruin and hope for the best. Dragging his legs over the icy ground, Leon hobbled for the keep's hallway. As he neared, soft whimpering caught his ear.

Was someone crying?

Great, Leon thought. The hallucinations had started, too. Ignoring the muffled sobs, he hauled himself inside the dark space.

"Who's there?" a voice whispered.

Leon jumped. His eyes darted about the shadows, but he couldn't see anything besides rubble.

"Not real," he said. He was about to take another step when he heard a girl's scream.

"No, don't come in here!"

Leon blinked. "Huh?"

"I-I said, don't come in here," the voice repeated. She sounded around his age. "Please. You mustn't see me."

Leon blinked. He'd had hallucinations when coming off before, but none had ever spoken back like this.

"I...I can't stay outside," he said, trying not to feel stupid for talking to something that might not be there. A sudden thought occurred to him, and his eyes widened. "Are you a user, too?"

"A what?"

Leon frowned. She seemed unfamiliar with the term.

"It doesn't matter," he said. "Look, if I promise not to look at you, will you let me in? It's an emergency."

A long pause followed.

"I'm sorry," the girl said at last. "I don't mean to sound so selfish. As long as you don't look, that should be all right."

Breathing a sigh of relief, Leon scrambled inside and collapsed into a hollow of rubble. With jittery hands, he fished out his tin and opened it. He dabbed his thumb into the sparkling powder, then licked the sweet dust.

At once his shaking ceased. Leon closed his eyes, waiting for the Fae's magic to kick in. He would gain supernatural abilities, like the fabled heroes of the Old Tales. That was the lure of Fae Dust. A while ago it had even been standard issue in the Brigade, for it turned the lankiest soldiers into unbeatable warriors.

That was before they'd discovered the 'aftershock'– when the Dust wore off. The ravaging pain, the uncontrollable fits, the vivid hallucinations: all thundered through at once, tearing mind and body apart. No-one had been known to endure for long, for the longer the period of abstinence, the worse the symptoms became. And the only known cure was death.

So Leon had to face the same torment, day after day after day. All because he'd taken that single dose for a stupid dare...

"What's your name?"

Leon jumped. He'd forgotten about the girl.

"It's Leon," he said, then bit his tongue. Idiot; he should've given a fake name. She could've been an agent for the Brigade. Then again, he'd just taken Dust right in front of her and she hadn't made a move. Maybe she was waiting to catch him off guard.

"I like that name," the girl said. "Named after the Royal Lion, are you?"

"Probably," Leon answered, raising an eyebrow. What was she talking about? There hadn't been a royal family since the castle had fallen into ruin.

"You must be," the girl went on. "Only the bravest would venture here."

"Or the stupidest," Leon muttered, rubbing the graze on his elbow. The bleeding had stopped, but it still stung. The girl laughed. Leon's cheeks flushed. "So, er, what's your name?"

"My name is Ruby."

"Ruby," Leon repeated. He managed a smile. "Nice. My sister's called Sapphire."

Ruby sighed.

"It used to be tradition for the daughters of the royal line to be named after the jewels set in the crown," she said. "But my mother gave me this name in spite of my lowly birth."

Leon raised an eyebrow. The way she spoke– it was weird. She seemed so...so...*old-fashioned*. Yet she didn't sound much older than he was. Perhaps it wasn't that surprising. There'd been a good theatre run of one of the Old Tales this month, and it wasn't unusual for the archaic dialogues to persist in the teen hubs.

The thought of hanging out with friends made Leon's stomach knot. Some friends they were, leaving him in this mess. Not one of them had spoken to him since. It was as if they couldn't stand to be near him, as if he'd become tainted . That wasn't far from the truth, but the effects of Fae Dust weren't contagious in that sense.

"What are you thinking about?"

Leon made to turn, but quickly snapped his head forward. She'd asked him not to look.

"Sorry?"

"You seem quite thoughtful."

114

"Oh, it's nothing," Leon said, slumping against the bricks. His arm twitched, and he bit his lip. The reloading fit would start soon. That was the other thing about Fae Dust– even if you took it to avoid the aftershock, every dose came with reloading symptoms. They only lasted a few minutes, but if they caught you off guard, they could cause serious injury. Hence why Leon wanted a place to minimise the chance of hurting himself. This hallway wasn't great– too many sharp edges– but if he curled up and protected his head with his scarf, the damage would be bearable.

"What's wrong?"

"Just a bit unwell," Leon said, rolling onto his side and wrapping his scarf around his head. "I'll be fine in a few minutes."

"Are you sure? Maybe I can…"

"You asked me not to look at you. Could you do the same for me, for a little bit?"

"O-of course."

Leon's arm seized with cramp, and he gritted his teeth. He wouldn't scream like last time. His neck ached, wanting to turn to one side, but it was blocked by the stone floor. Dull throbbing pounded behind his eyes, and he screwed them tight. *Get on with it*, he thought, clutching his knees to his chest. The quicker the fit got rolling, the sooner it would be over.

Surprisingly, that seemed to be the worst of it. The pain slowly vanished and the tightness in his muscles eased. His neck stopped trying to fight his head and shoulders, and he lay there in a quiet daze.

"Are you all right?"

Leon pushed himself upright and rubbed his forehead. Thank God it had been a mild reloader today. Not like last time.

"Fine." His vision came back into focus, and for a second he thought he saw the hem of a dress, but it passed. He took in a slow breath. The deed was done. He could go home and pretend he'd been out for a walk.

"I'm glad."

Leon hesitated. Heat rose in his cheeks, and he tucked his scarf beneath his collar.

"Um, thanks." Her words were soothing, touching a part of his heart he'd locked deep inside. A sudden tightness welled in his throat. How badly he wanted to spill everything to her: the constant secrecy, the lying to his family, the crimes he'd had to commit just to get enough Fae Dust to see him through the month. Someone, anyone, to share this burden with.

But he knew he couldn't. He couldn't trust anyone. It'd only lead to trouble. Sighing, he thrust his tin into his pocket and crawled to his feet.

"You're leaving?" Ruby sounded disappointed.

"Got to get home," Leon said, straightening himself out. As he fastened his buttons, the echo of the church bell reached his ears. "Damn, it's that late?"

He was making for the door when Ruby asked, "Will you come and talk with me again?"

Leon stopped in the doorway. That was an odd request. Maybe she really was trying to get his guard down. But what choice did he have? Tomorrow he'd need another dose, and there was no other place to hide safely. And somewhere deep down, in a place he'd shielded away, he felt he could trust her.

"Yeah, I can do that," he said. "Sorry, I've really got to go now."

"I understand." The girl sighed. "I look forward to seeing you again tomorrow."

Leon shrugged as nonchalantly as he could, glad his back was turned. Otherwise Ruby might've noticed a blush on his cheeks that wasn't due to the cold.

It was already dark when Leon returned to the castle the next day. Sapphire had seen his grazed elbow and drowned him in questions, threatening to tell their father, too. Fortunately she'd then left for riding training, allowing Leon to escape. Still, his father would be home within the hour. He'd have to make this quick.

He found the frosted hallway and stepped inside, armed with a tatty blanket. Even if yesterday's reloading fit had been mild, he didn't know what today's would be like.

"Ruby?" His voice echoed in the silence. A brittle wind played through the hall as if to question his presence. He continued to wait, but the girl from the day before didn't answer. His face clouded. *Knew it*, he thought angrily. It *was* a hallucination. He threw his blanket down and sat on it, prizing his tin open, then licking the residue off his finger.

The magic took hold, and he took a deep breath. He was bursting to do something, like run up a wall or climb the keep again, but he knew better than to leave his hiding place. In the warehouse it had been easier to burn his energy. He used to practise throwing copper pipes. Once, he'd managed to lob one the entire length of the building, through a window and over the adjoining rooftops, where it skidded down a fire escape and smashed into a Renovator's car. That had been deeply satisfying, for it was shortly after they'd announced their bid for the castle. They never did find out what caused the accident.

"I'm sorry, Leon. I didn't mean to be so late."

Leon vaulted to his feet, taking up a fighting stance. It probably looked impressive, but it made Ruby giggle.

"Did I scare you?" she asked.

"O-of course not," Leon said, sinking onto his blanket. He folded his scarf over his face, hiding his blush. Silence descended, and he licked his lips. *Say something.* "Er, so, how are things?"

"I'm all right," Ruby said. "Better than yesterday."

Leon nodded. "You were crying, weren't you?"

"Yes," Ruby murmured. "I didn't realise you could hear it. I was just so lonely."

From the corner of his eye, Leon caught a glimpse of a pale hand. He fought the urge to turn.

"I know the feeling," he said, fixing his gaze onto the ceiling. "Everything's twice as hard when you've got no-one to share it with."

Another silence, though this was more peaceful than awkward. Leon's eyes never strayed, but he could feel Ruby watching him. It wasn't a feeling he disliked.

"It seems you're no stranger to pains of the heart," she said.

Leon managed a wry smile. "You're probably the only person who talks to me besides my family." He clenched his fist. "No-one looks my way anymore, not since...since I started using. Not even those I once called 'friend'." He had to stop himself thumping his hand on the ground– he'd shatter the slabs. "I've got nobody to turn to but myself."

"How awful," Ruby said.

"*They* were the ones who started me off in the first place!" Leon's temper got the better of him. "Stupid losers, all of them. Abandoning me like a piece of meat!" He wrapped his arms around his legs.

"It hurts to be left alone," Ruby said quietly. "I was separated from my love, all because others couldn't understand the bond we shared. He was the prince; it was unforgivable for him to be with a commoner like me. I was taken from him, and I was powerless to change my fate."

Leon lifted his head. There she went again, talking about some prince and a royal line. Yet despite his scepticism, he sensed the torment behind her words– emotions not easily faked.

"That's harsh," he said, deciding to play along. "What happened to him?"

"I heard he looked for me for a time," Ruby answered. "Yet the years passed and he never found me. Eventually he gave up and disappeared. He has to be long dead by now."

Leon frowned. Her story was getting weirder and weirder. If it had been years since their separation, why did Ruby still sound so young? Either she was a good actor or it had really happened. He still hadn't seen her. Maybe she was older than he thought.

"Ruby, just how old…"

His question caught in his throat and he clutched his chest, unable to breathe. His neck flung backwards and his spine arched painfully. His head glossed the stone on his right before it was thrust forwards onto his chest. His body twisted into a heap, and he pinned his left leg down as it tried to kick the rubble.

"Leon, what's wrong?" Ruby's voice was panicked. "What's happening?"

Leon couldn't answer. His back went into spasm again and he cracked his head against the wall. Moist warmth trickled down to his collarbone, accompanied by stinging pain. Coloured spots flashed before his eyes; hoarse moans flew from his throat. The foul taste of burning rubber filled his mouth, and saliva dribbled from his lips.

Something cool and gentle touched his brow. The tightness in his back and legs eased, and he muttered gibberish. His whole body felt drained and sleepy.

"I know this," Ruby whispered. "This is Fae magic, poisonous to humans. I can help you. Try to sleep."

Leon fought to open his eyes. He couldn't do that. If he fell asleep here, he'd freeze to death. His father would find the house empty and start snooping. It would all be over.

"Can't," he croaked, making to sit up, but pressure on his chest stopped him.

"Just for a few minutes," Ruby said. "I promise I'll keep you safe."

Leon continued to struggle. He couldn't let this happen. He barely knew the girl– she could have no end of things planned for him. Capturing a Fae addict was worth a hefty price to the Brigade. The drug alone was worth thousands. Perhaps that had been Ruby's plot all along.

Icy gentleness stroked his cheek, and his eyes closed. The darkness soothed the pain, and he fell further into the abyss.

No! Stay awake, you idiot!

"Please rest." Ruby's breath lingered at his ear. "I don't like to see you hurting. It will only be for a moment. Let me help you."

The last of Leon's strength left him, and he passed out.

"Leon, are you awake?"

Leon's eyes slowly opened. Dried blood caked the side of his neck, and his head throbbed. It must've been a bad reloader this time. As his vision came into focus, he thought he saw a ghostly hand on his arm. It soon disappeared, though, and he blinked.

"Yes," he murmured, grasping at the rubble to help himself sit up. At least his arms and legs were under his control again.

"Thank heavens," Ruby sighed. "The Fae's magic is dangerous– you mustn't use it like this."

A blush crept onto Leon's cheeks. It seemed she *did* know about Dust.

"I can't help it– I have to," he said. "It'll be even worse if I don't take it."

"Is that why you come here?" Ruby asked. "To keep this pain from your family?"

Leon bowed his head.

"They'd kill me if they found out," he said quietly. "And I'd get arrested."

"I see," Ruby murmured. "I'm sorry."

"Don't be," Leon said. "Just… just don't tell anyone about this, okay?"

"I won't, Leon."

Wincing, Leon leant against the rubble and checked himself over. The cut on his forehead was sore, but aside from some scratches and muscle strains, he hadn't injured anything else. He tried to stand up, but pain shot through his legs and he sank down. He needed to rest a bit before he could go home.

"You know, I think I may be able to help you," Ruby said suddenly.

"Oh?"

"My mother taught me a protection spell against the Fae," she answered. "It might be enough to remove their magic from you."

Leon scoffed.

"Ruby, I know you mean well, but there's no cure for this," he asserted. "Especially when…"

Abruptly footsteps echoed from the hall, and Leon tensed.

"Ruby!" It was a man's voice. "My lady, where are you?"

Leon's blood ran cold. Was this a trap after all? He couldn't be discovered! He grabbed the wall and tried to stand again, but he collapsed to his knees. His heart burned with bitterness. She'd been planning this, stringing him along, waiting until he was too weak to escape…

"Leon, it's all right. Cervantes will do you no harm," Ruby said. Leon felt her cold touch on his shoulder, soft and soothing. He wished so deeply he could see her face. "But I need to go. Will I see you again tomorrow?"

Leon wanted to refuse, but that familiar warmth in his chest told him otherwise. No matter what his mind thought, his heart knew he had to return.

"Yes," he said at last.

"Good." Ruby's hand left him, and he listened to her drifting footsteps. She stopped a short distance away, still within earshot. "My apologies, Cervantes. I didn't realise the time."

"My lady, you mustn't remain here," the man's voice warned. "The Queen is watching! Come back upstairs, quickly now."

"At once, Cervantes," Ruby replied.

Then there was silence. Leon sighed, rubbing his eyes. He had to be losing his mind. In fact, he would've put everything down to pure hallucination if she hadn't gone and *touched* him. It was an odd sensation, too, without warmth or pressure– just a gentle coolness, like a spring stream. And it had definitely helped ease the fit.

The church bell gonged, and Leon swore. His father would be home. Picking himself off the floor, he grabbed the blanket and hurried out into the open. He wrapped his scarf around his head, hoping to disguise the cut. Tin snug in his pocket, Leon ran through the main gate and down the hill.

He never noticed the amethyst eyes watching from the keep window.

It was very late the following evening when Leon hiked up the hillside again. His parents had seen his injuries and tried to stop him, thinking he was doing some reckless stunts with friends. It was only thanks to a lot of pleading and favour-swapping with Sapphire he'd managed to get out of the house at all.

As he headed back to the hallway, he clutched a single rose. He wanted to thank Ruby for helping him with his reloading fit, and since it was almost Valentine's Day, he felt it was a suitable gift. He hoped she would trust him enough to let him see her now.

"Leon, I'm here."

Leon stopped at the keep entrance. Ruby's voice had come from behind him. He turned around, and gasped. Ruby was standing beside the castle gate, her body bathed in moonlight. As he'd suspected, she was around his age. She was a little shorter than him, with soft features and long brown hair. She wore a simple white dress, and her eyes were deep maroon, like her namesake.

Leon continued to stare, mouth agape. Ruby swept her hair back and walked over to him. Quickly Leon broke his gaze, cheeks burning.

"H-hi," he stammered.

Ruby smiled.

"When you didn't come on time, I feared you'd met trouble," she explained. "So I kept a lookout for you."

"That's...um...you didn't have to." Leon seemed to have forgotten how to speak. A thorn from the rose pinched him, and he winced. Get it together! "Oh, I, um, I brought this for you." He swallowed, fighting back nerves. "To...to say thanks."

Ruby glanced at the flower. For a moment her eyes danced, but they soon became downcast.

"It's very beautiful," she acknowledged. "But I can't accept it."

"Why not?" Leon asked.

Ruby turned away. "I...I just can't."

"Of course you can!" Leon reached for her hand. Ruby tried to step back, but she was too slow. Leon's fingers passed straight through hers, and he froze. Ruby gasped, holding her hand to her chest. Her eyes filled with tears.

"I...I shouldn't have come out," she whispered. She ran back towards the passage, sobbing.

"Ruby, wait!" Leon cried, rushing after her. He was buzzing with questions. His hand had passed straight through hers...was she a ghost? But then why didn't she look translucent?

Or was this all a hallucination, conjured by his lonely heart?

The moment he reached the hallway, his questions ceased; his mouth was pooling with saliva. Groaning, Leon crouched on the floor, knowing what was coming. Bile soured his mouth and he spat it out, forcing himself to take deep breaths. He'd left it too late. He needed to take the Dust, now.

He fumbled for his tin, hands shaking. It slipped from his sweaty fingers into the rubble. Swearing, he dived after it. It was stuck between the bricks. The blood drained from his face.

No, please, no!

In desperation he reached again. It was just too far, and the more he groped around, the further he pushed it between the stones. The nausea became overwhelming, and his head began to spin.

"Ruby…" he croaked. "Please, come back…"

The wind moaned through the cracks of the passage. Leon closed his eyes, trembling, the sweat pouring off his face. The pain in his side intensified, and he began writhing. His cheeks flushed with fever and his vision grew blurry.

Help…me…

Coolness suddenly wafted over his back, and he stilled. The pain remained, but not as raw, countered by the gentle cold. He managed to open his eyes, and was greeted by darkness. Soft light glowed behind him; he turned his head slightly. Ruby was kneeling beside him, stroking his side.

"Ruby," Leon whispered.

"I'm sorry, Leon," Ruby answered. "I…I couldn't bear to see you in such pain. I will try and remove some of the Fae's magic from you."

Leon sighed. How could someone he barely knew care more about him than the friends he'd known for years?

Gradually, his shaking subsided. When it became bearable, he left Ruby and crawled to the pile of rubble. He tossed aside the stones until at last the tin came in sight. He pulled it into his hands, and moments later he was licking the dust off his finger. He sighed, resting back against the stone floor. That had been a close one.

He stared at the ceiling, able to process his thoughts again.

"Why did you run from me?" he asked.

Ruby remained quiet. Leon ran a hand through his hair. "Look, I'm sorry I reacted like that. I…I wasn't expecting…"

"A ghost?" Ruby finished.

"Um, yeah," Leon mumbled. He rolled onto his side so he was facing her. Ruby placed her hands in her lap, averting her gaze. "Is that what you are?"

Ruby closed her eyes.

"I'm not sure myself," she said at last. "It's a long story."

Leon sat up. "I'm listening."

"I'm part of the castle's curse."

"Curse?"

"It all began when the prince and I fell in love." Ruby's eyes grew distant. "I was only a maidservant, but I spent a lot of time with him, and he returned my feelings. But his mother despised our relationship. The prince decided we should run away and be together, but the Queen discovered our plan." She paused and took a breath. "She was a powerful mage, and declared she would make my spirit eternal so I would be forced to watch my love grow old and die, and we could never be together. The prince tried to free me, but he was too late. Everyone in the castle at the time– the servants, even the Queen herself– were transformed into spirits, and so here we remain, forever bound to these ancient walls."

"So you've been here all this time?"

Ruby nodded, her eyes streaming with tears. "It's been five hundred years. My prince is long dead, yet still the Queen watches, hiding me from outsiders, continuing my sentence of loneliness. I will never be free again."

Leon's mind reeled. He'd never heard of this curse before. But his heart filled with disappointment. Despite the short time he'd known Ruby, he'd grown to like her, and it hurt to realise he could never touch or see her outside the castle. Bringing the rose was the worst thing he could've done.

"I'm so sorry," he said, lost for words. "I didn't know."

"It was my fault," Ruby answered. "I didn't realise you could see me. If the Queen finds out about you…"

Leon shook his head. "No, I'm glad I heard you crying, so I could talk to you. I just wish…" He let out a breath, looking at his tin. "I wish things could be different. For both of us."

Ruby simply nodded.

"Let me try again," she said. "I'm certain I can take the rest of the Fae's magic away from you."

Leon sighed. She'd definitely done something to his addiction; she'd soothed away a lot of his symptoms, and he hadn't even had a reloading fit this time. Not unheard of, but rare enough. Besides, he had nothing to lose and everything to gain.

"All right, what do you need to do?"

"Lie down and close your eyes."

Leon settled back down on the ground again. As he made to close his eyes, though, the passage began to rumble. Yelping, Leon sat up and braced against the wall. *So much for not having a reloader…*

"Leon, I'm sorry, you must go!" Ruby cried.

"What?" Leon glanced to the passageway.

"Leave the castle, now! The Queen is coming!"

Ruby made to push him, and Leon felt the prickling cold of her fingers against his chest. Their eyes met briefly, and he nodded at her unspoken question.

"I'll come back," he said. "I promise!"

He raced into the freezing night. The gate was right ahead of him, but as he approached, he heard Ruby scream. He stopped dead and turned back.

Ruby was lying on the frosted ground, her eyes closed, while another woman in a cloak stood above her. Her black hair contrasted with her amethyst eyes, and Leon shivered. She reached down, grasping Ruby's arm, and twisted. Ruby moaned.

"Stop that!" Leon roared, running back towards them. "Let her go!"

The woman paused and looked up.

"Ah, so you're the one she's been pining for," she said. "I see now. You see us because you bear my blood."

"What are you talking about?"

The woman laughed.

"I do not have to answer you, child," she stated. "You have no business here. Leave."

"Ruby doesn't deserve to be punished like this!" Leon retorted. Courage he'd never known swelled in his chest, and he growled. "The man she loved, your son– he's dead! You got what you wanted, now release her already!"

The woman's eyes narrowed. Before she could answer, Ruby murmured and opened her eyes.

"Leon…" she whispered. "Forget me…the Queen…will…"

Leon made to rush to her, but the Queen blocked his path.

"Why do you care for this wretched nothing?" she snapped, throwing Ruby behind her. "Eternal loneliness is her punishment!"

Leon stood his ground.

"She's my friend!" he shouted. "Leave her alone!"

The Queen sneered. "Foolish child, you hold an empty sentiment. You may feel affection for her now, but you will age and rot and die like my son, while she remains tied here. You will only break her heart further." She raised her hand. "Forget that you ever came here, boy."

Leon felt his arms and legs twitch as if a seizure were starting. He tried to resist, but already his feet were marching towards the gate.

"No– Ruby!" he yelled. Against his will, his legs carried him past the gate and down the hill.

When he reached the bottom he fell over, the magic gone. Snarling, he jumped to his feet and tore back up to the keep. He didn't care how late it was getting.

He reached the castle again, panting. All he could find was his abandoned rose in the rubble.

"Ruby!" He frantically searched the keep hallway, calling her name, but there was no trace of her or the Queen. A tear escaped him, and his shoulders sagged. He was too late.

Ruby…

"Sir Leon?"

Leon whirled round. A short, portly man stood before him: the servant who had warned Ruby the previous evening.

"Sorry," Cervantes said, bowing. "I didn't mean to startle you."

"Where is she?" Leon blurted. "What's the Queen going to do to her?"

Cervantes sighed. "I cannot take you to her now." He wrung his hands. "But if you return on tomorrow's eve, there may be a way to save her. Save us all, and let this castle rest in peace."

Leon blinked. "What? How?"

"I cannot explain now." Cervantes' body started to fade. Leon grasped at his arm, but as it had with Ruby, his hand passed through. "Just return…on tomorrow's eve…"

The servant vanished and Leon was left alone. He stared at the castle flag, his fist clenched.

I'll come back for you, Ruby.

Unfortunately, Leon's luck had finally run out. On his return home, he found his parents awake and waiting. They immediately shut him in his room. They hadn't found the silver tin of Dust, but Leon's castle visits had aroused their suspicions enough. He tried to explain, begging and pleading for freedom, but they ignored him. Then exhaustion took over and he fell asleep.

Now, with the morning sun boring through his eyelids, he rose from his curled position on the floor and renewed his assault on the door.

"Let me out!" he cried. He hammered and hammered till his fists were raw– and then, at last, he heard a response.

"You're not coming out until you've learned your lesson," his father's stern voice called. "We told you not to go back to the castle, and you deliberately disobeyed us!"

"Dad, I'm sorry!" Leon wailed. "I didn't mean to upset you!"

"Yet you went ahead and ignored us anyway!" his father rumbled. "You've been acting strangely these last few days, always trying to slip off in the evenings. Just what are you hiding, Leon?"

"I'm not hiding anything, I swear!"

"Son, we can do this the easy way or the hard way," his father answered. "Tell me the truth and I might let you out sooner."

"I told you the truth already!" Leon screeched. His father's timing couldn't have been worse. He needed to get back to the castle tonight or he might never see Ruby again.

"Then accept your punishment!" his father shot back. "You can have your freedom when you go back to school on Monday."

"No!" Leon kicked his door. "Let me *out*!"

His cry was met with silence. His father had gone downstairs. Closing his eyes, he sank against the door and buried his face in his hands. Poor Ruby. He should've done more to help her. If he hadn't been so late yesterday, maybe the Queen wouldn't have discovered them. Wouldn't have taken her away from him.

Eventually his back began to hurt, so he went to lie on his bed. He didn't want to think what would happen if he didn't get his Fae Dust in the evening. He'd hidden the tin in its usual spot in the garden, but if he was stuck in his room, he had no means to get it. And if anyone caught him, he'd be facing a worse punishment than this by far.

The daytime hours slipped by. Midday became early afternoon, then early evening turned late. His mother came up to offer him dinner, but he refused, too dejected to care for hunger. The aftershock would be coming soon, and he'd be on the floor, helpless. His parents would come to check on him, and then...

A knock sounded on his door.

"Leon?" It was Sapphire. "Leon, can I talk to you?"

Leon pulled his pillow over his face.

"No," he mumbled.

"I found something in the garden."

Leon's breath caught in his throat. He scrambled off his bed and pressed his ear to the door.

"Put it back," he ordered. "Now."

His answer was his door lock clicking. His door opened and Sapphire was there, in her pyjamas. But she wasn't holding anything. Before Leon could say as much, Sapphire pushed him further into his room. She might've been younger, but her gymnastics made her very strong. She stepped inside and pressed her back to the door, closing it.

"I thought that would get your attention," she said, smirking.

"Saph, this isn't a joke!" Leon grabbed her arm, but she twisted out of reach and pinned him against his bookshelf.

"I want to know the truth," she said.

Leon swallowed. Maybe she *had* found the tin. "What truth?"

Sapphire rolled her eyes.

"I saw you carrying a rose yesterday," she said. "You've been seeing someone at the castle, haven't you? That's why you've been going off every night."

Leon froze."Um, well, I…"

Sapphire pulled a face. "I don't know why boys have to hide stuff like this. Are you too embarrassed?"

"No way!" Leon snarled. "But…it's complicated."

"I guessed as much," Sapphire said. She tapped him on the nose. Leon scowled, irked his younger sister could bully him so much. "She must be really missing you right now." She bent close to his ear. "So, I'll unlock your door tonight and let you see her. And you can do my weekend chores for the next two months."

"All right, all right!" Leon mumbled. "Just don't tell Mum or Dad."

"Deal!" Sapphire winked. She let go of Leon, then slipped out of the door and relocked it.

Leon walked over to his window, feeling hopeful again. He didn't care what price Sapphire demanded, as long as he could return to the castle tonight. Ruby had spent five centuries suffering with loneliness; she deserved her peace.

And he was going to give it to her, no matter what.

Sapphire was true to her promise, but it was almost midnight by the time Leon reached the castle. He'd taken a long time to get to his tin in the garden, thanks to a severe chest pain and dead leg, but now he'd taken his dose and endured his reloading fit, he felt ready for anything.

He entered the castle grounds and wandered around the rubble. His rose remained where he'd left it, its petals black with frostbite.

Looking up, he spotted the flag; a strange light came from the window above it.

Movement on the ground caught his eye, and he glanced to the hallway. Empty. Leon frowned. He crept closer, his breath fogging the air.

"Sir Leon?"

Leon spun around, bracing his fists. The short, fat figure of Cervantes stood before him, dressed in rags. Leon lowered his arms, and the servant smiled. "At last, you've come! I feared you would not make it."

"Sorry I'm late," Leon apologised. "I'm here now."

"Indeed," Cervantes said. "You are our only hope of ending these centuries of pain. Follow me."

Cervantes drifted inside the keep, and Leon walked after him. He had to pick his way through the frosted debris. Eventually they came to the remains of the main stairs. Cervantes paused, and Leon watched. Slowly, golden light began to gather over the ruins. It settled on the lowest step and then spread upwards, forming a translucent staircase. Cervantes clapped his hands, while Leon gasped.

"I hoped this would happen," Cervantes said, beaming. "You must have royal blood in your veins."

"Why?" Leon asked.

"Only the royal line could command magic like this," Cervantes answered.

"But I'm not…"

"You want to save Ruby, don't you?" Cervantes cut him off. "That desire is enough. That's why you heard her crying, why you are able to see us at all. The Queen's spell keeps us hidden, but your power is equal to hers and broke through her illusion. So only you can break the curse." He gestured to the magical staircase. "Traverse these steps and find the flag that hangs outside. It is the source of the spell. You must destroy it."

"Okay," Leon said, "but can't I just climb outside and reach it that way?"

Cervantes shook his head."You cannot just remove the flag," he said. "You need to cut it with a special dagger."

"And where can I find that?"

"The Queen keeps it on her person."

"What?" Leon exclaimed. "Then there's no way…"

"You have the greatest chance against her," Cervantes said. "As I said, you have capacity for magic, too. You can defeat her." He bowed his head. "At the very least you can try. Let Ruby and the castle rest in peace."

Leon nodded. Although he wanted to keep seeing Ruby, and although she was his only chance to escape his addiction, he knew the Queen would only continue to hurt her. She deserved her freedom.

Squaring his shoulders, he charged up the translucent staircase, his steps sending ripples through the light. He could still see the ruins below, and he tried not to concentrate on the drop.

The staircase ended at a rotten door. Golden light seeped through its cracks. Leon gritted his teeth. He pushed at the wood, which was strangely warm. The door swung inwards, and he stepped into a wide chamber. It was empty, save for the swirls of light and dust swarming in the air. A pool of moonlight sat just before the window, and he caught the edge of the flag dangling above it.

Leon stepped forward and the light changed colour. The gold became silver, and the room distorted. A fireplace, some chairs and other décor appeared, and then he saw Ruby in the centre of the floor. She was doubled over, her ankles and wrists chained, and she was shivering.

"Ruby!" Leon dashed over the tiles, but before he could reach her, something leapt up and knocked him down. Leon gasped, the wind knocked from his lungs, as a huge, drooling dog pinned him down. He struggled to push it off, but it was much too heavy. Certainly no ghost.

"I told you not to return!" the Queen's voice rattled. She emerged from the corner of the chamber, wielding her dagger. "Now pay the price."

The dog growled, sinking its paws deeper into Leon's chest. Leon choked, struggling to breathe. It must've been a stray, now under the Queen's magic. Frantically he groped in his pocket, searching for his tin of Fae Dust. It was his only chance.

He flicked the tin open with one hand, raking his fingers in the powder. Then, as the dog tensed its claws, he freed one arm and licked the Dust off his fingertips. Strength pulsed through him, and he elbowed the dog aside. It skidded across the floor and hit the wall. Whimpering, it curled into a ball, fearful.

Leon got back to his feet, his senses heightened. He'd taken three times the normal dose; he could fight an entire army. Yet it would come at a hefty price. He had to end this before the reloading symptoms started.

"Give me the dagger," he warned.

The Queen's eyes narrowed."Never," she hissed.

Yelling, Leon charged. He struck at the Queen, but his fist passed straight through her. He recovered quickly and snatched at the dagger in her hand, but the same happened again.

A dark smile spread on the Queen's lips, and she raised her hand. Leon sank to the floor, held down by an invisible force. It grew stronger and he gasped, fighting to breathe. Leon gritted his teeth. How was he supposed to take a dagger he couldn't touch? He pressed his shaking hands to the stone floor, desperate to break free.

"Leon!" Ruby cried.

Her voice lent him courage, and he began to rise from the floor. He couldn't let her down!

"Impossible!" the Queen exclaimed. She tried to renew her hold, but Leon was too quick. He bolted to the wall where a rusted sword hung above the fireplace. He snatched it free, then lunged at the Queen. It struck her side and she howled, clutching the wound. At least this wasn't an illusion.

"Let her go!" he bellowed, slashing once more. His blade caught the Queen's hand, and she dropped the dagger. Eyes wide, Leon dived for it, dropping his own weapon.

As his fingers clasped the hilt– now solid– his vision went black. A burning raced up his spine; a piercing ache stormed through his skull. He hit the floor, grasping his temples. *No, no, not now!*

Leon screamed, his arms stretching out against his will. The ligaments cracked, and then his neck jerked, slamming his head onto the floor. Blinded by darkness and pain, he could only shriek as tears poured down his face, his head ready to explode.

I can't stand this, make it stop, make it stop!

"Leon, no!"

Jangling footsteps rushed across the floor. Leon couldn't even tell which direction they came from. Then an icy touch caressed his lips. It spread to the thunderstorm in his head, calming the violent pulses. The muscles in his neck and shoulders went floppy, and he lay on the ground. Gradually the darkness receded and the light returned. Ruby was crouched against his chest, her face inches from his. Her eyes were tearful, but when she saw Leon's were clear, she smiled. "The Fae's magic, you mustn't…"

Leon found himself smiling back. He quickly sat up, looking around. Ruby was still chained; the Queen knelt a short distance away, nursing her wounds. The chains had cut into Ruby's ankles and wrists, and she was bleeding. Leon wished he could touch her, if only to soothe her pain.

Something pinched his hand, and he glanced down. He was still holding the dagger. His jaw tightened. This was something he *could* do.

"I'll set you free, Ruby," he promised. He rose to his feet and started towards the window.

"No!" The Queen snapped her fingers, and the dog started barking. It bolted to Leon, its teeth sinking into his calf. Leon howled, dropping to his knees. Blood dripped onto the stones. He grabbed the scruff of the dog's neck, trying to get it off. Without the help of the Fae Dust, though, he wasn't strong enough.

The Queen gloated, staggering towards him.

"You'll never defeat me," she growled.

Leon scowled, clutching the dagger tighter. He didn't want to do this, but he'd run out of options. Feeling sick, he angled the blade downward and stabbed the dog. It loosened its grip but didn't let go. Yelling, Leon kept stabbing until he was able to kick it away. The Queen bolted, her bony hands outstretched. Leon leapt out of the window, landing on the rubble outside.

The Queen got a hand to his ankle, but Leon was already hacking at the flag. The dagger sliced through the red cloth, and it fell towards the ground. The wind picked up, carrying it towards the gate, where it burst into flames.

"No!" the Queen shrieked.

The keep walls began to rumble. Leon clung to the shifting bricks beneath him, but they were sliding and cracking. He lost his grip and fell. The last thing he saw was the frosted ground racing towards him; then the world turned black.

A moist tongue stirred Leon back to wakefulness. He groaned, trying to move away, but it was persistent. He opened his eyes to find the dog eagerly licking his face. He scrambled to sit, and the dog sat on its forepaws, tail wagging. Its wounds had healed, and it seemed to have forgiven him for his earlier assault.

Leon blinked, checking himself over. Other than the bite on his leg, though, he didn't sport any injury. Yet he'd fallen almost thirty feet onto solid stone and ice…

He struggled to his feet, rubbing his sore leg, and looked around. The dog barked, curling around his feet. The front keep wall had collapsed, and the flagpole was gone too. The light from earlier had vanished, and he could only hear the wind singing through his ears.

He was alone again.

Leon closed his eyes and let out a long breath. While he was pleased he'd broken the curse, a deeper sadness eclipsed his heart. His friend was gone forever, and he hadn't even had a chance to say goodbye. He stared at the damaged keep, biting his lip.

I'll miss you, Ruby.

Hands in his pockets, he felt for the silver tin. He was back to where he'd started, still addicted, still isolated. However, as he searched his pockets, he couldn't find the box.

Leon's eyes widened, and he turned his coat inside out. The tin was gone. His face paled. Had he dropped it during his fall? He pushed the dog aside and ran back to the rubble, picking through the bricks, searching for a metallic gleam. Yet without proper light and without knowing when he'd lost it, the tin would be impossible to find. He cursed. A whole month's worth of Fae Dust, gone!

Something touched his shoulder, and he froze.

"Are you looking for something?"

Heart in his mouth, Leon almost fell onto the rubble. He caught himself on his hands, then looked round. A young woman was standing behind him, her eyes a dusky maroon. She was holding a silver tin in her hands. Leon's jaw dropped. He tried to speak, but he only managed a tiny croak.

It couldn't be...

The woman smiled. She helped him stand, and for the first time Leon caught her scent: like rose petals and lavender mixed together. She touched Leon's cheek. Leon held his hand over hers. Her fingers weren't a ghostly whisper of cold any more, but real, solid, warm.

"Is...is it really you, Ruby?" he whispered.

Ruby nodded. "Yes. You saved me. I'm free now, free to live out the days the Queen stole from me." She rested her hand against his chest. "Now, it's my turn to save you. Hold out your hands."

Leon raised an eyebrow, but did as he was told. Ruby stepped back and opened the tin. She poured the powder over his palms, then clasped her own over the top. She murmured words Leon didn't understand. The powder started to glow, and he stared. A tingling sensation ran from the small of his back through his shoulders and arms, joining with the powder in his hands.

Finally Ruby released him, and the powder turned to silver light. It rose from his skin, and the tingling sensation went with it. The light hovered for a moment, then drifted away into the wind until there was nothing left.

"There. I've removed all the Fae's magic from your body," Ruby said, holding his hands again. "It will never hurt you again."

Leon's eyes filled with tears. After almost a year of this constant, hopeless misery, he was finally free!

He pulled her close and didn't hesitate. He pressed his lips to hers and closed his eyes. Ruby stiffened at first, but soon returned his kiss, and a surge of warmth flowed through him. When he pulled away, both his and Ruby's cheeks were flushed.

"Thank you," Leon whispered. "I…"

"It's all right, Leon," Ruby hushed him. "I know." She curled up against his shoulder. "It's finally over."

Leon wrapped his arms around her.

"Sure is," he murmured. "Let's go home."

Illustration by Sophie E Tallis

THEY RISE AND WE SMITE
BY DAVID MUIR

Suzanna 'Susie' Owens sat outside the United Magical Investigations Agency's Human Resources department office.

She had spent a year behind a desk at the UMIA, pretty much ever since the agency began operating. And they were now about to put her into the field for the first time. She was going to meet her partner.

So many of the living legendary Mages, Wizards, Witches and Sorcerers had accepted posts as agents with the agency. Susie was excited to find out who she was going to be partnered up with.

It could be Ariana Gias, who was the most famous graduate of the Wizarding school she'd studied at, the Syndrian School. It could be Mashgahar of Mesopotamia, the great Illusionist, or maybe even Tania Howe, the most famous Pyromancer of America – an actress in the Mundane world.

Susie was ushered into the large office. It would do for a CEO of a major company, but it was partitioned off with twelve individual desks, all bought from IKEA, and one large one at the end that was obviously antique furniture.

Her mentor within the agency sat behind her desk, typing away at a report. Danika Lowe was a Canadian by birth and a witch by calling. Short, slim and blonde, that's what most people observed about her.

"I'm not sure yet who we are going to get to train you," Susie was told in the Franglish accent of the Montreal native. "The lists are being tightly controlled because of the rotation of positions within the agency. You know about the change of command, of course."

Before she could reply with an acknowledgement, the door to the office burst open and two men walked in. They were as different as any two men you may find in the world. One was tall, longhaired, muscular, and dressed all in black. The other was short, willowy, and bald, dressed in a riot of colours.

"I'm not working with you anymore," the skinny man told the tall man, his voice soft and wispy. "I see why nobody has lasted long with you. You are a bloody maniac."

"Calm down, you cry-baby," the other said, his voice distinctly Glaswegian. "How the hell was I supposed to know you couldn't turn water into ice?"

"I'm an Aeromancer, not an Aquamancer," the skinny man replied. "How the hell is it that Gabriel of Alba, the great all-knowing, doesn't know that?"

"I'm not all-knowing," said Gabriel, new head of the UMIA. It was a job he had been essentially doing since stepping down from the Council of Magic a year ago.

On the Council he had been the representative of the Magi race. As humans are closely related to the chimpanzee, the Magi are closely related to the Gorilla. Their genus artificially evolved by the God-King of the Heavens, to be used as foot soldiers in a war with his brother, the God-King of Hell, born and bred as the last line for the Light against the Darkness and Guardians of all.

Their evolution to resemble humanity was no mistake, in order to allow them to protect the evolving Homosapiens, and a direct effect of their intermingling with humans was the introduction of magic into human bloodlines. Essentially Gabriel and his family were related to every magic user in the world as his parents were each of one of ten bloodlines that could be traced directly to the First Magi and his offspring.

The willowy man turned to the head of Human Resources.

"I want away from him now," he said in a tone that brooked no argument.

"Tanrith needs a new partner," Yejosh Lobe, head of HR, told him. He nodded and left.

The fat wizard turned to Gabriel. "Sanir was killed in combat with a Priory. He decided they could take it on without backup."

"Idiot," Gabriel said with a growl, taking a seat in front of Yejosh. "What did you want to see me about?"

"Sir, Miss Owens is due to go out in the field," Danika informed him. "Perhaps the First Agent would be best to show her the ropes."

"A Greenback?" Gabriel snorted, and Lobe nodded. "Do I look like I have even the remotest amount of patience it requires to train a new agent, or in your own experience when have I ever had that kind of patience. You've known me long enough to know that I've got about a pencil width of patience for people who don't know how to do their job properly."

"Partners, like assignments, are assigned – not chosen." Dannika reminded him with a smile on her face, and Gabriel not so covertly flipped her off. "And besides, this time you can teach her by observing you doing all the wrong things, which means she'll know how to do things right.'

"You know what you can go and do don't you?" Gabriel asked her, throwing her the V-sign.

"Go suck a donkey's balls." Dannika retorted.

"That's quite enough from the pair of you." Lobe told them. "I would expect that type of bickering from a pair of neophyte wizards, not from two of the most experienced and powerful members of the magical community, notwithstanding the fact that you are the most senior agents we have."

"Sorry, Yojesh." They both said almost in unison.

"Now that's settled, I'm afraid Gabriel that this is going to be one assignment you are really going to hate," Lobe said, ushering Susie to take a seat beside Gabriel. "The Vatican has informed us that three of their priests, and a number of Magic users, have gone missing in Roma. The Pope asked for you specifically."

"They hate me in the Vatican," Gabriel said with a shake of his head. "I'm pretty sure the Pope is the one who hates me the most."

"It's not the first time he's called for you," Lobe informed him. "Normally the Council ignores the request, but this time he insisted you and no other. You leave for Roma in the morning."

"Why not teleport in?" Susie asked, her accent quite posh. Both of them looked at her.

"We need to enter the country legally. Otherwise, they can't have us involved in an investigation," Gabriel replied with a shrug. "Roman law."

They arrived at the Vatican the next day, expected and watched by every eye that they passed. Gabriel was dressed once more all in black: greatcoat, combat trousers, combat boots and plain T-shirt. Susie had dressed essentially the same, except she wore a bomber jacket, stiletto boots and jeans.

They were led into the public gallery above the College of Cardinals, which was in session. Italia was ruled from the Vatican by its politicians, priests, Bishops and Cardinals. Its Head of State, the Pope, was a life position.

"Do you understand them?" Gabriel asked Susie. She nodded.

"Latin is one of the languages the books of Magic are written in. I read, speak and think Latin like a native," she replied proudly.

He nodded. The man was trying to get a measure of her.

"Something about this year's crops not being as good as they had hoped," she went on. "They are worried that they may not be able to sell as much, which would then impact on how much they would be able to donate."

Gabriel snorted. "Relatively few Cardinals give a crap about the donations. They care more about what is in their coffers at the end of the year."

When the session was ended, the UMIA agents were led to the Pope's private office by his First Minister, who left as soon as they were delivered. Susie got her first look at the leader of the Catholic Church up close as he took off his robes of office. Pope Paul the Eighth, successor to Saint John Paul, was every bit the Slavic gentleman. He was, like his predecessor, a Pole.

"Gabriel." The Pope nodded to the Magi. "Who is this?" He threw his robe to his page, who deftly caught it. He wore a simple, grey wool suit along with his shirt and collar.

"Susie, my new partner," Gabriel replied. The First Agent wasn't a man to speak more than needed.

"Another one," the Pope snorted, and looked the Wizard up and down. "You go through partners like I go through First Ministers."

"Why are we here, Josef? I am a very busy man," Gabriel said with a sigh, using the Pope's birth name: Josef Andre Ostrowski.

"Come, come," the Pope said, motioning them to follow him through his private tunnels. "I'm surprised they sent you. They usually ignore me when I ask for you. Or is that you trying to make a point?"

"All cases are assigned randomly," Gabriel replied with a sigh. "Why me this time?"

"This concerns the Accords," the Pope replied as they were met at an exit by a car and a Swiss Guard protection team. Gabriel rarely – if ever – showed any emotion other than anger, but he was surprised by whatever the Accords were. The car drove them a mile across to the other end of the Vatican.

The building was ancient, much older than those around it. Gabriel knew where they were, and swept in ahead of them. When Susie and Paul joined him, he was talking to a man dressed half like

Gabriel and half in the uniform of a Roman Legionary: cloak, helmet and armour. They were talking in a language that Susie didn't know. It sounded like the Ancient Magi she'd been taught in school, but an entirely different dialect. While the Legionary was awed by Gabriel, he was still speaking in an angry tone.

"He's a Guardian," the Pope told her, answering her unasked question. "They are tasked with protecting the places of Magic in the World. Before this became part of the Vatican City, it was a place of Magical learning: the Great Library of Roma, where many of the volumes are of a Magical nature and many of them are of a dark nature. All the books that the Magi and the Council collected over the Millennia were taken to the Great Libraries, like Alexandria, Constantinople, Nalada and Ugarit. This is the last of them to stand. The others fell either by the hands of the Dark Lords, or due to misuse by their nations. The Guardians left them, and the books were moved elsewhere. We never made the Guardians leave as many did. We trust the Magi, not the Council."

"Why?" Susie asked him.

"The Magi have an unswerving, singular devotion to the light, which puts most priests to shame." Paul replied with a smile, as he took a seat. "My history with Gabriel goes back to when I was a Bishop in Poland, and he a young Pack leader. Before he became War Master. Before he even became the Cadre Leader. He and his pack were chasing a Dark wizard. Their actions were reckless. More people died than I thought were necessary for him to carry out his job. It is why I do not like him. But I respect his position – no rest for the Evil and the Wicked – and also his devotion to his gods and his people. They are a race apart, the Magi, and their history is bloodier than that of the Catholic Church and the Empire that once called this city their capital. He is excellent at his job, however much of a bastard he is. You would do well to learn everything you can from him. I trust no other to find out what happened to my priests or the Magic users who tend this place."

"How many of the Dark books are missing?" Gabriel asked Paul as he joined them.

"Twelve." the Pope replied with a sorrowful look on his face. "A couple I know only by name, like the Kandeharish Codex. Two of them I studied while in the Seminary when I considered joining the Fist, before I chose the quiet life of the parish priest. The Ashigura Grimoire and the Shondax Carta."

"Vampyres." Gabriel said with a growl of disgust. "I hate bloodsuckers."

"Will we require the assistance of the Hunters?" Susie asked them. The Pope snorted. Her partner just shook his head. "What?"

"Don't you know that you are partnered with the War Master of the Magi?" Paul asked incredulously. "The youngest ever leader of the Hunter Cadre. They still haven't replaced you in, what? Ten years?"

"It's been a year since I sat on the Council, so nine rounded up," Gabriel replied with a shrug. "You know how we are, Josef. Much more than I would like it sometimes. But no, Susie Owens of the Syndrian School, I am Hunter enough for now."

"The Swiss Guard is at your disposal." the Pope informed Gabriel, handing him the case file. "Good luck. And good hunting,"

The two UMIA agents were tailed by a team of Swiss Guard officers, including Tactical and Forensics officers, to the home of the first priest on their list. He was named Benedict Matthews, an American by birth, brought up in New Amsterdam. He was an Italian citizen now, having spent his entire priesthood – apart from his training – in the Vatican's many libraries.

Gabriel had ordered the Swiss Guard commander to keep his men on the ground and out of sight. He didn't want to spook Father Matthews, and didn't want the Holy Police – as he called them – traipsing through a Magical crime scene.

"Do you feel it?" he asked Susie as they moved nearer the door. She nodded. "At least we know there is Dark Magic involved."

"Do you think he was part of a Kabal or Priory?" Susie asked him. He shook his head. "Why not?"

"It's not something that's talked about, even in our world," Gabriel replied as he knocked on the door. "Father Matthews, we are with the UMIA. We would like to speak with you." No answer. "Father Matthews, if you don't answer, I have to assume that there is something wrong and I'm going to have to put the door in." Again, no answer.

Gabriel stuck his foot through the door at the lock, and lobbed a multiplying fireball into the apartment. Susie gave him a look.

"Can never be too careful." He held his hand out and the fireballs came back to him; when he closed it, they had disappeared.

"So what isn't talked about, even in our world?" she asked him.

Gabriel put gloves on and began poking through the sparse domicile of Father Matthews.

"Every potential priest is checked for Magical ability," he replied as he lifted up the couch. "None that have any ability to learn or use Magic are allowed to join the priesthood. Some remain in the Seminary and become the Magical arm of the Holy Order of God's Righteous Fist. The Council doesn't like the idea, but a knighthood of the church isn't something they can interfere with. It is, after all, a Mundane organisation, which just happens to have Magical users in it. It's like the Masons or the Knights of Saint Columba."

"What was the deal with the guy in the Roman armour at the Library?" Susie inquired, taking a look in the bedroom. It had a bed and a wardrobe, which had all the priest's worldly possessions in it.

"The Guardians are given a position either for life, or until the place is no longer protected," Gabriel replied as he went through the kitchen. "Decius has protected the Library since he left the Legions of Rome, almost two and a half thousand years ago. He's the last of his era to protect the place. Many have died in the attacks on the Library. All Guardians wear armour and cloaks, just like all Hunters wear black. The legwear and footwear adapt with the times. He is the most respected member of his Cadre. Even those who protect the Council Chambers and the Meeting Hall of the Triumvirate are not as respected as he."

"How old are you? Since you have the title War Master?" Susie asked him, suddenly afraid to know the answer.

"I will turn twenty-seven on March the sixth," he replied with a smile. "My coming was forewarned by at least twenty-seven separate prophets, sages, seers and the like. Read the Prophecies of Pythia and you'll get me. Gods, do I wish I could strangle her for the crap I've been through. Basically, I am the genetic reincarnation of the first Mage ever born with powers, and I happen to also be of his bloodline, which is weird in so many ways."

"I read the Legends of the Magi in school. Most Wizards believe your people are nothing more than that," Susie said to him, a little in awe of him too. "I never thought that they were true."

"All true, and much more besides," he replied with a sorrowful sigh. "Come, there is nothing to find here. The Magic is long gone."

They found nothing at the remaining priests' homes, which were all much like Father Matthews' in that they were sparse with few possessions. They were truly proper priests. It wasn't until they reached the home of Mario Bachelli, a native of Tuscany, who was one of the principal Curators of the Magical section of the Library, that they found what they had been searching for.

"There is more than a passing aura of black Magic on this place," Gabriel said, looking at it from the street.

He had the Swiss Guard enter the home first. He knew he would find something there, an artifact, or a tome of ancient and malevolent Power, and he would rather they get killed by any safeguards, than himself and Susie. As he always said Mundanes could be replaced since they bred like rabbits but Magic users like Susie and Magi like him couldn't. They entered the house and found more than they'd bargained for: Satanic writings (which was stupid, because Satan was dead, killed by another Prince of Hell a couple of hundred years earlier, during one of the Black Crusades), blood-covered walls with verses from dark texts, and a couple of the stolen books. Gabriel picked one up, almost fizzing with fury.

"The Book of Sherdis," he said, slamming it down and wiping his hand on the upholstery. "What do you remember about Vampyres from your school days?"

"The King or Queen of a Coven is always a Magic user," Susie replied with a strained look on her face. It was hard for her to remember this because Wizard training partitioned your mind. Her short-term memory was atrocious, and it didn't help that her Dyspraxia messed with it too. "The first Vampyres were involved in research on how to prolong their already long lives through Magic. They were trying to gain immortality."

"Which the Gods granted only to the Magi. Though there isn't any being on this planet with true immortality because even we can die," Gabriel said and nodded for her to continue.

"They found that blood could sustain them, but only the blood of humans could sustain them for more than a few days. They must drink at least a litre of blood to satiate the thirst. Only by draining a human's entire blood supply could they actually take off years from their own bodies," Susie recalled, gulping in a few places.

"They created thralls, from Mundane humans, so they would require less blood to keep themselves going, as they would feed off of them with psychic energy. The Council, upon discovering them, ordered the Vampyres hunted down, their research confiscated, and them and their thralls killed. But some of the research was hidden, and a few of the lower Vampyres and their thralls were never caught. Occasionally they appear, or someone recreates the research. Vampyres and Vampyres – the human version – can no longer consume food or drink other than alcohol. They favour the night places. I believe one of them sits on the Council of the Dark Lords."

"High Queen Amadastra," Gabriel growled, fire wreathing his arm. "How I would love to rip her shrivelled heart from her body. Questioning her would be fun."

"Agent Gabriel?" They were interrupted by one of the Swiss Guard officers. "We found this pile of papers that may of be some interest to you."

"Thank you," Gabriel said with a nod, going through the many fliers for a nightclub named *Cuore della Fuoco*, Heart of the Fire. "Well, we know where they hunt. For sure they are involved in Dark Magic of some sort. I say I place a call, and we do some Hunting."

The club was one of the places for the rock and metal music fans of Roma to frequent, though one of the few that wasn't underground. It was packed with men and women writhing and wriggling to the Goth metal band on the stage – a band that was doing the rounds in the cities of the most Catholic nation on the planet. It always made Gabriel laugh, when he spent time in Italia, how much contradiction there was there.

He and Susie sat about a half-dozen chairs apart, seemingly completely oblivious to each other. Susie would occasionally eye up a man or a woman. Both of them could certainly feel the Dark Magic that permeated the room each time one of the Dark Ones – which was a name that the Vatican and the Swiss Guard used for Vampyres – walk past or order drinks at the bar. Both noticed that they all returned to a group of tables that had been reserved by the management when they arrived.

Both magic users had changed. Susie was wearing a blood-red dress with a black cloak. Gabriel wore a Slayer T-shirt, fingerless gloves, black New Rock boots rather than his combat boots, and jeans instead of his combat trousers.

A woman left the group. She was curvaceous, with hard dark Italian features and long black hair. She dressed most provocatively, her breasts practically falling out of her corseted dress. If it wasn't for the blackness flowing from her, Susie would have found her attractive.

She walked over to Gabriel, tongue licking her lips as she got closer. She was sexually aroused by the Magi War Master. Susie could see that her fangs were beginning to jut out of her gums. The sight of it gave her gag.

"I have been watching you tonight," she told him, in a lisped hypnotic Italian. She worked her hand down the muscles of his upper arm. They were as hard as steel. "I can tell you are a dangerous man. You are the most attractive of the men here to me, because of the danger."

"Oh, yeah? And exactly how dangerous am I?" he said with a feigned intrigued smile. Only he knew it was fake.

"You are a very dangerous man," she replied with a smile, the fangs pushing through further. "In you I see a man who has death on his hands and in his eyes. It makes my loins purr."

"See, here's the thing," Gabriel said with a sigh, grabbing her with a hand wreathed with fire as he stood. She squealed as her hair began to get singed, trying desperately with her superhuman strength to get his hand off her, but it was clamped there. "I know what you are, and you make me sick."

"Help, you fools! He must be with the people our lord warned us about!" she screamed at her Coven. They all bared their teeth and began to move towards Gabriel.

In moments, each of them had a dozen Swiss Guard pistols trained on them. The pistols were loaded with either silver bullets with a white phosphorous core, or magic spells. Apart from the Coven, the staff and the band – who were now all cowering – the entire club was filled with Swiss Guard, UMIA agents and Magi Hunters. Gabriel gave Susie a nod, and she flicked the house lights up. He cleared his throat, and pulled the Vampyre woman so she was facing the front rather than his neck.

"Now, you should know who I am before you make a decision on what you will do," Gabriel said to them. "I am Gabriel of Alba, War Master of the Magi. That name should sufficiently kowtow the former mages among you. For those of you that were human, you are predators. I am the King of all Predators in the World."

"What do you want?" asked one of the male Vampyres, who he recognized as being formerly Father Matthews. "Tell us, and maybe we won't kill you and all these people with you, drain you of all of your blood."

"You obviously don't think I'll kill you, do you?" Gabriel asked him with a sigh. He shrugged as he incinerated the female then wiped the ash from his clothes. "All I want is your king, the one who you serve."

Another man stepped forward. "I am he."

Gabriel nodded to one of his men, who launched a fireball at the man. He was incinerated in seconds.

"See? That was a lie." Gabriel shook his head. "I do not like it when people lie to me."

"No one will tell you which of us is King. You will have to kill us all to find out," one of the women – one of the prettiest women Susie had ever laid eyes on – told him defiantly.

"That really is a shame, because if you did tell me, and I offed him without killing you, you would all return to being human." He clicked his fingers, and the room erupted in a hail of bullets, fire and death. When all was done, not a member of the Coven survived the encounter. There wasn't a single fatality among the security forces or patrons. The few Swiss Guards who had been injured, and a couple of the Mundanes who had been caught by either fire or bullets, were being tended by healers.

"Gabriel!" Susie shouted at him. "I can hear the King's roar."

"I can also," he said, bounding towards the door.

Outside, the sound that the King was making was near deafening, a loud and high pitched bat scream. What had been Mario Bachelli, a handsome Italian male dressed in the finest Italian handmade suit, stood before the Magi War Master, fangs jutting from his mouth, his nose more of a snout and his eyes ablaze with rage.

"You dare slay my children!" he roared. Gabriel knew it was meant to be frightening, but he found it a little like a two year-old's frightened squeak. "I will tear you limb from limb and feast on the blood of your people."

"See, I've heard that a couple of times. It has never happened," Gabriel sniffed and shrugged. "Okay there was the one time where we lost a couple of people but that's because they never listened to orders."

A fireball rebounded off a black energy shield two feet from where the Vampyre King stood. He began to change into a half-bat, half-man form, with the face and wings of a bat, but the legs and arms of a man. A dark energy ball flew from his own hand and rebounded off Gabriel's shield.

"Do you really expect to beat me?" Gabriel asked.

"I will end you, boy," the Vampyre replied, as a large sword with a blade of dark energy appeared in the monster's hand. Gabriel shook his right arm, and a twin-headed axe wreathed in Whitefire appeared in his own hand.

Susie began incanting spells of fire and lightning in an attempt to overwhelm the Vampyre's shield. The King cackled an altogether evil and crazy laugh and swatted her with the flat of his blade, sending her flying into the glass of a nearby shop. "Your pet Wizard did nothing to me."

"Yeah, well, your pitiful blade is not going to do a damn thing to me," Gabriel replied. He launched his axe at the Vampyre's shield – once, twice, thrice in quick succession – mighty blows that no mortal man could take. They rebounded each time, sparks flying as blade met shield, but still rocking the King back.

"Impressive," Gabriel said as the Vampyre launched his own attacks, swinging his axe in a flurry of blows, designed to distract and annoy which pushed the mage back. "Most impressive. But I doubt they'll help you much."

"Talk is cheap, Council whelp. I will destroy you," the Vampyre shot back.

"Did I forget to introduce myself?" Gabriel said with a grin, regaining his footing. "I am Gabriel of Alba, War Master of the Magi, and I am your end."

Gabriel roared as his axe and the sword met. His axe head caught the blade, and he snapped the Dark blade with a tug on the haft. In a single heavy blow, the Vampyre's shield collapsed.

"Nooooo!" the Vampyre King screamed as Gabriel side head kicked him, to put him off balance and began slicing off the Vampyre Lord's limbs, one by one. Then, with a back-handed swing, Gabriel decapitated him. The body began to turn to ash. Gabriel whipped his left hand up, and a whirlwind took the ash up into the air, higher and higher until it burned up in the atmosphere.

"Yeaeasss!" he said with a chuckle to himself, hanging the axe over his shoulder. "When you and your filth rise, and I will bloody well smite."

"Well, that was bloody good fun, wasn't it?" Susie said. Having lost her put-on posh accent; instead that she was Mancunian was evident. She had put a towel onto the shoulder that had been sliced open when she went through the shop window. "Are all missions with you going to turn out to be like this?"

"Pretty much," he replied with a shrug and a smile. "Let's get the healers to take a look at that, and go tell the Pope that we trashed the Vampyre coven in his backyard."

"He's not going to like the reports," Susie said to him. He much preferred her real accent; the posh one had been getting on his nerves. "He would like you if you didn't keep killing people."

"It was totally necessary this time, though," Gabriel said as they walked into the club. "Besides, if I didn't kill those that needed killing the planet would be overrun by Daemons and Devils that even we couldn't permanently hold."

"Well, that's a supremely happy thought." Susie said to him.

"There's an old law enforcement adage.' Gabriel snorted. "If you couldn't take a joke you shouldn't have signed on for the job."

A SIMPLE GAME
BY K A SMITH

So, Peiraeus was sealed, all shipping had ceased, but I had to see it for myself. The few people I met by the dockside wondered if any ship would ever come again. Their eyes had the same furtive look I had seen in the city, like trapped beasts. With the gates under constant guard, nobody in, nobody out, there was nowhere to go. The Spartans had retreated from our walls, in fear of the plague they contained, but Pericles had decreed that Athens be isolated, to save Attica from the pestilence that laid us waste. I turned my back on the sea, girding my loins for the grey trudge home.

Bodies lay in the streets. With the fresh air between the Long Walls behind me, the stench of Athens assailed my nostrils despite the scented cloth that covered half my face. I had forgotten how foul it was. I stood doubled over, gasping, hands clutched to my empty stomach, when a voice behind me called my name.

"Aristagoras?"

I turned, wiping at my mouth.

"I thought it was you." It was Platon. His eyes gleamed in the light of the torch he held as he looked towards Peiraeus gate. "Where have you been?"

I shrugged. "I took a constitutional, for my health."

He laughed, the first I had heard for days, then gave me a knowing look. "There is no way out, I can assure you, but where would you go? We're doomed. This is a judgement, and not the first. The Gods have found us wanting."

"The Gods?"

"Would Athena allow this? Would Apollo? If it were not the will of Zeus?" Platon came from a priestly family; for him the answer to everything was always the Gods. He made a sweeping gesture. "Use your senses, man, and tell me we are not doomed."

I saw no point in arguing; the will of the Gods seemed all too clear. "At least we will save Attica. Pericles has sealed the city, this will not spread."

"Huh!" Platon made that snorting sound of his. "Does the fool believe that the pestilence that afflicts us comes from within these walls? If violet-crowned Athens, beloved of the Gods, is suffering, will anyone be spared?"

I looked about me. In the darkness I could see little of the dereliction: the rotting corpses of man and beast, the daubed walls and smashed amphorae, houses left empty by death now broken by scavengers seeking not wealth but simply food. Here and there a burning dwelling delivered an offering of smoke and ashes to those below; nobody thought to put out a neighbour's fire these days. "I don't know, Platon. Why?"

"We Hellenes fight among ourselves, while the Mede strengthens his grip upon us with gold and sweet words. How long will it be before we worship at his altars and neglect our rightful Gods? We have no need for some Eastern Lord of the Sky; their mumbo-jumbo is nonsense, but we will fall into their ways before long, if nothing stops us. And Zeus will stop us. The wax will be wiped clean, so the righteous may remain to follow the old ways, the right ways. Those of us who have lived in arete will have nothing to fear, while those who have failed the Gods will be swept away."

"It sounds awfully, well, wholesale."

"You always did speak like a merchant, Aristagoras, but then you are one. I know you to be a good man, though, in spite of your shortcomings. You should go home and question your life; if you have honoured the Gods then you have nothing to fear. If not, I suggest you prepare yourself for Thanatos. You know, you don't look well."

"Thank you, Platon, for your reassuring words. I would invite you to dinner, but cook is indisposed. You know how it is."

Cook was dead when I returned – the last of the household to live, excepting myself. If this was the will of the Gods, then they were unforgiving indeed. Cook was the most devout person I knew. I had hoped that he might recover; he had seemed less fevered when I left him with a bowl of millet porridge and a jug of water by his bed.

Cleaning his body and preparing it as best I could took me until morning. I burned the soiled sheets and wrapped him in clean, then took him outside to lie with the others. I was only glad that my wife and sons had been spared this end, having died when the Spartans first invaded, except that perhaps they might have known a little more about cooking than I. I boiled some beans with a leek and some scrapings of smoked ham, then went to bed; try as I would, I couldn't eat.

Sleep did not come easily. I missed the noises of the city. I lay there thinking about the Gods. Heracles had fought Thanatos for the Soul of Alkestis, so perhaps I could contest for my own? I would challenge Thanatos to a game of backgammon; it was too simple to cheat, skill outweighed luck, and I knew of no better player than myself. I had honoured Hermes, as befits a merchant. I prayed to him for aid. "Please, Lord, let me contest for my soul. Intercede for me."

The sound of wood on wood awoke me.

"Who's there?"

A lamp flickered into life. A wooden board sat on my table; a figure stood in the half-dark, pale wings rising behind. "You want to play?"

"Thanatos?"

"This is wartime." A face limned by pale curls leaned into the light. "Besides, my brother is busy."

Ker was beautiful beyond imagining. I tore my eyes from her face to look at the chequered board with strangely sculpted pieces. "That's not backgammon ..."

DEATH ALWAYS COLLECTS
BY JEREMY RODDEN

It is my turn to die next. I don't want to die, but when one makes a deal with Death, He always comes to collect. Death doesn't care if the deal was with a couple of scared housecats trying desperately to save their owner's life; He has a quota to maintain. The Church will tell you that animals don't have souls. Death disagrees.

It began when my owner became depressed and decided a few bottles of pills would solve all his problems. That night, Death came for him. We saw Death standing over our master's body, preparing to retrieve his essence for His collection.

Popular culture says that animals can sense evil, such as dogs barking at ghosts. We cats can sense ghosts as well, but we aren't as noisy as our canine cousins. Death is no ghost, however. Nor is He particularly evil. We found Death to be unwaveringly neutral. He was there to collect a spirit – nothing more, nothing less. Death waits for no man or beast, so we had to think quickly.

"Take us, instead," I offered.

Skye shot me a sideways glance. She was never particularly fond of our owner like I was. At the same time, she sensed my desperation. We were middle aged. Our owner was barely more than an adult. He had one kitten – I mean, kid – to look after and his mate was expecting another.

"Yes," Skye assented. "Two instead of one, Death."

Death turned his cloaked head and saw us: two small Siamese cats. We stared right back into his beady red eyes. He nodded and responded, "Agreed. Soon." His voice was a raspy whisper. My tail twitched and puffed at the sound of it. Death left with our owner barely breathing but alive.

We spent the next year on edge, not knowing when Death would return for us. He returned on the one-year anniversary of our owner's suicide attempt. Skye and I braced for his icy touch but, inexplicably, he only took Skye. The owners cried as they buried her in the backyard, seemingly unaware that Skye took our owner's place.

It is fast approaching the second anniversary of our inverse Faustian deal. I know that Death will be here for me very soon. I await him like any other cat would: calm and stoic. I hope my owner makes our sacrifice for his life worthwhile. It is my turn to die next.

PHOENIX FEATHER
BY LINDSEY J PARSONS

Shrilate sucked cool spring water through pursed lips, his ears flicking back and forth with the action of his swallowing. The noise he was making cut through the silence of the highland valley, and his enjoyment was obvious in his relaxed stance.

Alex sat looking down at his mount with a mixture of frustration and guilt. *He's making enough noise to wake the dead,* he thought, running his fingers through his shoulder-length blond hair. The sun was well past its midpoint and heading fast towards the western horizon. This was a fool's errand and Alex knew it.

Summer solstice was fast approaching and it was traditional to give presents in celebration of another winter passed. Each summer Alex tried to outdo his brother and give their father the most exciting or unusual present, but Richard – being older – always came up with something better. The truth was, Alex always left it to the last minute and so had to make do with anything he could find in a hurry. Not this summer, though. He'd given it a lot of thought, and a Phoenix feather quill would be unbeatable in the present stakes.

Phoenixes only nest in the valleys of the highlands. He'd had to do a swap so he could take the Northern patrol, onto which he'd added an extra two days' marching – and on top of this, Shrilate was missing out on his rest day. In theory it had seemed so easy. Phoenixes lined their nests with their feathers, so all he had to do was find a nest and help himself to a choice of feathers. Yet in practice it had proved impossible. Phoenixes were rare and difficult to spot.

Shrilate looked up, startled, as an orangey-red flash crossed the valley downstream. Alex gathered his reins and urged his horse to give chase. Shooting forward, Shrilate accelerated to a fast gallop. They were gaining on it. Alex could see the bird's feathers as it wove between the trees, glowing like flames in the sinking sun.

Shrilate stopped dead and Alex almost fell off as he crashed forward onto his horse's neck.

"What the ..." Alex threw his reins down and crossed his arms over his head, trying to contain his frustration. "We were so close, Shril, what's wrong with you?"

 The horse just stood shaking his head and refusing to move. Perhaps he's hurt? Placing his hand on the shiny black neck, Alex let his mind connect with his horse's. Shrilate felt there was great danger to the right of where they stood and was compelled to head that way. Alex sighed. They had lost the Phoenix now anyway, so they headed right.

As they reached the edge of a clearing, Alex could hear crying. At the foot of a tree to their left lay a small boy, his leg twisted at an unnatural angle. Shrilate started shaking with fear and from somewhere to their right came a deep, rumbling growl. The rank smell of hot, damp fur reached Alex's nostrils just as the undergrowth parted and the most enormous mountain bear he'd ever seen appeared.

There was no time for thinking. Alex kicked Shrilate forward and they shot out into the clearing between the boy and the bear. The horse pirouetted and leaped back the way he'd come, flicking mud up into the bear's face as he went. Ignoring the boy and roaring with anger, the bear gave chase.

Considering his size and bulk, he was quick and he was gaining fast. His massive shoulders easily broke through bushes and undergrowth that Shrilate had to step around.

Just as the bear got so close he was snapping at Shrilate's haunches, they broke out into a wide open valley. Leaping forward with sweat running down his flanks, Shrilate flew along the valley floor and they started to increase their lead.

Halfway along the valley, the bear gave up the chase and lumbered off to have a drink from a nearby stream. Standing in his stirrups, Alex whooped a victory cry at him before heading back to find the boy.

Still lying at the foot of the tall pine tree, with tear streaks down his cheeks, the boy looked to be less than ten winters old. Alex dismounted and knelt next to him. "Did you fall out of the tree?"

The boy nodded. His leg was still twisted at a crazy angle; he was breathing fast and looked very pale.

"I can fix this for you, but it will hurt to start with because I will have to straighten your leg." Alex waited for the boy to nod again before placing his hands on the broken leg. Concentrating on the break, he summoned the magic from deep inside himself, letting it flow through his hands, pulling it up through the ground and out of the air. Pure magic energy flowed through him and into the boy's leg. With a quick, sharp movement, he pulled the leg straight again and concentrated the magic on knitting together the bone and repairing the flesh. The boy half gasped and half screamed as Alex moved his leg, but relaxed as the break healed.

"There you are, good as new. You were lucky I came along." Alex grinned at the boy; the magic was still buzzing through his body, making him feel warm and alive. "I'm Alex, what's your name?"

"Roy," the boy said, prodding his leg with a look of awe.

"Well, Roy, let's get you home and on the way you can tell me what you were doing up a tree in the middle of nowhere." Alex lifted Roy onto Shrilate and climbed up behind him. Roy didn't say much, other than which village he came from, and Alex didn't notice. He was deep in thought about what he could get his father now his plans had failed.

Reaching Roy's home, Alex explained to his parents what had happened.

"You'd better thank Alex for his kindness," Roy's father said, but Roy had disappeared.

"I'm sorry, he's very shy." Roy's father looked embarrassed. "He spends all his time roaming around on his own, chasing fire birds."

Just then, Roy reappeared carrying a large Phoenix feather. Offering it to Alex, he said, "Thank you."

Illustration by Sophie E Tallis

THE DREAMING MOON
BY KAY KAUFFMAN

Anna Martoka sat bolt upright in bed. Her breath came in short, ragged gasps. Her heart hammered away in her chest. She shook uncontrollably, but her fiancé, John, simply snorted as he rolled onto his side, still sound asleep. *Why can't I sleep in peace like that?* she wondered as she crawled out of bed.

Anna threw on a sweatshirt and padded out to the balcony off the bedroom. She crossed her arms against the cool night air as she sat down in the oversized deckchair near the railing. A full orange moon had just begun its ascent. *A dreaming moon*, she mused as she tried to slow her still-racing heart. *No wonder I haven't been getting any sleep lately.*

A dreaming moon, her mother had once explained, was a rare occurrence and only affected certain people. A dreaming moon produced intense visions, often forcing a person to confront their inner demons. But occasionally, a dreaming moon produced premonitions. Anna was certain that's what she had experienced.

She watched the moon rise higher in the sky as she considered what she'd seen. It was that boy again, the same one she'd been meeting in her dreams every night for weeks now. The other dreams had been pleasant, filled with happy meetings and leisurely walks and much joy. But this dream was different, more disjointed, darker.

She could still feel the straps that had bound her arms and legs; the acrid stench of woodsmoke from the fire that burned in the hearth still hung in the air. The boy had saved her from torture at the hands of a dark man, but he was beaten soundly for his efforts.

Mama, I wish you were here, she silently cried. *I know you could help me make sense of these dreams.* She sighed as the boy returned again to her thoughts, for this time he was mourning. His brother mourned with him, as did the dark man from her previous dream.

Anna hugged her legs and rested her head upon her knees. She closed her eyes for a moment and the young man's face appeared again. He was smiling this time, laughing as he wrapped his arms around her. She could almost feel the comforting warmth of his strong arms and the shape of his name on her lips as joy bubbled up from the pit of her stomach and erupted in laughter.

When she opened her eyes again, the moon was nearing its zenith. A cool breeze sent shivers down Anna's spine as she sat up and stretched. The moon had changed from orange to gold and as she looked at it, she shivered again. This time, though, it had nothing to do with the wind. She turned around, expecting to see John watching her from the doorway, but no one was there. "Weird," she murmured. With one last glance at the sky, Anna went back inside, eager to be rid of the moon.

Tulo sighed, frustrated, as he climbed out of bed. It had been weeks since he'd gotten a decent night's sleep and his exhaustion was obvious. Bekol had mentioned several times that he looked positively haggard. He was both touched and annoyed by his brother's concern. *If only he had a cure for this insomnia,* he thought.

Such thoughts were pointless and he knew it, but still they came. The only thing that could cure his sleeplessness was news of Anná and at this point, that news was unlikely to come. After fifteen years, she was probably dead. That's what everyone else thought. But not Tulo – he couldn't bring himself to believe that. *No, she's alive,* he assured himself. *She's alive. I can feel it.*

A golden moon shone brightly through the room's lone window. Old tales of dreaming moons surfaced from distant memory and he wondered if there was any truth in them as he looked deep into the night sky. Thoughts of Anná soon reclaimed his attention and he wondered if she, too, were looking out on the moon and wondering.

Tulo's eyes closed, but he still saw the moon. It cast an eerie glow over a young woman curled up in a chair on a balcony in some distant land. *Anná!* He knew her immediately. He reached for her, but she was too far away. He called out to her, but she remained still. He whispered her name and then her eyes slowly opened. As their eyes met, a shiver raced up Tulo's spine.

She was alive! And soon they would be together, he was sure of it.

AUTHO NIGHTS CRITIQUES
BY RICHARD A. WENTWORTH

Welcome to Autho night critiques. Up next is J.C, the last time he and Sam met, some words about age had come up, so this might be an interesting, epic exchange.

Sam stands on the critique mound and J.C. steps into the receiving box. The crowd becomes still with wonder.

Wait, he appears to be shy, not ready to face Sam!

Yes! Sam, (Da—Da—Dummm) so shy, so innocent, and with surgical skills of precision, tearing into his story and riddled it with helpful suggestions.

Sam stares him down, turns her back to J.C. She stares into the stands, waves and chuckles.

Not sure if I like that laugh…MOHHAA-HA-HA.

Okay, now, J.C. finally steps into the box and digs in. Sam slowly turns, and gives the catcher a brush—off nod. OH, OH, she is smiling. She nods her head and delivers the critique.

I do not believe it—a zodiac slider crosses the plate. I thought she retired that one a while ago. We have to go to slow motion… see it came up so fast and J.C. was caught by surprise. J.C. frowns, steps out of the box and waves at Sam.

Wait…not sure what is happening. I could have sworn I saw some guns in her hands (man, even the slow—mo did not catch it.) Must be the heat of the moment, but it is only a pen.

J.C. steps into the box. Sam stares him down, straightens, ready to deliver another....

Hold on, J.C. steps from the box and Sam's manager, Lisa (the Ice Queen), comes running out to huge applause.

Oh, man, J.C. is in big trouble now. The Ice Queen offers words of wisdom to Sam and... wait...

Zoom in...can you read what they are saying?

Yes! OH, NO, this should be entertaining. The Ice Queen gives Sam a hug and...

No, wait, something is happening... Sam is nodding and smiling, not a good sign for J.C.

The Ice Queen steps back and heads for the dugout.

J.C. glares at the Ice Queen. She stops, points a finger at him, (not very nice, Ice Queen) and gives him an icy stare. Then she gives a thumb down.

She is laughing: you do not see that too often. I do believe we might be seeing an Idaho Fast/Freezing knuckle critique waiting to be delivered.

I do not know if J.C. has ever faced one before, and I'm not sure, if he can handle it.

J.C. steps up and gets ready; Sam delivers the critique and the crowd lets out a gasp.

We have to go to slow motion to capture this moment in history.

J.C. stands poised, but as the critique zooms past for an epic strike; he appears to be frozen by fear. No...

Wait, he is down. Now that is one hair parting: newbies occasionally need to be put in their places. Oh, No...the medic has rushed out and is carting him off.

Poor kid, I don't have the heart to tell him that Sam will be the attending doctor when he wakes up.

DWARFS R US
BY WILL MACMILLAN JONES

The dilapidated workshop on the nondescript industrial estate looked much like any other rented industrial unit. Similar rubbish drifted in windswept piles around the rusting sides of the building. Pools of water collected outside and carried a suspicious floating oily scum, although the oily scum floating about inside the unit were themselves strangers to water. An aura of desolation and indolence floated over the roof. Only the stacks of empty pizza boxes and the small mountain of beer cans betrayed the fact that these occupants were to a degree different from the other tenants on the estate. Or perhaps they didn't: it was that sort of place.

The faded sign over the closed doors read DWARFS R US. It featured a cheerful, smiling dwarf carrying a spanner: a sight calculated to deceive customers and attract those government agencies trying to stop misleading advertisements. The doors were shut tight, to discourage customers and similarly unwelcome visitors. The half-starved dog tied loosely in front of the entrance was mute testimony to the paucity of Revenue Inspectors in those parts.

The wind howled mournfully and a drizzle of rain tried, unsuccessfully, to avoid falling. Also unsuccessful at avoiding falling was the heavily booted witch whose broomstick again misfired in the critical landing phase. The oily scum lurking in the pond boiled in sudden terror at her arrival; the dog broke its lead and fled. Slowly a pointed hat rose, like Venus, from the waves. Unlike Venus, the remainder of the witch following the hat was neither a little lacking in the clothing department, nor possessed of a sweet smile. What might pass on a dark night for seaweed was in profusion, however.

"Why would anyone leave a puddle that deep near the damn doors?" muttered the witch, and hopping on one foot she removed a substantial boot from the other. She turned the boot upside down and swore at the stream of water that poured out. Replacing the boot, she strode up to the door and knocked, well, booted the door until a small hatch opened in the door and a face appeared.

"We're closed for rivet Rivet RIVET," muttered the face through a beard. As frogs don't have beards, he became clean-shaven rather quickly. The witch tapped her foot a couple of times, but the cold water splashing around her ankles dissuaded her from continuing.

Inside the workshop, a common business conversation was taking place as the nominal supervisor slammed down the phone on a customer.

"Did yer tell him that his cheque came back?" asked a nearby dwarf, putting a piece of pizza down on top of a pile of unpaid invoices.

"Yes."

"Well, what did he say?"

"So did the faults you said were fixed."

"Rivet, rivet!" complained the frog from behind the door. The supervisor sighed, and walked warily to the small hatch.

"May we help you, madam? And could you see your way clear to restoring our colleague here?"

"I'm not happy that I've had ter come back here," declared the witch.

There was a certain level of muttered agreement on the other side of the door.

"What seems to be the trouble?" asked the supervisor, elected unanimously to the position of customer care consultant by everyone else.

"Me broomstick. It keeps cutting out and dropping me from a height."

The dwarf decided not to comment that it hadn't chosen enough height to stop her being able to complain. Like three thousand feet.

"When does it happen most, madam?"

"Landin'. And taking off. Sometimes when I'm just cruising, too."

A mental image of the middle-aged witch cruising traumatized the assembled dwarfs, some of whom began to sidle towards the rear of the workshop unit. The supervisor spun round.

"Stay where you are, you lot!"

"But that's Grizelda the Witch, an' she's in frog mood," replied one, dropping his spanner in fright.

"It's still lunch time, and I haven't finished my pizza," another complained. The supervisor bowed at the witch, turned to his recalcitrant colleague and glared at him from a distance of almost two inches.

"Do you want to tell her that?"

"Rivet rivet rivet!" suggested the new frog, hopping up and down anxiously.

A further dwarf – in appearance they were more or less interchangeable, and regular customers normally differentiated them by careful study of the pattern of ketchup stains on their overalls – opened one of his pockets and removed a small parcel of courage he had been saving for a rainy day. He then carefully opened the visitors' door, considerately closed the bear trap that lay just inside, and pulled the barbed wire to one side to allow Grizelda to enter without snagging her clothing.

Snorting, the witch stepped carefully through the door and looked around the inside of the workshop unit. Stands stood along one wall, bearing broomsticks in various stages of repair. Several had been there long enough to acquire their own spider colonies. She thrust her broomstick towards the nearest dwarf.

"Tek it!" she ordered. The dwarf stepped back, but Grizelda stepped forward, until he reluctantly accepted her offered broomstick. He looked vaguely surprised that it didn't try to bite him and looked around for a repair stand. The witch nodded in triumph, then frowned when oil dripped onto her boot from the shadowed, shrouded shape that was lifted above her head on a ramp.

"What's that?" she demanded.

"Um, special job that, a bit hush-hush."

Grizelda snorted, and lifted a corner of the thick sacking. A gleaming black sleigh runner appeared, and an anxious dwarf jumped forward. Grizelda glared at him and lifted a little more of the cloth, before dropping it back down again. The dwarfs all relaxed.

"Whose is this, then?" asked the witch.

"Notsanta's."

"I can see it's not Santa's, his is bright red."

"No, it's Notsanta's."

"Notsanta?" The witch cracked her finger joints, and the echoes ran all around the workshop, terrorizing the spiders.

The supervisor looked all around, but mainly for effect, and then lowered his voice. As he was only four feet high to begin with, the witch had to lean forward to catch his words.

"You know how every force in the universe has an equal and opposite reaction?"

"Like Ying an' Yang?" asked Grizelda, a bit nervous that the conversation was about to get technical.

"I thought they were American comedians?" asked one of the dwarfs.

"Nah, that's Cheech an' Chong," replied another.

"I thought they were the Marx brothers?"

"Don't start on Marxist jokes, Karl will moan at you all afternoon."

Grizelda glared at them, and they shut up.

"Anyway," continued the supervisor, "Santa is a force. And that belongs to his opposite. You don't want to meet Him on a dark night, I can tell you."

"Why?" demanded Grizelda, confident that she was the most dangerous entity in the area.

"'Cos everything He's got is jet black, and you can trip over Him an' His gear."

"What is it He does, then?" asked Grizelda.

The supervisor shook his head. "You don't want to know."

"Yes I do."

The supervisor looked around again.

"You know that Santa has a list of who's naughty or nice?"

Grizelda nodded.

"Well, Notsanta gets to visit all the girls who've been bad."

Grizelda's expression didn't change.

"I thought that were Santa's job – and why he's always got a smile on his face," she said.

The supervisor leant forward and whispered in her ear.

"Ah. Right. OK, I'll keep out of His way then. If His vehicle is in here, where is He now, then?"

"Probably still in the pub," replied the nearest dwarf.

They all stepped carefully away from the silent, shrouded shape on the ramp. Oil dripped down and smouldered on the concrete. Grizelda looked at her boot, but the oil had failed to make an impression there. She smirked slightly and then turned her attention back to the supervisor.

"You told me that it were properly fixed last time I were here with it."

"Well, we were sure it were fixed."

"Then why does it keep on misfiring?"

"Look, lady, the thing is so old you've got to expect problems. Why don't you buy a new one? You'd get a warranty an' everything, you know."

"It's not old. It's matured," objected Grizelda.

"Like a wine?"

"It certainly has a whine when it's running, that's true."

A second dwarf approached carefully. "I replaced all the bristles last time you were in here, madam. And the time before that we scarfed a new section into the handle. But every time we put new bits in, the problems come back. I think you've got a virus."

Grizelda sneezed, and the dwarfs jumped back a pace. "I've had an head cold for a couple of weeks, it's true." She pulled out a handkerchief that, properly treated, could have replaced the research section of the government's biological warfare department for the next decade. After blowing her nose, she selfishly returned it to her pocket instead, to the general relief of the dwarfs.

"Not that sort of virus. I meant in the operating system." The supervisor turned to his co-worker. "Have you run it through a spellchecker, Fred?"

"Did that last time."

"And?"

"That cheap new spellchecker you bought keeps defaulting to Chinese, and I think the spells were coded in Yorkshire. It kept trying to order chicken fried rice and Peking Duck from the nearest takeaway."

"I see. Useless."

"Yes, 'cos we've only got the pizza place and the fish 'n' chip shop."

Grizelda started to draw a deep breath, then – as the stale aromas hit her – changed her mind.

"I'm going for a cup of tea in the village. I'll be back in two hours, and I want it sorted out by the time I get back," she announced.

The dwarfs exchanged glances, and breathed a collective sigh of relief, as the door slammed behind her. One opened his mouth to speak, and four hands slammed across it in a reflex action. The door slid silently open, and the witch's head poked back in.

"Sorry, forgot something," she said innocently, then nodded at the frog at her feet. The reconstituted dwarf leant heavily against the wall, breathing hard, as Grizelda vanished outside.

The dwarfs looked at each other and then at the offending broomstick. The lucky bearer of the broom held it gingerly, as though it might bite, and with relief popped it onto one of the special repair stands that stood nearby. The dwarfs clustered around it. One, with no regard for his personal safety, sucked his own teeth.

"Right!" said Fred. "We need some action an' we need some ideas."

"I've always got some ideas," called a fresh voice from the door.

"Oh no, not him as well," groaned he-who-had-been-frogged.

"Just what we didn't need," agreed the supervisor, putting his hand on his wallet in a protective fashion. "Dave, the spare part salesman. Who forgot to reset the bear trap, then?"

"Such a cheery welcome I always get here!" announced Dave, grunting slightly as he edged his big bag of samples past the barbed wire at the door. His grin and flashing white teeth seemed to stand out brilliantly in the gloom of the workshop, as did the gold chain around his neck. The bracelets clinked solidly under the sleeves of his jacket.

"Who's going to offer me a cup of tea?" Dave demanded.

There was a pause. Then most of the dwarfs remembered that the kettle was at the back of the workshop, and all but the unfortunate supervisor shot off out of reach. The latter practised running on the spot for a moment, until he realized that Dave had a tight hold on his overalls, and he couldn't escape with the others.

"This," Dave said with the manic cheerfulness taught to all high-pressure salesmen, "is your lucky day, chief!"

The dwarf looked dubious.

"I've got some samples I can let you have of some new potions for broomsticks and some self-spell-restoring bristle lotion!"

"Oh yeah? Is it any better than the last lot you left us?"

"Why do you ask? It's new! It's got to be great!" enthused Dave.

"Well, we used one of the last add-ons you tried on us."

"And?"

"The user complained. She said she flew round inverted for two days."

"So?"

"We had to buy her a new pointy hat. And some thermal underwear."

"You'll not have any trouble with this batch, I promise you. Look at what I've got here!"

Despite himself, and the noises from the back of the workshop where six dwarfs were fighting over who was going to fill the kettle, the supervisor looked into the open case.

"What's that?" he asked, prodding a padded envelope. Dave maintained his fixed smile.

"The only free item there," he replied. "It's a service pack update for the Spellcheck Machine you leased last year. Fixes a couple of small glitches, you'll probably not even have come across them!"

"You mean the fact it defaults to mandarin?"

"The future's orange," Dave assured him. "I keep hearing that on the telly."

"No, mandarin the language," complained the dwarf.

"Oh, that. Big market for us, China."

"All them tea cups you keep breaking."

Dave dismissed the criticism with an airy wave of an arm. The dwarf ducked, and winced as one of the heavy gold bracelets clanged off his once shiny mechanic's helmet.

"Just put the disc in after I've gone, and all will be well. Now, let me show you this!"

Dave reached into his case and reverently brought out a small glass bottle and a large book.

"Latest thing! You dust some of this onto the bristles and they get magically regenerated! The broom flies a bit faster, it's more economical and the owner gets some extra kudos for being in tune with the environment."

"What's that book for?"

"Oh, that's the application manual and the terms, conditions and exclusions. You don't need to worry about that!"

Wincing slightly from the weight, the dwarf picked up the tome from the floor and flicked through it, squinting at the lettering.

"It seems to be written in mandarin, too," he objected.

"Business is business, chief. It's the coming market, the business language for this century, and we all have to be fluent in modern practice."

"This is a traditional business, though, this is."

"Well, I can see that," agreed Dave, looking around at the cobwebs growing over some customers' personal transport devices. He accepted the tea reluctantly offered by one of the returning dwarfs and drank gingerly. With an extraordinary effort of will, he managed not to wince at the sugar level, and put the mug down on a nearby shelf.

"Try this!" he urged, grabbing a small box from his case.

"What is it?"

"In-flight entertainment. Straps to the front of the broom."

A dwarf pressed a button on the box, and the workshop echoed to a strange, eerie noise. The dwarf pressed the button again, and silence returned. Dave spread his gleaming grin around for effect.

"Whalesong!" he announced. "Environmentally sound, too."

"Sound would drive me mental, right enough."

"What about this? Again straps to the broom, you can sell it as an add-on when you use some of that dust on the bristles."

"What's it do?"

"Beeps loudly to tell you that a speed camera is close by."

Several dwarfs nodded with appreciation.

"Then the rider can zap the camera, instead of the other way round," one approved.

"And," smirked Dave, "the 'piece de resistance'!"

"What is it resisting?" asked Fred.

"Nah, that's us, resisting buying it," the supervisor replied.

"Special new formula," Dave said in honeyed tones. "Go-faster stripe paint. Paint this on the handle, you get an extra twenty mph until the paint wears off, and then you can sell a second application."

"How long does it last?"

"Depends how thick you apply it."

"You've got ter be thick to apply it at all," protested Fred.

"It does what it says on the tin – jar – pot, though," Dave assured them. He pulled out his order pad. "I'll put you down for half a dozen, then, shall I? A case of the bristle powder and some of the Traffic Alerts and a few pots of anti-drag stick polish ..."

One of the dwarfs had, quite fearlessly, stuck his head into the case to examine a packet that caught his eye.

"Here, what's these red buttons in this box?" he asked.

Dave looked a little uncomfortable. "That was a demonstration line, but I'm not supposed to sell them. They actually *did* work properly."

The dwarf mechanics' faces registered disbelief.

"What are they?"

"Emergency stop buttons. When pushed, the broom stops," Dave explained.

"What was the problem?"

"We had customers coming back, flying off the handle at us."

"Why?"

"The broom stopped so fast that they flew off the handle."

Dave went back to writing on his order pad and placed some samples on the shelf beside the door. He looked again at the cup of (almost) tea, shuddered, and offered the supervisor his pad and a pen. Muttering in his beard, the dwarf signed the order form, ignoring as best he could the complaints coming from his wallet.

"I'll leave you these samples, see you next time." Dave waved genially to the dwarfs and, his bracelets flashing, stepped back out past the barbed wire. A moment later, his wrist shot back in and grabbed his smile. As the door shut behind him, the dwarfs heaved a sigh of relief.

"Right," said Fred. He grabbed an armful of the new samples and turned to glare at the offending broomstick. "What say we try some of this lot on it, then?"

"Or all of them on it?"

"Good idea!"

The dwarf mechanics advanced on Grizelda's broomstick, which quivered on its stand as the weight of their glares fell upon it.

The stand containing various assorted cakes quivered on the counter, until Grizelda withdrew her glare and turned it onto the café owner instead.

"Tea!" she demanded.

"Yes, luv. Sugar on the counter, there."

Grizelda swept an imperious glance around the small room. Apart from one table, the place seemed empty.

"You aren't very busy," she commented.

"No, luv." The café owner leant forwards across the counter. Grizelda leant forwards to meet him, and he recoiled quite quickly.

"It's that chap there. In the black cloak an' hood … He keeps glaring at the folk who come in, and they leave quick."

"Won't work on *me.*"

"Er, no, I can see that. I'll bring your tea over, shall I?"

"An' a couple of them scones."

Grizelda turned on her heel and stomped noisily across the café floor to a table near the window. The window was obscured by a poster for a recent gig by the Banned Underground, but two weeks of being fixed to the café window had rendered the poster nearly as squalid as the Banned Underground themselves. Grizelda, with a shudder, pulled at one corner until it fell off the window. She looked out through the grime to enjoy the rain-washed vista, shuddered and turned back. The café owner approached with her tea and scones and a pot of jam.

"Turned out nice again," he observed. Grizelda just looked at him and he turned away.

"Two customers I get today," he muttered to himself, "and they are both miserable gits."

The hood jerked slightly and the café owner found himself lying on his floor, nose embedded in a large sticky blob of ketchup. There was the suspicion of a snigger behind him, but the café owner ignored that and with enormous dignity – and a red nose – marched off.

"Pleased ter make your acquaintance," remarked Grizelda, conversationally.

"Do you know who I am, then?" asked the hooded figure.

Grizelda sipped her tea and pulled a face. She tipped a large part of the sugar bowl into her cup, stirred it vigorously, and nodded in satisfaction.

"I saw your – vehicle, let's say, in the workshop."

"Oh, right. I see. Does it not worry you?"

"Why should it? I'm not a child."

"In my official capacity, I can visit adults too."

"How is that? I thought you only happened to children!" demanded Grizelda.

"I used to be a teacher, before I got the job of Notsanta instead of the pension. So when the contract terms were being finalized I included School Inspectors in the target group too."

"Well, I'm not one of them."

"Lucky for you," remarked Notsanta darkly, and with little regard for his personal safety drank more tea.

"What were up with your sleigh, then?" asked Grizelda, curious.

"Well, my reindeer aren't like the ones that red-dressed bloke gets. His are friendly and approachable. Mine are more than likely to not just bite the hand that feeds them, but eat it up to the elbow as well. As a propulsion system, they are definitely outmoded and I keep trying to get an upgrade."

"Hum, I could see that. No traction control."

"Right. Anyway – purely out of spite, I'm convinced – they keep kicking seven bells out of the sleigh runners, and messing with the onboard guidance system by peeing into the sensors. I mean, it was bad enough anyway – kept going the wrong way up one-way streets – but when it has a five hundred yard positioning error too … well, you can imagine the complaints we got when kids were getting me instead of the other one."

"Humm, I could see that," agreed Grizelda.

"And when I visited some poor innocent lawyer …"

"Isn't that a contradiction in terms?"

"Probably. I mean, how was I to know he wasn't a School Inspector? He looked nasty enough to me. Still, the fuss he kicked up made them send the Notsleigh in for its first proper service in years. Should be done soon."

Grizelda recalled the silent, shrouded and deserted shape on the ramp. "How long?" she wondered.

"Another three months, they tell me. That's three months I'm going to be sat in this café."

There came a choked wail of despair from behind the counter, where the café owner was still engaged in a life or death struggle with the ketchup on his nose.

"Three months? I'll be ruined!"

"So will my insides be if I drink your tea for three months. Don't worry, I'll move on next week," sneered Notsanta.

The café owner subsided behind his counter and looked at the small array of cleaning materials there. With a sigh, he dismissed them as useless, picked up some sandpaper instead and applied it to his nose.

Grizelda tried her tea again, pulled a face and put the cup down.

"Nice meeting you, I think," she said to Notsanta, who nodded. Boots clumping on the floor, she left the café for the walk back to the garage.

"Oi!" called Notsanta as the door closed behind her. The café owner rose from behind the counter with the sandpaper covering most of his face.

"More tea!"

"Right!" said Fred. "Just time ter put this stuff on before she gets back!"

"Before who gets back?" asked Grizelda, quietly, into his ear.

Fred froze, which all things considered was possibly his safest course of action. Grizelda stepped back and then walked all around her broomstick, whilst the assembled dwarfs stood and watched her in horror. Or terror. Or both, for good measure.

"Am I a bit early, then?" she asked innocently. "Don't let me stop you working."

"Right," said Fred and, as he watched in horror, the small paintbrush he was holding pulled his arm towards the broom and started painting stripes along the handle. Grizelda nodded approvingly and several of the dwarfs started to breathe again.

"So," smiled Grizelda (no one was fooled by the smile, in fact several dwarfs started to edge away) "is it finished, then?"

"Well, madam," muttered the supervisor. "We've done all we can. If it don't work better this time, you really will have ter buy a new one."

"I see. Well, I suppose that if you really have done all you can, I'd best take it for a test fly."

"Right," said Fred.

Grizelda held out her hand and the broomstick slid from the repair stand into her grasp. Again, she nodded approvingly. "Whatever you did to it, it feels better at the moment. No!" She held up a hand as a dwarf started to speak. "I'll find it all out for meself."

The witch carefully eased out of the door and then took off slowly into the darkening sky. Behind her, the door slammed shut and was quickly locked from the inside.

"Right!" said Fred and started for the rear exit.

"Where are yer going so fast?" called the supervisor after him.

"I'm going home. Now. Quick."

"Why?"

"Because Karl went and installed that Emergency Stop button, and I don't want ter be here when she tests it out."

The remaining dwarfs looked slowly at each other, then at Karl. Then they all started running for the back exit.

Outside, over the lake, Grizelda's cloak streamed out behind her as she tried a power dive, followed by a sharp turn on pulling out of the dive over the shore of the lake.

"Wheeeeeee!" she screamed in delight at the increased performance of her old broomstick. "Wheeeeeee!" she screamed as her hands slipped on the newly polished stick. Twenty feet above the dark waters she sped across the lake, the go-faster paint stripes sparkling with power; the glossy finish of the wood improved by Dave's anti-drag polish, but a little slippery still in her hands.

"Now, I wonder what this red button here does?" she wondered. Out over the dark, cold waters of the lake, she leant forward to try it out.

*

The characters appearing here are on special leave (or possibly have gone AWOL) from The Vampire Mechanic, the third in the Banned Underground series by the same author. The Alliance of Worldbuilders would like to thank Red Kite Publishing Limited for sanctioning their involvement, or maybe just failing to object loudly enough. Rumours that Grizelda threatened to turn the publisher into a frog if he disagreed are, well, just rumours. Probably.

WYRM
BY A. F. E. SMITH

From the window of my tower, I watch them come. Men on horseback, men on foot. Thin men, fat men, dark men, fair men; some cloaked in rich embroidery, some in the more sober garb of prosperous merchants, a few wearing little more than rags. All are armed in accordance with their station: swords, axes, pitchforks, stout sticks.

They are here, like the knights of old, to slay a dragon and win the hand of a princess.

I look at my hand, white-knuckled against the stone. The nails are chipped and dirty, the skin scratched, the cuff at the wrist frayed. It doesn't look much like the hand of a princess. But I suspect few of my would-be suitors will mind – not with the dazzle of my father's gold in their eyes and the lure of his throne before them. They seek to step into a dead man's shoes by ridding the kingdom of the creature that killed him. And until one of them does, this tower will be my home.

That was what the noblemen of my father's council decreed, after he was found broken and bloody in the Wyrmwood. No doubting what had done it: the tracks were there to read, earth gouged by clawed feet and rocks singed with flame, trees felled by the creature's passing. A dragon had returned to the kingdom, where such had not been seen for nigh on a hundred years. And so for my own protection, the noblemen said, I must remain locked within these walls until a champion can be found to destroy the threat. For my own protection, and also for theirs – because who would attempt to slay a dragon without promise of reward?

Not that I am much of a reward.

Once I might have dreamed of marriage. Of children. Of love. But those dreams are long buried. Since my father's death, I rarely dream of anything except the dragon: talons tearing into tender skin, fire raging through flesh. Those images haunt me. Yet I have a duty to my people and my kingdom. To be their queen, to fulfil the role I was born to, I must marry.

And so I watch the men arrive, the still green arches of the Wyrmwood beyond them, and wonder how many must suffer before the dragon is finally conquered.

Buried too deep to be found, the wyrm slumbers. Flame banked, claws sheathed, it lies coiled. Dormant. Waiting.

It dreams of screaming. Of blood and agonised pleas. Of the swift, hot satisfaction of rending limb from limb.

It dreams of vengeance.

Once the aspirants are gathered in the great hall, Lord Elgan – the oldest and kindest of the noblemen – comes to fetch me. Consternation crosses his face when I step out into the light of the stairwell. I have made no attempt to disguise myself, to wrap myself up in fine fabrics and perfumes and cosmetics like a birthing-day gift tied with a bow. I am going to them dishevelled and unadorned, clothed only in an old gown and my grief.

"Your highness. Do you think perhaps – a comb –" Elgan falters, and I smile at him. Or at least, I show my teeth.

"They will take me as I am, Elgan, or not at all. Would you have a king who cannot see beyond the surface of things?"

"No. No." As I said, he is kind. He holds out his arm for me, and adds in a half-whisper, "Though nothing could ever hide your likeness to your mother."

My pain swells into something that makes me stumble. Five years, and I feel her absence as keenly as ever. If she hadn't died, I wouldn't have to marry now. If she hadn't died, my father too would still be alive.

Were she to return from the dead, I doubt she would even know me, no matter the likeness between us. The gulf between the twelve I was then and the seventeen I am now is almost too wide to bridge.

"So Father always said," I agree with Lord Elgan. "And would that it were not so."

We are at the doors to the great hall. Before Elgan can ask me what I mean, I step forward and fling them open. He scurries round me to make the formal announcement.

"Her most Royal Highness, the Princess Meaghan!"

Silence. As one, the men turn. I stand without speaking or moving, letting them see my bitten nails, my unkempt hair, the marks of sorrow on my face; and I watch their eyes. Those who grin with greed, looking at me as they would a trophy, I discount straight away. They don't have the strength of will to defeat the dragon. Likewise those who glance away, embarrassed on my behalf; if they can't endure a woman's grief then I doubt they can endure much else. That leaves less than a handful, men who regard me gravely and steadily. Men who face me as equals. Men who might kill a wyrm.

I number them to myself: red hair, dark hair, no hair. Three, then. Red-Hair is a nobleman's son, one I vaguely recognise, but he doesn't appear cocky as he studies me – only thoughtful. Dark-Hair is of merchant stock, solidly built with a stolid gaze; his lack of discomfort may stem from a lack of imagination, but I'll give him the benefit of the doubt for now. No-Hair is a warrior through and through, shaven-headed and carrying enough steel to fill an armoury.

Perhaps he is here for the sport, but at least he's looking at me as if I'm a person, not a prize. Three. Three possible chances out of fifty.

As I turn to go, the random shifting of the crowd opens a line of sight clear to the back of the hall. There, a man leans against the wall and watches me from beneath his hood. A fold of his cloak covers his mouth and nose, but I can see his eyes. They are alive with amusement.

Maybe make that four.

I nod to Lord Elgan, and he takes my arm to escort me back to my tower.

The wyrm sleeps, but lightly. Now it has been awoken once, little will be needed to wake it again. A shout, an arm raised in anger, a man trespassing where he shouldn't – all will be met with swift and bloody retribution. The wyrm knows nothing of weakness. The wyrm defends itself.

Let them bring their weapons. Let them bring their desire for dominance. The wyrm is fire and scale and claw. The wyrm is stronger than them all.

The next day, accompanied by two of the noblemen, I stand in the long gallery and watch my aspirant champions training in the courtyard below.

"Fewer of them than yesterday," Lord Rhain remarks. He is a brusque man with a thin moustache. "Looks like you scared some of them off with last night's display, your highness."

"If they are that easily scared then I hardly think they would have the courage to face a wyrm," I point out, and he glares at me.

"We need those men. Who knows how many attempts it will take to kill the beast?"

"I notice Lord Telor is not complaining." I incline my head towards the red-haired nobleman on the other side of me. "But then, I have just increased his son's chances of becoming king."

A flush rises in Telor's pale skin, but he says nothing. Forgetting himself, Rhain grabs me by the upper arm and swings me to face him.

"This is not a game, Meaghan!"

"Let go of me," I say icily, though my flesh has melted into quivering fear at his touch. "I will be your queen, Rhain. Learn some respect."

Slowly he removes his hand and steps back. "I apologise, your highness," he says. Then, with a calculating glance from beneath sparse brows, "But you cannot be a queen without a king."

This is true, and so I say nothing. The laws of our kingdom dictate that a woman cannot rule alone; hence the noblemen's fear. Hence my need to marry. Until the dragon is slain and my hand is claimed, we are weak – a ripe plum waiting to be plucked by a greedy hand.

Fists clenched, I turn back to the courtyard and study the sparring men in silence. Black-Hair's solidity turns out to be stupidity after all, and so I discount him. Red-Hair is deft and swift, but he fights as if he is performing in a mock-mêlée here at court: perfect, polite, *honourable*. If he wants to be a king, he must learn cunning.

I turn my attention to No-Hair. As I would have guessed, he dominates the sparring ground. Already the other men are skirting warily around him, unwilling to risk incapacitating injury in what is merely practice. As his current partner falls back, winded, he turns in a circle and rattles his weapons with a grin.

"Come on, fellas! Who's next?"

Silence. He is strong. Perhaps he will be the one to –

"I'll try you." A man steps forward from his leaning-post against the wall, shedding his cloak behind him. His hair gleams silver in the weak sunlight, but his dark, almost black eyes are familiar from last night. The hooded man.

"Not afraid I'll break you, little 'un?" No-Hair asks in gentle mockery – and indeed, Silver-Hair is slight beside him, barely more than my height and slender with it.

"Terrified," Silver-Hair says, smiling. "But I'll take my chances."

They salute each other, and the bout begins. No-Hair is clearly the stronger and more experienced of the two, but Silver-Hair is ... I have no better word than *slippery*. He is agile, but more than that: he is never quite where I expect him to be. Time and again, he should be beaten back by one of the shaven-headed warrior's blows, yet time and again he is successful in evading it. Watching them, I am torn. A king should be a capable warrior, yes, but he should also be capable of trickery. Though Silver-Hair is outmatched in arms, his cunning makes him the other man's equal. That is to be admired.

Finally, though, he is cornered and disarmed, knocked off his feet to sprawl on the ground. No-Hair leans over him, touching the blade of his short sword lightly to his throat. "You concede?"

"Well ..." Silver-Hair's leg lashes out, quick as thought, and No-Hair is tripped off balance. Scrambling to his feet as the other man falls, Silver-Hair catches the weapon and spins it round to point back at its owner. "Perhaps not. Do you?"

No-Hair grins up at him. A murmur ripples through the watchers. Yet before anyone can react further, a third man steps forward: one who last night looked at me with greed in his eyes.

"Enough of this! We are here to kill a dragon, not play with each other. Tomorrow at dawn, I will find the wyrm and destroy it!"

He puffs out his chest, grinning, as the men's attention turns to him; as cheers and mocking shouts alike surround him. With a shrug, I walk away down the gallery.

I already know he won't succeed – and even if he does, he won't get me.

The wyrm watches the man advance, axe held in a two-handed grasp. An axe! As if he is going to fell a tree or chop off a chicken's head ready for the pot. His face blanches as he takes in the full scale of the wyrm, fully twenty-five feet from nose to tail, but he keeps coming. A vision of gold shines in his eyes. And they say dragons are treasure-hungry.

When he is close enough, he swings the axe in a clumsy arc towards the wyrm's neck. He thinks this is going to be easy; he should think again. The wyrm's horned head sends the weapon flying from his hands; one vast clawed foot kicks against his chest, knocking him over, pinning him down. A jet of flame scorches his cheek. Now he is writhing and screaming, desperate to escape, gore flowing freely from his lacerated flesh. He was stupid and arrogant, and now he will pay the price.

Yet there are worse things than stupidity and arrogance.

The wyrm wrenches its talons free, leaving the man torn and bloody but alive. It watches him limp from the clearing, clothing and dignity in tatters. Then it stretches – a long, satisfied stretch – before returning to its sanctuary.

"From now on, I want to decide who faces the dragon," I tell the noblemen. "Clearly not all these men are capable of it."

"What makes you think you are qualified –" Lord Rhain begins hotly. I give him a look, and he curbs himself. "Forgive me, your highness, but you know nothing of the masculine arts. How can you possibly tell who is best suited to the task?"

"Conquering the wyrm will require more than skill in weaponry," I say. "And so will being our king. Both require intelligence. Courage. Guile. Is that not so? Surely it is better for me to select the likely champions than for them to select themselves."

Silence. With an inward sigh, I switch from logic to emotion. "Besides, I am to be married to the victor. It's only fair that I should have some say in who that victor might be."

"Of course, of course," Lord Elgan says. "After all, Rhain, it makes little difference. One man faces the dragon every day until it is killed: that doesn't change."

Rhain sighs. "Very well."

"Good." I look around the table at each nobleman in turn. "Then our aspirants must be involved in more than weapons training. Here's what I want them to do ..."

Over the next few days, I hold a series of events: frivolous things, games and conversation and dancing. And as the men struggle with these new situations, I search for the qualities I expect in a king. I watch Red-Hair navigate each occasion with courtly ease and a complete lack of awareness that he is under observation; I watch No-Hair blunder through, awkward but supremely determined; I watch Silver-Hair watch the others and laugh. I try to decide which of them will be the one to succeed. And in the meantime, each morning I select a different man to attempt the Wyrmwood. They all come back bloodied and bruised. But they aeedll come back alive.

The noblemen begin to grumble.

One day, after a long and tedious performance by a visiting troubadour, it is Lord Telor who escorts me back to my tower. Before we are halfway, he looks at me sidelong and observes, "My peers are unhappy."

"They should turn their ire upon the men," I reply. "Not upon me."

"Princess Meaghan ..." He spreads his hands. "Whatever you are doing is not working. I beg you, let my son Gwern be the next to face the dragon."

I shake my head. "He is not ready."

"Is he any less ready than the others you have chosen?"

"Your son is clever and elegant," I say. "I have no doubt he is brave. But he lacks cunning. I would not send him to be mauled by the creature before he has learned what he needs to learn."

"Please, your highness." Telor looks at me imploringly. "Gwern would make an excellent king. He is of noble birth. And I have seen that he doesn't displease you."

What does noble birth have to do with it? I want to ask, but I suppress the question. Telor will haunt me until he gets what he wants; I might as well give it to him now. Let Red-Hair go in search of the wyrm. It's possible he will succeed, but even if he doesn't, it can't hurt for Telor to owe me a favour.

"Very well, Lord Telor," I say. "Gwern will be next to make the attempt. But remember: this was your desire, not mine."

The red-haired man stops at the edge of the clearing and offers a courtly bow, though his hand remains on the hilt of his sword.

"I salute you, mighty wyrm. May the best of us win."

His politeness is pleasing. Yet there seems little reason for him to be polite. The wyrm did, after all, rip his king apart.

It charges, but the red-haired man is nimble. He skips to the side; the blade flashes down. The wyrm roars and backs away, leaving a shattered talon lying on the moss. Grinning, the red-haired man scoops it up.

"When I am king, your skin will adorn my throne room."

Not so polite. Turning its head, the wyrm belches a vast cloud of flame in his direction. The man screams, rolling on the ground; the air fills with the stench of burnt cloth and singed flesh.

"Please –"

A second flame rolls over him, red as his hair. Sobbing, he scrambles away, still slapping at the small fires that cling to his clothing.

With any luck, he won't set the whole of the Wyrmwood alight.

The evening after Red-Hair returns from the Wyrmwood with burns all down one side of his body and a bloody talon clutched in his fist, I hold a ball – though I do not dance. I stand at the side of the room, dressed in a long black gown and gloves, and watch the ladies of the court dance with the aspirants. After a time, someone comes to stand beside me. I glance at him out of the corners of my eyes. It is Silver-Hair.

"Will you dance, your highness?" he asks me, catching the look. I shake my head.

"Not with you."

I wait to see if my rudeness will anger him – if he will storm off or lose his composure or be rude in return – but instead, a laugh tints his voice. "Then I hope you don't mind if I don't dance either."

I turn to face him more fully. "What's your name?"

"Owyne."

"I'm Meaghan."

"I know."

I scan his face: the light of amusement is still in his eyes. "You are always laughing. What is it that you find to entertain you in my father's death and the threat of a dragon laying waste to our kingdom?"

"In that, nothing," he says. "But in all this –" he gestures around the ballroom – "a great deal."

"And why is that?"

"Because I believe the man who wins the right to sit beside you as an equal will be selected as much by you as by any dragon-slaying skills he may possess. Some of the others complain that we are wasting our time on froth and frivolity when there is a dragon to be slain. But I've watched you assess us. You're trying to decide who deserves to share your secret."

My gloved hands clench into fists. "What secret?"

"Presumably, how to defeat the wyrm," Owyne says. "I can't believe you'd size us up like cattle for anything less."

I give him a brittle smile. "Sorry to disappoint you, but I have no such knowledge. If I did, I would certainly have no need of champions to perform the task for me."

Go on, I tell him silently. Say there's a difference between principle and practice. That I might know, but it will take a man to act. Something to make me dislike you.

"You might," Owyne says, leaving me simultaneously relieved and disappointed. Then he adds, "I can just imagine what Lord Rhain would say if you went to him with the key to the kingdom's survival. *Nonsense, Meaghan. What we need is a great big man with a sword.*"

That surprises a guilty giggle out of me. It's the first time I've laughed since my father's death, so it sneaks out somewhat furtively. Nevertheless, it is a laugh. I clap a hand over my mouth; Owyne's fingers settle lightly on the back of my wrist, drawing my arm down again.

"Laugh," he says. "No-one will fault you for it."

Reflexively I step back, out of his reach. "I will."

"Why?"

Because if it wasn't for me, my father would still be alive. I shake my head. "I have to go."

As I turn, he reaches out for me again – and again his touch is light, as if he knows how much I dislike the contact. "Meaghan ... I want to help you."

"Do you?" I fling at him. "Or do you want to help yourself?"

He would have a right to erupt in fury, at that. Men put up with far less from their wives and daughters, and I am neither to him. Yet his expression is disappointed rather than angry.

"I won't even try to slay the dragon, if such abstention will convince you," he says. "I'll give up all pretensions to your hand. Just talk to me."

I look at him, searching for deception. For some trace of his ever-present amusement, something to prove he is laughing at me. But I find nothing except honesty.

"You want to talk? Fine. We can talk. Meet me in the summerhouse at midnight."

"But I thought –"

"Be there," I tell him, and walk away.

When the ball ends, Lords Elgan and Rhain escort me back to my tower. Once they have locked the door and placed a guard, I change my gown for a shirt and a pair of breeches – though I keep the gloves on. Then I climb out of the window and down the ivy that covers the entire western wall. I glance up at the sky: it is already past midnight.

When I reach the summerhouse Owyne is waiting for me outside, lantern in hand, his hair reflecting the moonlight. He turns at my approach; I see the flash of his smile through the darkness.

"I thought you weren't coming."

I shrug. "You thought wrong."

He holds the door for me, then follows me inside. The lantern goes on the ceiling hook, and he regards me curiously by its gently swaying light.

"So now you're here, can you tell me *how* you're here? I thought you never went anywhere without an escort. I thought your tower door was locked at night."

"It is," I agree. "But the window isn't. Next time the noblemen want to imprison someone for her own safety, they should make sure there isn't a climbing plant growing up the outer wall with a stem strong enough to hold a grown man."

I admit it: I'm showing off. And I don't realise how much I'm giving away until he looks at me with eyebrows arched in speculation.

"Then you're not afraid of the dragon?"

"Put it this way," I say. "I'm not afraid to die."

It is meant flippantly, to turn his question aside, but the truth that underlies the words introduces an unintended note of bitterness. Owyne searches my face.

"Something has hurt you. What is it?"

I fold my arms in a tight barrier across my chest. "My father is dead. What else do you need?"

"When my father died, I mourned," Owyne says. "But I didn't lock up all my laughter. I didn't force myself to stop living."

"That's different."

"Why, Meaghan? Why is it different?"

"Because you weren't responsible for his death!" I blurt the words out, then wish I hadn't. I turn away, because there's no expression I could see on Owyne's face that wouldn't hurt. I don't want his condemnation. I'm afraid of his indifference. And I can't bear his pity.

"What happened?" He is calm. Just that. I can't read anything more from his voice at all, and somehow that helps me to speak.

"The day my father died, I'd gone to the Wyrmwood alone. I shouldn't have been there. I wasn't allowed outside the castle without guards, or anywhere without him knowing about it. But I needed to get away –" I choke as I remember what I was fleeing from. I don't want to talk about this. "He came after me, to bring me home. And he was killed."

He'd made me jump, I remember. He always had a noiseless step; I was never sure where he was in the passageways of the castle until we came face to face. In the wood, with the wind in the trees and birds calling from the branches, I hadn't heard him until his hand fell heavy on my shoulder.

"There you are."

I whirl, heart thudding in my chest. "Father —"

"You know you shouldn't be out here alone, Meaghan." His face is flushed, brows drawn down to meet at the bridge of his nose. "How many times do I have to tell you? It isn't safe."

"I'm sorry," I stammer. "I won't do it again, I promise."

"You're too independent." He isn't listening to me. He's frowning at me as if seeing something – or someone – else. "Your mother was the same."

The birds have fallen silent. I back away a step, fear creeping up my spine. "I know, Father. Come on, let's go home. Please."

But it's too late.

I'm shaking. I tuck my hands into my armpits, bow my head and close my eyes tight, but the memories keep coming.

"You saw it happen?" Owyne asks, an edge of horror in his voice. I almost forgot he was with me. I nod, pressing my gloved fist into my mouth to suppress a whimper. The blood … I can't stop remembering the blood …

"Then how did you escape, Meaghan?" It is a whisper. I look up. He's close, hands outstretched as though he wants to comfort me but knows I would reject it. I draw in a single, shuddering breath.

"I'm sorry, Owyne. I have to go."

The next morning, I allow No-Hair to set out in search of the dragon. Then, as I have every morning since the aspirants got here, I climb down the tower wall and head off into the Wyrmwood.

This man is bristling with weaponry. Sword, shield, knives, mace, flail. He wastes no time on conversation. He simply attacks.

The wyrm swipes at him with a taloned foot, but though it leaves gouges in his breastplate, it does not stop him. Fire blazes over his shield, but the man casts it aside before the heat can touch his skin. Then he is running along the length of the wyrm's body, beyond the reach of its teeth; even as the wyrm gathers itself together for another strike, the sword sinks deep into its hind leg.

The wyrm bellows. Its barbed tail swings round, knocking the warrior to the ground. A heavy foot descends on the man's chest, crushing metal into flesh. He chokes and splutters, fighting for breath. The wyrm presses harder.

He shed the wyrm's blood. He brought his aggression into the forest. He must be destroyed.

Glazed over with pain, his eyes plead for life.

After a long, reluctant pause, the wyrm lifts its foot.

As soon as the pressure on his chest eases enough for the man to move, he drags himself upright and staggers away, wheezing with every breath. Once he has gone, the wyrm turns its head to look at the sword still protruding from its leg. Wounded and in agony, it does the only thing it can think to do.

It retreats back inside the form it came from.

I run through the forest as fast as my legs will carry me. With every other step the wounded one buckles, sending pain shooting through me until my whole body is hot with it. I just have to reach the tower. If I can reach the tower, I will be safe.

For now, I won't even think about the prospect of climbing back up to my window.

The castle grounds are deserted, the remaining men at their training. Before I am halfway to my destination, my leg crumples beneath me and I fall to my knees. The blood roars in my ears. Dizzy spots dance before my eyes. Ahead of me, the tower rears up, as vast and inaccessible as an iceberg. I can't make it.

I haul myself back to my feet and head for the summerhouse.

By the time I get there, I am half stumbling, half crawling. I shove the door open and fall over the threshold, leaving smeared red footprints in my wake. Inside, I drag myself over to the far wall and prop myself against it, willing the world to stop spinning. I'm shaking, but I manage to tug off my gloves and explore the wound with numb fingers.

This serves me right. This serves me right.

The daylight coming in through the cobwebbed window flickers as someone passes it. I hear a muffled exclamation. Before I can cover myself or hide or shout a denial, the door opens and Owyne walks into the room.

"Meaghan! What –"

He takes in my bloody leg, and his expression changes. The air seems to solidify around us for a moment. Then, very slowly – as if I'm a wounded animal – he crouches down so that his head is level with mine. His gaze flickers to my missing fingertip and back again.

"It's been you all along," he says softly. "Hasn't it?"

I don't say anything. I can't. My heart pounds in my skull.

"It explains one thing," he says. Still soft, so soft. "I always wondered why your father was the only one the dragon actually killed."

His gaze is sad and knowing. He knows too much. My hands come up to cover my ears, but I can't block out the memory.

"You look so much like her." Fingers touching my hair. That hot intensity in his eyes.

"Father, don't." I push his hand away. He catches my wrist. Then my other wrist. Grip bruising. He pulls me towards him.

"Cari," he whispers against my lips. "How I've missed you."

"No, Father, it's me, Meaghan –"

Then his mouth is hard on mine. His body pinning mine down. Fear and revulsion and fiery outrage running through me. He promised – last time, the time before – he wept and said it was a terrible mistake and it would never happen again. Yet here he is, breaking me once more. Breaking me. My bones melt. My heart shatters. My skin dissolves. And then – and then –

The wyrm stirs. Memory floods through it, of the first time it emerged: how it took over the puny girl body that contained it, so small and helpless, and forced it to change. Nails became talons, hair became spines, skin became scales. Softness and weakness were transformed into size and strength.

Anger became fire.

The man had been hurting her, but now he was afraid. He tried to run. The wyrm caught him easily, sharp teeth sinking into his shoulder, shaking him like a limp rag. Gobbets of flesh and gore sprayed across the clearing. The man screamed and struggled, until the wyrm's talons sank into the softness of his belly and spilled out his guts. Then the scream became something else, something inhuman. And when the wyrm snapped his spine, it faded into an incoherent gurgle. Still the wyrm tore at him, rending his limbs and ripping his flesh until the earth beneath him was black with blood –

The recollection is compelling. The wyrm begins to wake.

I'm rocking back and forth, trying to jolt the memory loose from my head. I force myself to stop. Owyne touches my arm, and the dragon surges inside me. I don't know what looks out from my eyes, but he snatches his hand back as if bitten.

In a way, I wish No-Hair had killed me. Easy enough, to let his blade pierce my heart; to lie down, a beast forever, and sleep in the Wyrmwood.

I don't deserve easy.

"It's all right," Owyne is whispering, over and over. "It will be all right."

I turn on him. "Of course it won't! I killed my father. *I killed him.*"

"Because he hurt you." Our noses are almost touching; I can see myself reflected in his dark eyes, tiny and distorted. "Because he –"

"He was my father!" Using the wall, I push myself to my feet, away from him. Fierce emotion flares inside me, guilt and anger and pain and *the wyrm is stirring, the wyrm is opening slitted eyes and lashing its tail –*

A man calls outside, close by. "Owyne? You there?"

He's coming in. He'll find me. Everyone will see me and know my shame and I have to run, I have to get away –

It has to attack. It has to fight. And if it returns to the Wyrmwood now it will have its chance.

The last thing I hear before the wyrm takes control is Owyne's voice raised in alarm, providing me with a cover that may ultimately prove futile.

"Come quickly! The dragon has taken the princess!"

The wyrm crouches in the forest all night, veins humming with fear and fury. It could flee. It could fly away and never return. But a wyrm's purpose is to fight. To tear apart all who seek to take what is not rightfully theirs. To strike before it is struck.

As the first light of day touches the topmost branches, the latest champion appears on the other side of the clearing. His silver hair shines in the shade of the trees, matching the sword he carries. The wyrm charges forward, tail lashing, then stops in confusion. The man is placing the weapon on the ground. He is standing up and spreading his hands.

"Meaghan," he says softly. "What must I do?"

The wyrm looks at him, unblinking, as the raging fires inside it cool to a simmer. It should kill. It should destroy. And yet …

Very slowly, it stretches out its neck until its head is resting on the verdant moss. Its spines retract beneath the skin, leaving the throat vulnerable, offering the man a clear path to strike. Smoke rises from its nostrils, thin and straight in the still air.

The man picks up his sword again. The wyrm watches him, unmoving, as he walks steadily forward until he is within a blade's distance. He reaches out to place a palm against its warm scaled neck, perhaps gauging the best place for the blow to descend.

"Are you sure?" he whispers.

The wyrm closes its eyes.

The sword falls.

A girl lies in the Wyrmwood, in the clearing where her father died. A deep cut bisects her throat. Blood drenches her clothing and soaks dark into the moss beneath her. Beside her, a man stands with a scarlet-stained blade and waits, hope and sorrow in his eyes.

Around them, the forest is soundless.

After some time, other men begin to arrive at the clearing, ones and twos and clusters. Thin men, fat men, dark men, fair men; some cloaked in rich embroidery, some in the more sober garb of prosperous merchants, a few wearing little more than rags. They stop at the treeline and fall silent, bowing their heads.

"The wyrm?" one of the lords whispers, and the silver-haired man turns to face the gathering.

"Slain," he says softly.

"Then you are our king …"

"No." A wry smile crosses his face. "Meaghan is your queen. She was the one to rid the kingdom of the dragon."

"But – but she is dead …"

The silver-haired man glances back over his shoulder. "Think again."

The girl's chest rises and falls. Her eyelids flicker. Her hands move slowly across the moss, wiping away the wyrm's blood. Somewhere, a bird is singing.

She opens her eyes.

Illustration by Sophie E Tallis

THE WISHING TREE
BY SOPHIE E TALLIS

Evan sat on the branch, swinging her legs, something she had done a thousand times before, as she had done since she was a child. The Wishing Tree continued to whisper to her, soothing, caressing, each tender shoot and leaf urging her onwards. The pounding rain lost its power here. Nothing ugly could touch her in this magical place. Shards of moonlight slipped through the swaying canopy. She sighed. She could lose herself here, utterly. If happiness was a place, something tangible you could grasp or just be in, this was it.

She was vaguely aware of the acidic glow of the streetlights from the top of Hillrise and the distant hum of cars on the motorway. For so many people, this small neglected wood was no more than a dumping ground. Fly-tipping mounds, the cliché of broken shopping trolleys, used condoms, porno mags, beer cans and dog shit littered its dells and grassy knolls ... but it was still beautiful.

From an early age Evan had been drawn to the Wishing Tree, though she never knew why. Only *she* was able to climb its awkward gnarled branches. Only she had ever been brave enough to reach its fingers stretching ever skyward, then dangle like a deranged monkey while her friends screamed and cackled below. She had been invincible. But age tears down such possibilities, age tells you to tread carefully ... age puts the fear in you.

Evan watched the breeze catch the leaves around her, making them dance in the broken starlight. She closed her eyes and raised her arms in the air. She thought of the huge condors of South America, gliding on the thermals with their monstrous wings. The feel of the warm air under them, forcing them up. Only her balance could stop her from falling now. She looked into the gloom beneath her feet. At this height and with the rusty railings below, she knew if she fell she would kill herself.

The tree continued to whisper. She felt the soft wind pushing against her and the dappled light shifting over her eyelids. She had the overwhelming desire to let go.

That afternoon had passed in a haze. As always, Evan had trudged up the street to the bend in the road where she could see her house, sitting proudly at the end, and could see which cars were parked in front of it. An old rambling cottage, it sat on the corner of Wolfridge Street and the lane that led up to The Square. Its overgrown brambled garden, lined with old trees, stretched down the road toward her. She looked at the cars outside. Her father was still in and her mum hadn't come back from work yet.

Evan stood for a moment, deciding what to do.

School had finished at 3:30; it was now 5:39. She couldn't spend any more time wandering about, in case her mum phoned. She walked briskly, passing the overhanging holly and the three cars that had been left rotting in the garden for as long as she could remember. The radio was blaring in the kitchen as normal. She lifted the latch of the gate, hoping to avoid the usual squeak, but left it ajar in case she had to run. She stopped by the back door. Silence. She couldn't hear him: no fridge door clattering open and shut, no screeching of chair legs on the quarry-tiled floor. Evan turned her key in the lock – she'd perfected how to do this with no sound at all. She stood in the small lobby, listening through the stable doors.

It was deathly quiet.

She closed the back door behind her. She'd chance it. With any luck he'd be kipped out on the couch in the living room, glued to whatever sport was on, or he'd be upstairs sleeping it off and snoring.

The kitchen was empty. The dog didn't greet her. He must be in the living room with it. She instinctively looked in the bin at the empty cans there. Ten or twelve by her count.

Suddenly she heard a noise. *Shit, he's awake, he's coming!* Evan grabbed her bag and, as quickly and silently as she could, crept up the old cobbler stairs and along to her bedroom. If she was quiet enough, he wouldn't realise that she'd come home yet and he might piss on off to work or whatever.

She closed her bedroom door and sat on the edge of the bed, listening, perfectly still. The fridge door went again. The radio was turned up. She could hear the muffled voice of her father – probably speaking to Fluff, their dog, or to someone on the phone. Yes, now the back door was opening and he was calling Fluff to go out to the toilet before he left. She waited.

Eventually the dog came in. Evan waited for the shuffling her father always did, trying to eventually sort himself out for work. She knew she was safe as long as he didn't come upstairs. If he came upstairs, he'd walk along to her room to check if she was in.

He was in a hurry today. The back door slammed. Evan relaxed. She was safe.

She waited for the gate to go, then the predicted heavy footsteps back up to the door because he'd forgotten something. The keys in the door again, scraping chairs in the kitchen, heavy footsteps up the other stairs and the thud of him in her parents' bedroom. *Shit, please go down, don't come along!* Good, good … the steps were going down again.

"Evan? Evan? Are you in?" came the voice suddenly, calling up the old stairs.

She kept silent. Shit, shit! He was coming up. Panicked, she looked for somewhere to hide. Suddenly the stable door clattered shut and the back door slammed again. Keys locking it now, then the gate, then his car. *Wait, wait for the car to start and watch it leave. Wait ... wait.*

The street lights glowed red as Evan peered out of her window, keeping herself low, and watched as her father drove off.

Great! Relax. He's gone.

She closed her eyes. The Wishing Tree was talking to her again, soothing and calming her. The Wishing Tree was always there for her, whispering the answers to her English test, telling her what to say to the bullies at school, warning her of danger. Oh, how she loved it ...

She had relied on it more and more over the past few months, as the world around her seemed to slip away. Only she knew the secrets of the Wishing Tree; only she had been lucky enough, special enough, to be chosen. Every wish she had wished had come true, *every* one! She had only one more wish to ask ...

The evening came and the lights of the village glittered in the cold night. Mum's voice echoed over the answer machine. Staying overnight for a two-day conference – Evan had forgotten.

"... We're going to go down for dinner in a minute."

"Oh, right. How's the room?"

"You know, basic. It's all right. Is Dad there?"

"Uh ... no ... He's popped out to Tesco's to get some more milk," Evan lied. "D'you want me to get him to phone when he's back?"

"No, don't worry, we'll probably be at dinner then. You've seen the dinner in the fridge?"

"Yes, thanks."

"And there's salad to go with it if you want."

"Thanks."

"Are you all right? You're quiet tonight."

"Yeah, I'm fine."

"How was school?"

"It was fine, Mum ... honestly, everything's fine."

The phone went dead for a moment.

"Okay, well, I'll be back tomorrow. It'll probably be around six or seven, though. I'll phone you if it's later."

"Okay, have a nice dinner."

"I love you, sweetheart."

"I love you too, I'll tell Dad you phoned ... Have a good day tomorrow ... I love you, Mum."

"I love you too. God bless. Sweet dreams, darling."

"Love you ... bye, Mum ..."

"Sweet dreams." The phone clicked off.

"I love you," whispered Evan.

She held the receiver in her hand and pressed it against her forehead.

She could hear the tick of the grandfather clock in the kitchen and the hum of the fridge. She went downstairs and switched off the noise of the radio. She loved listening to the sounds of the house, the familiar creaks and groans she'd grown up with, in a home that she had loved and feared in equal amounts.

She glided the bolts of the back door across and turned the key. Double locked. Safe. He would have to use the conservatory now. This old house held so many memories, so many secrets, such magical joy and nostalgic happiness and such terror. Evan stood, her back pressed against the stable doors, taking in the view. The cracked quarry tiles, the pine cupboards that never quite fitted together. The solemn stretch of the Victorian sideboard, its dark smooth wood and the brass handles of its heavy drawers.

In summers past, her mother would stand by the window watching her children play in the garden, chasing each other between runner bean canes and past tended borders full of pansies, sweet peas and love-in-the-mist. Evan remembered the constant wail of the radio

217

and the shrill beating of the electric mixer. Her mum was always baking. The oven was always on. Wire racks loaded with hot jam tarts or cooling sponges, dishes half full of icing or buttercream, flour on counter tops, broken eggshells next to the sink ... and always water splashed on the floor.

"Mother's been in the kitchen!" they'd joke.

Evan touched the mixer, wiping her finger across the rim of the bowl, feeling a thin layer of dust under her skin.

Things change.

She didn't understand why, but she knew they did.

Evan switched off the light and left the kitchen in darkness. It was raining. She could hear it clearly now, pounding on the roof of the conservatory. Even in light rain, the sound was so loud the cat would be too frightened to go in. Now, it was thumping down, hitting the PVC like so many fists. Evan found rain to be cleansing, a way of freeing oneself from worries. But rain like this ... the sheer violence of it half frightened and half excited her. Standing in the midst of such an onslaught had a way of forcibly emptying any thoughts, filling the head and body with only the pounding noise.

She smiled.

She was glad it was raining. *Like tears*, she thought ... *tears for me?* She walked into the living room, the womb of the house. This, the smallest of rooms and the oldest in the cottage, with its low uneven ceiling and castle-width walls, was dominated by a fireplace far too large for the room, but somehow it worked. The leather sofa, now over 30 years old, bore more creases and lines, but had the warm steady comfort of something lived in: something that had seen and witnessed the best and worst of life and had still survived.

The Wishing Tree whispered again.

"Yes, I know. A fire, that's what we need."

A fire had already been laid in the hearth. Evan lit the paper sticks, watching carefully as the embers spread until she was sure the fire was lit and well on its way. She didn't know why, but she wanted the house to be warm. With any luck, when her father returned at two or three in the morning, pissed as a newt, he would come in here and just pass out on the couch. She knew he wouldn't check upstairs, so she had plenty of time now.

The smoke curled its way up the black chimney as flickers of flame caught light. The fire was blazing. Evan sat for a moment in its warm glow. The rain had stopped.

She glanced out of the window: it was still light. Only just, though. The Wishing Tree was waiting ... and the promise of yet more adventures. She wanted to reach it before dark.

She quickly kissed the cat and dog, then opened the conservatory door. She could smell the chimney smoke mixed with the fresh scent of rain. She closed and locked the door behind her. The house was warm and safe.

Now, sitting up in the tree, the sky was black and amidst the rustling tree branches she could hear rain coming once more. Perfect ... Magic Time!

Climbing higher in the tree, Evan smiled and swung her legs again. She had never felt so happy, so light. The Wishing Tree was calling her, calling her to its branches, to its loving embrace. She placed the heavy rope around her neck.

It was time to go.

HOW TO CREATE A VILLAIN OR LET SLEEPING CANDEMONS LIE BY JEREMY RODDEN

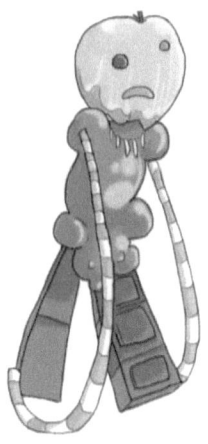

Art by Cami Woodruff

"Hello? Are you in there?" Roy G. Biv called into the darkness of the monster's cave at the base of Marshmallow Mountain.

"No!" The monster's hollow voice echoed in the cave entrance.

"Then who just answered?"

"It's a recording –"

"Oh, come on, Candemon," Roy interrupted. "Do we really have to go through that gag? Can you just come talk to me?"

Roy heard the Candemon shuffling to his feet. He took a few steps back from the mouth of the cave and nervously adjusted his rainbow-colored bow-tie. He forced a smile as the monster emerged from the darkness. The Candemon's pupil-less hard-candy eyes stared straight ahead.

"It's a beautiful day!" Roy cried. "Are you coming to the party at my castle?"

"What party?" the Candemon replied.

"I mailed you an invitation last week." Roy pointed a finger at the mailbox outside the cave that had C. Demon written on it in rainbow colors. The 'o' in demon was a little, red heart. "Um, you didn't have a mailbox so I made one for you. Then I put the invitation in it."

The Candemon walked awkwardly toward the mailbox on his candy-bar legs. He raised his candy-cane arms in the air . . .

SMASH!

. . . and destroyed the mailbox. "I hate parties," the Candemon said in his unique, empty-sounding voice. He turned back to the cave and began walking back inside. The entrance of the cave framed his candy-apple head, making it look like the Candemon was wearing the mountain as a hat.

Roy giggled at the mental image. The Frankensteinian candy monster turned back to Roy and tilted his head to the side. "Is something funny?"

"Erm, no?" Roy replied. "But, how can you hate parties?"

"I've never been invited to one."

Roy heard a tinge of sadness in the Candemon's voice and grew hopeful. "But you just were! By me!"

The Candemon scratched his head with one of his candy-cane arms. He glanced at the shattered mailbox. "Why?"

"Because you live on my Candy Island! I want everyone on Candy Island to be able to have fun and be happy."

"But why now? You've had other parties."

Roy looked up at the Candemon. He had to, considering the monster was over twice Roy's height. Roy felt his gaze fall on the upside-down gummy bear that served as the Candemon's torso. Something about the gummy bear's face being the Candemon's crotch always bothered Roy a little bit. The gummy bear's dead eyes looked just as vacant as the monster's proper ones.

"My eyes are up here," the Candemon said.

Roy hadn't realized that he was staring at the gummy-bear face. He quickly raised his eyes to the candy-apple head instead. "Sorry," he mumbled.

The Candemon crossed his arms over his chest. "And what fun and happiness is there for me, Roy?" Roy looked at the Candemon more intently. "And stop feeling sorry for me. I can feel your pity when you look at me."

He was right; Roy had always felt sorry for the Candemon, even though many of the other residents of Toonopolis feared and hated the creature.

"I'm sorry." Roy reached into his pocket and retrieved a handful of jellybeans. He offered a white one to the Candemon. "Jellybean? Freshly picked from the forest."

The Candemon reared back. "Two problems with that, Rainbow-Boy," he said. "Problem the first: me eating candy is pretty much cannibalism. Problem B: I hate the white ones because I always end up with nasty buttered popcorn."

"Oh, I guess . . . hey, wait a minute?" Roy sputtered as he realized the conflicting information within the Candemon's problems.

The Candemon laughed.

Roy's eyes opened in surprise. He had never heard the Candemon laugh before. Granted, it was a bit of a creepy, echo-y laugh, but a laugh nonetheless. Roy laughed too. "So you'll come to the party, then?"

The Candemon reached out with one of his arms. Roy flinched as the Candemon playfully flicked Roy's gnome hat to the ground. "We'll call it a maybe," the monster replied.

Roy picked up his hat and smiled. After placing his hat back on, he waved his fingers at the shattered mailbox. A stream of rainbows flew from Roy's hand and the mailbox was magically restored. "Bring your invitation."

Roy skipped away from the Candemon's cave happily, feeling hopeful that the Candemon might finally be able to join the rest of Candy Island's citizens in celebration. Now he just had to tell Princess Polipo that she was going to have a special guest at her Sweet Sixteen party.

"But Princess, you need to keep wet or your tentacles will dry out," said one of Polipo's royal guards.

"It's my party and I'll dry if I want to!" Polipo replied.

Roy heard the tail end of the conversation between the octonoid princess and her guard. He sighed. It sounded as though the Princess was continuing to be very demanding. She was standing on a stage in the center of Taffy Towers in a pink gown. The Rainbow PEZ Road ran underneath the stage and to Roy's throne behind it. She looked almost like a regular girl because her tentacles only barely poked out of the bottom. Roy felt her stare when she spied him. It was not a pleasant stare.

"Roy! Where have you been?!"

"Princess," her guard started, "you should not be impolite to Roy. It's rude to ask about his personal business."

"It's my party and I'll pry if I want to!" she replied.

The guard sighed and mouthed 'I'm sorry' to Roy.

"Don't worry, Cal, it's okay," Roy said. "You really should wear something that will not get ruined when you get wet, Princess. You'll get cooked out here in the sun."

"It's my party and I'll fry –" Her eyes drifted away from Roy and her face grew red.

Roy followed her stare. She was looking at an ice cream sculpture that was being carted in by a few of the party's caterers. Roy was impressed by the size and detail. It looked exactly like Princess Polipo, down to the pink fondant coloring her tentacles. Roy felt a breeze as the princess ran past him toward the sculpture.

"I'm really sorry, Roy," the guard said out loud.

"Don't worry about it, Cal."

"Um, I'm Ceph. Cal is my brother."

Roy felt his ears warm. "I'm so sorry, Ceph! I always get you two mixed up!"

Ceph narrowed his eyes and pressed his lips close together. He looked angry. "Are you saying all octonoids look the same?!"

Roy took a step back. "No . . . I just . . . you and Cal . . ."

"Oh stop it, brother." Roy turned and saw an identical-looking octonoid guard behind him. Ceph's twin brother Cal looked annoyed. "We really don't have time for this."

Ceph broke into a laugh and patted Roy on the shoulder. "My brother's right, Roy. We have to make sure everything is perfect for Polipo," he said with a bit of venom in his voice. "Can you keep an eye on Princess Pain-in-the-butt for a moment?"

"Sure, Ceph. I have big news for her. A special guest!" Roy gave a thumbs-up to the twin guards as they walked away. He found Princess Polipo giving the ice cream sculptors an earful.

"– And my nose isn't that big! And my hair is chestnut, not brown! You are ruining my party!"

"Um, Princess," Roy called.

"What?" she cried over her shoulder. "Roy, these idiots are ruining everything. This is supposed to be the best party ever. All of my friends from Underwater City High are going to be so jealous. It's supposed to be epic!" She pointed a finger at the people holding the ice cream copy of Polipo. "They hate me. They want my party to suck!"

Roy shooed the caterers away and drew Polipo's attention. "I'll make sure they fix it, Princess. Don't worry."

"Good."

"Now can you let me modify your dress so you won't dry out? It will look exactly the same, I promise."

The princess rolled her eyes. "I guess."

Roy waved his hand, sending rainbows to encircle Princess Polipo. He wiggled his fingers and then threw his hands in the air, the rainbows flying into the sky as he did. Polipo looked exactly the same.

"Feel that?" he asked. "I added some magic mist into the fabric on the inside of your dress to help keep your tentacles moist."

Polipo swirled in her dress, allowing the hem to spin in the air. She actually looked like she was going to smile. Roy didn't hold his breath.

"I have a surprise for you," said Roy. "You're going to have a special guest for the party."

"Ooh! Did Daddy get The Flatkey Boys to perform for me?!"

"Er, not exactly. But you will have a guest no one else has ever had. It's –"

BAHWOOOO!

Roy was interrupted by a trumpet blast from one of the royal guards. The sound of an octonoid conch shell was unmistakable. One blast of the trumpet called the octonoid guards.

BAHWOOOO!

Roy asked Polipo, "What does two conch blasts mean?"

"An attack," Polipo said. She yawned and shrugged her shoulders.

"But who would be attacking your part – oh no!" Roy realized who the guards thought was attacking the party. "Stay here!"

Roy didn't waste time running and used his magic to teleport to the location of the royal guards. What he saw proved his fear correct. Cal and Ceph were squaring off with the Candemon. They both were holding tridents and pointing them at the candy monster.

"Stay back, fiend!" one of the twins shouted.

"You are not going to crash our Princess's party!" said the other.

The Candemon's hard-candy eyes swiveled back and forth between the two guards. His mouth was curved into a crooked line. "I was invited," he cried.

"Yeah, right. Who would invite an ugly monster to Polipo's Sweet Sixteen party? Get him, Cal!"

"You got it, Ceph."

The two octonoids charged toward the Candemon, who lifted his candy-cane arms in defense. Roy immediately cast a rainbow between the two sides, causing Cal and Ceph to crash into it and collapse.

The Candemon turned to Roy. "What is this all about, Roy? You invite me then send guards after me? What cruel trick is this?"

"No, it isn't like that, Candemon. I didn't have a chance to tell them you were coming yet." He helped the octonoids to their feet but made sure to keep the rainbow barrier between them and the Candemon. "Cal, Ceph: I invited him. He is here as my guest."

"Why would you invite such an ugly creature to Princess Polipo's birthday party?" asked one of the twins.

"Because," Roy answered, "he is part of Candy Island and deserves to be invited to the party." Roy walked through the rainbow barrier to stand beside the Candemon. "Why should he not be allowed just because of what he looks like?"

Cal kept a wary eye on the Candemon but addressed Roy. "It's not just that. It's the other thing . . . you know."

Roy waved his hand dismissively. "That's just a rumor. How do people know that his creator is dead anyway?"

Ceph replied, "Everyone knows, Roy. That creature shouldn't even exist in the Tooniverse anymore. He's stayed alive with some sort of trickery or evil."

"Everyone knows," Cal echoed.

"Well, I don't know," Roy said. "And on my Candy Island, you will not attack my guests. Put down your weapons so I can lower the barrier."

The guards angrily stabbed their tridents into the Rainbow PEZ road, sending bits of the rectangle candy flying into the grass to either side. "Fine," said Cal, "but you have to explain this one to the Princess."

Roy smiled. "I will."

The guards picked up their tridents and scuttled away. Roy waved his hand to lower the rainbow barrier and stood face to gummy bear with the Candemon again.

"I think I should go," the Candemon said. "This was a bad idea, Roy."

"No, it isn't. I promise it will be okay. I'll protect you and make sure you are welcome. Do you trust me?"

The Candemon stood silent and motionless for a moment. Roy could feel the hard candy eyes trying to stare through him. He never let his smile falter, even though he felt quite uncomfortable.

"I trust you, little gnome. And it better not be mislaid trust."

"Yay!" Roy cried. "Stay here. I'll go talk to the Princess and her guests to make sure they know you're coming. It's been crazy with all of the preparations and you came sooner than I expected. It'll be okay."

Roy turned on the spot and ran back to the center of Taffy Towers where the party was to take place. Judging by the look on Princess Polipo's face, someone had already told her who her special guest was.

"Roy! HOW COULD YOU?!" Roy reeled from the screech. He knew sirens that wish they could wail like that.

"Princess, he is your special guest. I thought you'd be happy."

"Happy to have that hideous monster ruin my party? Everyone else is trying to ruin it already. And now you, too? It is disgusting. My party is supposed to be beautiful and perfect!"

"And one of a kind, right?" Roy immediately saw that he had struck a chord with the princess. Her mouth curled into a smirk of entitlement. As spoiled as she was, Roy knew that Princess Polipo was not unintelligent. "A party like none of your friends from school have ever had or will ever have. A party that people will talk about for years to come?"

The princess's smirk moved into a full-blown smile – the first smile Roy had seen on her all day. "You're right. No one has ever had a pet monster to perform for their party. Especially one as gross as the Candemon. I have to tell Jessica. She is going to be so jealous!" The princess ran away before Roy could correct her about the Candemon's status at the party.

What can go wrong? Roy thought to himself. At least she won't have the guards attack him . . .

Roy walked through the party that was going at full steam. He spied Princess Polipo talking to a very strong-looking pair of teenage mermen wearing UCHS letter jackets. He assumed they were members of the school's underwater football team. The princess seemed to be enjoying herself.

In a corner of the party, he found the Candemon sitting by himself holding a very tiny cup of punch. Roy could never read emotions on the Candemon's face, but he looked both sad and comical at the same time. Roy approached the Candemon and said, "How are you enjoying the party?"

"No one has tried to stab me with a trident in the last hour or so."

Roy chuckled, thinking the Candemon was being sarcastic. The lack of response from the Candemon made him wonder if that was the case. "Well, that's progress, right?"

"I still don't understand why I'm here, Roy. All this happiness around me only makes my isolation hurt more. Why are you trying to hurt me, gnome?"

"I am not trying to hurt you. I want you to be part of the joy. I want you to be happy like the rest of my Candy Island citizens."

The Candemon made a motion that Roy thought was a shrug. It was hard to tell. "I am only a citizen here because that's where they sent me when I was sorted in Sorting Square all those years ago, Roy. I could just as well belong in Gothicville with the rest of the monsters."

"I have never known the sorters to get a location wrong, Candemon. And I've been here a long, long time. You belong here. Both on Candy Island and at this party. Come, let's go dance!" Roy took one of the Candemon's candy-cane arms and brought the monster to his feet. The Candemon's eyes grew a little wider, obviously startled by Roy's strength.

As Roy led the Candemon to the dance floor in front of Princess Polipo's stage, the crowd parted to make way. The music stopped abruptly as they reached the center of the floor and all around them fell silent. Roy ignored the stares and whisperings and began dancing.

"There's no music, Roy."

"There's always music in my head," Roy said. He then removed his hat and a very fast-paced jig echoed inside Taffy Towers, bouncing off the tall, colorful walls and filling the room with upbeat dance music. Roy encouraged the Candemon to dance by holding his candy-cane arms and shaking them back and forth the way one would do with a toddler at a wedding.

Roy was so engrossed in trying to help the Candemon fit in, he didn't notice one of Princess Polipo's football-player friends moving in behind the Candemon until it was too late. Roy went to shout at him, but was pushed out of the way as the other merman teen charged into the Candemon's gummy-bear stomach.

"No!" Roy cried. But it was too late. The Candemon's unstable chocolate-bar legs were already off balance and the monster tumbled backwards over the bent-over merteen.

CRASH!

The Candemon fell headfirst into the large ice cream sculpture of Princess Polipo and destroyed the entire centerpiece. He was covered in ice cream and various toppings and struggled to get to his feet.

Roy flew to his side. "Candemon? Are you okay?" He turned to the princess, now standing in the center of the dance floor with her face turning red from laughter. Roy could tell the boys had committed the prank at her request. "Why would you do this, Princess? He is your guest!"

"No, Roy," she said. "He's your guest. He is *my* entertainment. Like you said, people will talk about this party for years. The party where the Candemon finally got put in his place." The hatred in Princess Polipo's voice gave Roy a pain in his chest.

The Candemon finished flailing in the mess of ice cream, toppings, and shattered table to find his footing. He slowly stood and the ice cream fell from his candy-apple head to the ground. He was shaking. Roy couldn't tell if it was from embarrassment or anger. Probably both, Roy wagered.

The Candemon spoke, his voice surprisingly calm and flat. "So this is why I was invited. I see now, Roy. I see why I was brought here." The Candemon's voice did not match his body language. He was still shaking. The stomach of the upside-down gummy bear was beginning to have a golden glow.

"What is that?" asked Roy. "Why are you glowing? I hear a sound." Roy took a step away from the Candemon as the golden glow grew stronger. He could hear a voice slowly starting to emanate from the Candemon's chest.

"Help me," a faint female voice cried. "Help me out of here."

"O M G," cried the gathered teens from Underwater City and various guests from Candy Island. "It's true!"

"SHUT UP, ELEANOR!" the Candemon screamed, silencing the murmuring of the crowd. The golden glow immediately dulled to a very small spark, barely noticeable unless one looked closely.

"So the rumors are true, then." Roy let his smile fade away. It actually hurt his face to not be smiling, he found. "That spark. That glow is . . . your creator's essence? You captured her essence when she died so you could live on?"

The Candemon's face contorted into a twisted smile. "Not all of us get to live forever like you, Roy. We aren't all Originals. But I do get to live forever. As long as Eleanor doesn't die, I live. Don't you see?"

"That is awful!" cried Polipo. "You really are a monster, inside and out!"

"I'm no more a monster than you, Princess Polipo. I just accept what I am. And since you and Roy plotted so well to get me to this party to 'entertain' you all, how about a demonstration?"

Roy stood motionless as the Candemon shook the remaining debris from his body and roared. He spat molten marshmallow at the crowd and encased half of them in a white prison. He charged at the two football players and knocked them into the air. "Batter up!" he cried as he swung his arms like a bat, propelling the strong merteens into the stage, bringing the entire setup to the ground in a heap.

Roy snapped out of his trance and shouted, "NO!" He raised a hand and instantly trapped the Candemon inside a rainbow ball. The monster smashed at the ball but couldn't break it. His widened eyes showed shock at Roy's power. "Stop," Roy mumbled.

"But isn't this what you wanted, Roy? Isn't this why I'm here? Let me continue giving this little brat her unforgettable party." He pointed an arm at Princess Polipo, who was cowering next to the rubble of her Sweet Sixteen stage. "Let me continue to entertain her. She looks entertained, does she not?"

"Stop it, Candemon."

"You're the one who brought me here. This is your fault, Roy."

Roy raised his hand to the sky, causing the Candemon-filled rainbow ball to also rise. "You're wrong, Candemon. Everything about you is wrong. You still existing is wrong. I knew the rumors. I thought that, even if they were true, you could coexist with other creations. How different were you, after all?"

"More different than you could imagine, Roy G. Biv. I'm immortal. I'm closer to you Originals than these fleeting creation toons you love so much."

"No you are not. Go home, Candemon. You were right. You don't belong here." Roy flicked his wrist and flung the Candemon's ball out of Taffy Towers and toward the horizon. The monster's screams slowly faded as the ball hurtled away from the destroyed party.

Roy could hear him calling, "I'll be baaaaack."

"Are you happy, Roy?" Polipo cried from the wreck. "You ruined my party. Why would you invite that monster?"

"No, Polipo, you ruined your party. You and your friends being unwilling to accept someone who looked different and had a different background than you. You brought this upon your own party."

Polipo bent down to stare Roy in the eyes. "But you saw it, Roy. You heard him admit that he was an Anomaly. You even said yourself that him existing is wrong."

Roy plopped on the ground and let out a long exhale. "But it isn't our place to right that wrong, Polipo. He shouldn't exist but he does. Better to just let him alone. The Tooniverse will right the wrong in time. It always does."

"But . . . what about my party?"

Roy looked around at the destruction, including half the crowd mumbling from encasements of solidified marshmallow. "It will be remembered for years to come, as you wished. Especially by the Candemon. Whatever happens in the future, just remember your role in creating your own enemy, Princess. He was content being left alone. It was you and I that pushed him, figuratively and literally."

"But what could he possibly do to us, Roy? He is no match for your power."

"Let's hope we never find out." Roy stood and began sweeping debris with his foot. "Now let's clean up. I think your party is over."

*

Read more about Roy G. Biv, the Candemon, and Princess Polipo in Toonopolis: Gemini, book one of the Toonopolis Files.

THIS ONE SAFE PLACE
BY J. C. RUTLEDGE

It takes a hero of special calibre to have their name bestowed upon a land. Traeslen was such a hero. He had been out hunting when he discovered an army from the north encamped at the far end of what was then known as Trade's Lane, a pass through the mountains of the South Twin Range.

Traeslen ran for days and nights until he came upon Fandomore, his village that stood watch to the south of the pass. Try as he might to warn his people, none would listen. What army could brave Demon's Run, the vast desert north of the mountains? Even the merchants would not dare the risk at this time of year. It was impossible, they said, and lost no sleep over it.

Despairing though he was, Traeslen took up his sword and bow and returned to Trade's Lane alone. He found himself a defensible position where he knelt and prayed. When the army arrived, he unleashed his fury upon them. He singlehandedly held off the entire army until, pierced by several arrows and many blade wounds, he finally fell.

It was then that the gods stepped in, raining fire upon the army until they lost all will to fight and fled. The battle was won and from that day forward Trade's Lane was known as Traeslen Pass, after the hero who stood alone with his faith against an army and won.

Or so legend tells.

"That was ten years ago!" Rablin Gress argued. "We were under orders from the king, but he could never get the people to accept us. Apparently he couldn't even pass on his beliefs to his son. This new king has put a death warrant on all practitioners of the magical arts. Yet here we still are, protecting the very people who would butcher us if they knew what we are!"

"It doesn't matter!" Edwin Whiste shouted. "It is our duty to protect these people."

"Duty!" Rablin raged, spittle foaming at the corners of his mouth. "Don't talk to me of –"

"Rablin, Edwin, please. We do have guests here," Moriga Thurar cut in, her calm voice immediately silencing the two men.

Liksemos Ardron watched the exchange, his head oscillating between the debaters. Rablin was an older man, his beard long and sweeping. He alone of all those gathered at the table wore the pointed hat with the wide brim that marked their craft, the arrogant fool.

Edwin, on the other hand, was middle aged and balding. He always seemed to be glaring out from behind his square spectacles. According to some at this table, he didn't even belong here. He wasn't much of a wizard – he barely even dabbled in the craft – but he had a passion for books rivalled by none, and they needed a librarian.

Liksemos himself was just in his twenties, with black hair and a neatly trimmed beard. He took pride in his appearance, ensuring that he could comfortably walk among the non-magical populace while still able to easily fit in with his magical brethren. Sometimes he wished the rest of the coven would take the same care.

"I am sorry to have caused such a fuss," said the elf at the head of the table, brushing his chestnut hair behind his pointed ears. "My companions and I were merely wondering about any possible treasures left behind after the battle in Traeslen Pass. I was unaware it would bring up a subject of such dispute."

"No, there are no treasures left," Moriga said. Liksemos had no idea how old she was. She had raised him since his parents had been burned at the stake for witchcraft more than fifteen years ago. Back then she had been old enough to be his mother, yet she didn't seem to have aged a day since. "The villagers claimed them long ago. Some are hoarding them, believing that in time the relics of Traeslen Pass will be priceless. They're probably right," she laughed.

"The greedy –"

"Rablin, enough," Moriga insisted. "We all know your feelings, you don't need to share them again. Now, if I may, I would like to call this meeting of the coven to order. Firstly, I would like to once again thank Liksemos Ardron for lending his house to our cause."

"My home is yours," Liksemos said generously. It was true enough. He had spent years building a business within the community that allowed him to conceal the movements of both himself and the coven. Sometimes he felt that the witches and wizards spent more time in his home than they did in their own.

"It is very kind of you," Moriga continued. "Next I would like to welcome our guests this evening: Theckni, who graciously provided this delicious spread for dinner."

"Please," the elf at the head of the table said. "I merely cooked the food; you were the ones who provided the materials."

"Indeed, and what a splendid job you did," Edwin chimed in.

"Yes," Moriga agreed. "Also, I would like to welcome Agitha Hathlen, a travelling research witch. Our guests provide us with our first order of business for tonight. Theckni and his companions are the adventurous types, travelling, exploring and gathering treasure. As they have an elf in their group, as well as an experienced wizard, they have requested sanctuary to avoid persecution during their short stay in Fandomore. Are there any objections to granting them this?"

There were mutterings of agreement. After Theckni had cooked them such a delicious meal, they wouldn't deny him their protection.

Liksemos considered objecting, only for a moment, because undoubtedly he would be the one hosting them. Alas, he had chosen his role in the coven and it was too late to change his mind about it.

"We would also like information on local legends, if you can provide it," Theckni added. "My friend, Sir Hurmal, has a particular interest in dragons."

"Our library is at your disposal, provided you take care of the books," Edwin Whiste offered.

"Excellent. Moving on, then," Moriga said. "Agitha Hathlen, please come forward." Liksemos was always impressed by her ability to keep meetings on track. What he wouldn't give to have someone like her on one of his business committees, but she had no interest in such mundane affairs.

A young blonde woman awkwardly rose from her seat at the table and made her way to the middle, where Moriga was sitting. Her steps were slow and heavy, one hand laid protectively over her bulging stomach.

"Hello," she started nervously. "I'm Agitha. I've spent most of my life travelling, gathering information and writing books about this wondrous world around us. I was always told I was too curious for my own good, but it has led me to so much information – you wouldn't believe some of what I've discovered!" She coughed, noticing that she'd gotten carried away in her excitement. "Anyway ... it seems my curiosity got the better of me –" she patted her swelled stomach – "and now I'm afraid my travelling days are over. I hope to retire as a witch, buy a house and raise my child, but ... to do that, I need money I don't have."

So that was why Moriga hadn't given him more information about the guests, Liksemos thought, pinching the bridge of his nose and shaking his head. Money. All of the coven's money went through him – though it would be more accurate to say that it came from him – and once an expense had been accepted by the coven, there was no way he could say no to it.

"I was hoping that your coven might be interested in buying my books, to provide the money I need," Agitha continued. "I'm sure they will be valuable to your collection and, in exchange, I will pledge that a child from each generation of my line shall be sent to you to be apprenticed. In this way I might help you in your duty to protect Traeslen Pass." Her eyes drifted around the table, pleading with everyone present to help her.

"It is our duty to protect all books," Edwin said without hesitation. "We will gladly purchase them from you."

"Hold on a moment," Liksemos said, grasping at straws. "No offence to you, sister, but I think we need to know a bit more about these books before purchasing them. We can't just buy the scribbling of anyone who happens to pass by."

"Well," Agitha said, gaining confidence as she continued, "I have several books on plants and a few on spell components. There are a couple of spell books devoted to travelling and researching safely. Then there is my pride and joy! I call it Creatures Beautiful and Deadly, and it is a compilation of everything I know about any creatures I have come across. But it's more than that! It's a learning book. When someone is reading it, it gathers all the information they have on creatures and adds to its compendium! It will always be growing and adding to its knowledge, making it my most valuable possession."

Liksemos knew immediately from the mutterings up and down the table that he was out of luck. The last book alone could seal the deal and, if he wasn't careful, bankrupt him if the coven chose.

"Any objections to assisting Agitha?" Moriga asked. There were none. "Very well. Liksemos?"

"We will purchase your books from you and allow you to stay here until you secure your own residence," Liksemos said, trying to hide a sigh. "I will also offer you a position in my company so that you may continue to provide for your family." *At least then I'll be getting something back from my investment*, he added to himself.

"Thank you, thank you so much!" Agitha said. Had it not been for her burden, she would have skipped back to her seat. No sooner had she sat down than Rablin burst from his chair, outraged.

"I've had enough of this playacting!" he shouted. "Buying books, making deals for children from each generation to be trained by us – it's a joke!"

"Very well, Rablin," Moriga said, heaving a sigh. "Your petition is next on the agenda. You may have the floor."

"Brethren, look around you." Rablin began pacing around the table, ensuring he made eye contact with every member of the coven. "Look at how thin our numbers have become. Why are we still here? Oh, I know why we came. The old king sent us here to defend Trade's Pass, promising us that he would stop the persecution of our kind. We have defended the pass since then – we stood watch over Traeslen – and what has happened? The pass was renamed for the man who singlehandedly defeated the entire army with the help of the gods!

"We were there, brethren. We know that the gods have done nothing for our world since the end of the God Wars, and we have been the better for it. It was us, not the gods, who rained fire upon the enemy and sent them fleeing! Yet here we are, ten years later, still hiding for fear of being discovered.

"I ask you, why? The new king has sentenced us to death, something the people of this country have been doing for generations. Liksemos, *you* know! Your parents were killed for their craft! As was your wife, Edwin, and Moriga's brother. Enough, I say! If these northerners want this country so much, let them have it. I'm through protecting these people who wish nothing but death upon us! Brethren, I invite you to come with me, to find a place where we can live openly and without fear. Who's with me?"

The room was silent. Each member of the coven had their eyes fixed upon the table, unwilling to meet the burning gaze of Rablin.

"None of you?" Rablin's voice resonated with defeat. A tear was running down his cheek. "How can you keep this up? Moriga?"

"I made an oath, Rablin," Moriga said evenly, meeting his gaze. "I made an oath to defend the pass and these people until my dying breath. Nothing can make me leave."

"Edwin, think of your wife."

"I'm sorry," Edwin said. "My books are all here. I couldn't possibly move them all and someone must protect them. I'm staying."

"Liksemos!" Rablin pleaded. "You had just asked for my daughter's hand in marriage before they dragged her off and drowned her in the pond! Surely you, of all people ..."

"No." Liksemos's stomach was clenched and he couldn't draw his eyes from the table. He knew the poor man was crying now and could barely bring himself to speak above a whisper. "My life is here. My commitments are all here. It's what she would have wanted."

"Fools!" Rablin screamed. "You will all burn! They will come for you. They know nothing of how you've protected them and they would still burn you even if they did!"

There was a crash as the door slammed open and Rablin vanished into the night. Silence reigned over the room for quite some time.

"Well," Moriga said at last, the softness of her voice directly contradicting Rablin's rage, "that draws a conclusion to our meeting for tonight. I wish it could have ended on a better note."

Liksemos saw the rest of the coven out of his house, saying farewell to each of them and wishing them well. At last he was left alone with his guests.

"That was quite interesting," Theckni commented, "though rather aggressive. It is sad to see your coven has fallen upon such hard times."

"What a horrid man," Agitha said. "How could a wizard become so miserable? He should be revelling in the world around him!"

"Rablin is ..." Liksemos struggled to find what to say. The man had nearly been his father-in-law, but had changed so drastically in the past few weeks that he hardly knew him. "He has his reasons," was the best he could manage. "Agitha, there is a room for you on the third floor. Theckni can show you the way, I believe his companions are –"

An explosion from outside shook the house. Liksemos burst through the door to see what was happening. "No, no, no!" he cried.

The thatched roof of one of the village houses was on fire, but it wasn't any normal fire. Magical blue flames danced around the house, billowing black smoke into the air. Above the house, wreathed in the growing cloud of smoke, stood a wizard on a magic carpet.

"It is Rablin, is it not?"

Liksemos nearly jumped out of his boots. How had that elf come up behind him so silently? He was about to answer when Rablin began to speak.

"How do *you* like to burn, fools?" he bellowed at the villagers scurrying below. "Drown my daughter, will you? Well, we'll see about that!"

A bluish orb appeared in his hand, then sped towards a second house. It never made it. A black hole appeared out of nowhere and swallowed it up.

"That's enough, Rablin." Moriga's voice drifted through the night. No matter how hard he looked, though, Liksemos couldn't find her.

"You dare to interfere?" Rablin screamed, nearly falling off his carpet as he spun round and round trying to find her. "Show yourself!"

"Come down from there and I'll show myself," Moriga's voice said with infuriating calm.

Rablin was on the ground in an instant, his rage driving him onwards. He stumbled from his carpet, running into the village square and climbing onto the scaffold where so many of his friends had been burned.

"Where are you, woman?" he screamed.

"I am right here, my old friend," Moriga said, stepping into the square from a cloud of smoke. "Can you not restrain yourself? You have broken our sacred trust. You must submit yourself to justice."

Desperately Liksemos cast his gaze around the village, looking for friendly faces. He caught sight of several witches and wizards hurrying away from the scene to the safety of their homes. Why did they run? Moriga needed their help!

"Justice!" Rablin laughed. "This *is* justice!" He cast another spell at a random house, but Moriga was able to intercept it before it hit.

"No, Rablin," she said sadly, shaking her head. Did she look older? "This is revenge, not justice. If you don't come with me, I'll have to take you by force."

"Take me by force?" Rablin spat, walking down the steps of the scaffold. "Who was it that led the defence of Traeslen Pass? And you think you can take me by force? You and what army?" He rasped out a spell, sending a beam of fire straight towards Moriga.

Liksemos lunged forwards, but found a restraining hand on his shoulder.

"Look," Theckni said softly, pointing to the growing crowd of villagers. "Why do you think your friends do nothing? They know they cannot risk exposing their craft. You must allow Moriga to handle this alone."

She was holding the fire off easily enough, but Liksemos could see she was in pain. Her shock at what Rablin had just done was plastered on her face.

"You don't know what he's done!" Liksemos insisted.

"Yes, I do." Theckni's voice was full of sadness. "He has commenced a blood duel. You could not help her now, no matter how hard you tried."

Liksemos opened his mouth to argue, but the elf was right. Rablin's spell was feeding on Moriga's life energy to power his magic. It was forbidden and now that it had started, there was an open conduit of magical energy flowing between them. It couldn't stop until one – or both – of them was dead. All anyone could do was watch.

Finally overcoming her shock, Moriga stabilised her shield against the fire and launched a counterattack. It was a series of simple spells. Small orbs, each glowing a different colour, drifted towards Rablin. While he was countering them, she began casting a more complicated spell.

"Brilliant distraction," Liksemos muttered. For the first time it looked like Moriga would win, but then Rablin found the pattern of the spells and countered the rest of them earlier than anticipated.

The flames veered off from Moriga and surrounded Rablin, shielding him just in time as a column of ice spewed from the witch's hands. The ice hit the fire, instantly enveloping the combatants in a cloud of steam.

Lights flashed – the steam changed colour – various spells went flying off into the night. Liksemos entirely gave up trying to keep track of the spells, instead choosing to put up a quick shielding spell to prevent any of the rebounds from harming the observing villagers.

Ah yes, the villagers. They were clustered around buildings, peeking around corners to watch. Liksemos was glad of it, because it made it safe for him to watch, but why did they do it? They were obviously terrified and they had to know they were in danger, yet still they watched.

The curtain of mist lowered, revealing Moriga with a glowing bubble surrounding her. Rablin was hammering on it with spell after spell, all of them bouncing off, but with each hit Moriga winced. Her shield was getting weaker and Rablin knew it.

The end of the battle was swift. Moriga's bubble burst and she collapsed to the ground; Rablin let out a triumphant laugh and gathered his magic for his final spell. He was halfway through casting when he began to scream.

It was a short scream, because that's all he had time for before he was gone – just gone! It took Liksemos a moment to figure out what had happened. Rablin had overstepped his bounds! Moriga had lured him into casting more and more powerful spells, until his own magic consumed him. Liksemos couldn't wait to congratulate her on her victory.

Except ... she was now surrounded by the villagers. They picked her up and carried her over to the scaffold, where they tied her to the stake it supported.

"What are they doing?" Liksemos protested. "She just saved them!"

"They are doing what they believe to be right," Theckni said. "They fear magic above all else. Who can blame them after that display?"

"No." Liksemos rolled back his sleeves, preparing to cast. "This is wrong. They can't burn someone who just saved their lives. I won't let them."

"Wait, my young friend." The elf stepped in front of him. "Stop and think. Moriga's life was forfeit the moment she revealed that she was a witch. You know this. She knew this. Yet she still stepped forward to defend these people from Rablin. Would she want you to kill them to save her, when she has already traded her life to protect them?"

In that moment, everything became clear to Liksemos. He knew why no one else had stepped up to help bring Rablin down and why, as he looked around, none of the coven were visible. They were afraid and ashamed. They didn't want to see what was going to happen.

"Also, now that she is gone, who will lead your coven? They need someone strong and reliable or they will fall apart. You know this."

Liksemos stood tall and nodded. He knew. Moriga had always intended for him to lead the coven once she was gone. He just hadn't expected it to be so soon. And he wished Theckni would stop talking about her as if she were already dead. He wished he would stop giving the same advice Moriga would have.

"You should return to the house," Liksemos told the elf, stepping around him and fixing his gaze on the villagers piling fuel around the scaffold. "Blood is in the air tonight; if these people find an elf about, you'll wish burning had been your fate."

"Will you not join me?" Theckni asked.

Liksemos shook his head. "Someone has to see this. She deserves that, at least."

The elf nodded and silently returned to the house, leaving the young wizard alone.

The villagers piled fuel higher and higher. After what they had just seen, they weren't leaving any chance that this witch could survive. They had to kill her while she was weak. At last they set the fire. Flames leaped and danced around the unconscious form tied to the pole. There was no sound except for the crackle of fire. The villagers watched in silence.

Liksemos also watched in silence, but only after he'd cast a charm that would ease Moriga's pain, if she was even aware enough to feel it. Inside he was boiling with turmoil, but he didn't let any of it show. He had to act like what he was – an upstanding pillar of the community who wouldn't get his hands dirty, but would see this through to the end. Any villager to cast a look his way would get a solemn nod, nothing more. The secrecy of the coven would be preserved.

Eventually the crowds began to drift away. The witch was long dead and the fire was burning lower, but Liksemos wouldn't leave. He stayed until the fire had burned itself out and the wind was playing in the cooling ashes. Only then did he turn back to his house.

He looked up at the three-storey building. Tomorrow he would have to contact the builders to design a fourth – maybe even a fifth – level. A plan was forming in his mind. He had a lot of work to do and he would need the extra space. He'd keep building his home until it towered over the village, even the mountains, if he had to.

These villagers had burned his parents, drowned his future wife and now they'd killed the woman who had raised him. He hated them with every breath he took, but Moriga had brought him up to be their protector. So he would protect them, but he would also protect his own people. He would give witches and wizards a solid, safe home in Fandomore. By the time the people found out they were there, they would be too afraid of how many there were to act against them.

Perhaps, eventually, that fear would turn to respect and magic would become an acceptable practice.

Until then, all he could do was remember those he'd loved, and hope.

Illustration by Sophie E Tallis

FINAL ENTRY
BY KAY KAUFFMAN

"The date is…aw, hell, I don't know. Does anyone even care what the date is anymore? It must be nearing winter – the darkness comes sooner and lasts longer these days.

"It wasn't always like this. We used to care about dates and times. Life was peaceful; people were happy and safe. Now such things seem trivial. Safety is a fairytale. And the Targons are the monsters under the bed."

I pause. There's a noise in the distance, a kind of scuttling sound, and it's coming closer. "Jean is dead. Targon bastards ate 'er. And Benny… They got the others, too. Now I'm the only one left.

"I remember reading a play once, a very long time ago, about a man who tried to escape his destiny. He believed he could beat the gods and his hubris destroyed everything he held dear. Funny, isn't it? Our belief that we could defeat disease has destroyed everything that we hold dear. Well, everything we held dear, anyway. There's nothing left worth caring for. Only survival."

Silence. No more scuttling. Somehow the silence is scarier. Silence means they're plotting something and when they're plotting, disaster is the only result. I look around, but all I see are shadows. The Targons love shadows. I know I should end my log entry already and get on with the task at hand, but I lower my voice instead and keep talking.

"It all started with the cure. After decades of research and billions of dollars and hundreds of studies, they finally came out with a cure for cancer. Well, a cure for lung cancer, anyway. But one cure led to another and then another and before long, a panacea. All it took was a shot in each hip and bing, bang, boom – no more cancer. It was wonderful.

"At first, everything was fine. People were living better, healthier lives. Instead of chemo, they got Targonal shots. No more hair loss, no more radiation therapy, no more waiting and hoping and praying for survival. Cancer patients around the world were given Targonal. Everyone rejoiced.

"But then the side effects emerged. The FDA pulled their approval, but it was too late. Benny had received the shots just before his thirtieth birthday, about six months before Targonal lost its FDA approval. He'd been diagnosed with melanoma. Two shots later, he was back to his carefree, happy self. But a few months after his Targonal injections, Benny began acting funny. He went from Mr. Gregarious to reclusive hermit almost overnight. Before long, he was downright feral.

"The government had rushed the drug into production. By the time its long-term side effects surfaced, millions of people had received Targonal injections. They tried to fix the mess they'd made, but there was nothing they could do – they'd all had Targonal injections, too, and it wasn't long before the government collapsed.

"The last time we saw Benny, he was almost unrecognizable. It's hard for me to say that – he was my best friend – but it's true. He looked more animal than human. The sight of him made my skin crawl – he was all matted hair and filth and muscle. I wondered at the change, but not Jean. She still saw him the way he used to be; she saw the slightly flabby but handsome man she'd fallen for at summer camp. She saw that same man right up until he ripped her throat out, I could tell by the look in her eyes."

I glance around, checking to make sure I'm still alone. I could swear I heard something behind me, even though I'm up against a solid brick wall. My arm is twitching; it's been doing that a lot lately.

"If the FDA hadn't fucked up, Benny and Jean and all the others would still be here and there would be no Targons. Hell, maybe we wouldn't be fighting for our lives. The Targons are smart – too smart. There's no way we'll ever be able to beat them. We are now the hunted, instead of the hunters. This is our fate. And cancer? No one cares about cancer anymore. No one lives long enough to get it.

"Rumor has it that the Targons live and hunt in packs. I keep hearing them; if I didn't know better, I'd say they were hunting me specifically. Not that it matters, I guess. We're all Targon fodder."

I fall silent as the hair on the back of my neck rises; I can hear something moving in the distance. I fire into the darkness, hoping to hit the bastards. Something skitters off to my right and I'm sure it's not a rat. Now the skittering is off to my left. There it is again, in front of me this time.

"This is it. I'm surrounded. I can see their eyes leering at me from the shadows, but I refuse to be their next meal. I ain't goin'down without a fight ..."

"Wow, that was some dream," I mutter as I swing my legs out of bed. *Targons? Really? What the hell was my subconscious on last night?* I get dressed and head downstairs for breakfast. The kitchen is empty, which is unusual because Benny is always up before me.

I sit down with a bowl of cereal and five minutes later, Benny ambles into the room. I look up to say hello, but the words die in my throat. My dear, sweet Benny stands before me, all matted hair and filth and muscle, and he looks ready to rip my throat out.

NIGHT OF A THOUSAND SPELLS
BY DAVID MUIR

He was not your typical baby, even for one of the Magi. His tufty down of hair was dark brown and his eyes already a piercing blue. Gabriel, his parents had named him. *Bloody idiots*, he thought to himself. Hardly a Magi name – it was the name of the Christian texts. *Messenger of the gods, indeed*.

He was the only baby in the nursery that wasn't part-human. He wasn't human at all.

The Magi were a race apart, as to gorillas what humans are to chimps, but artificially evolved by the God-King of Heaven to serve as his foot soldiers against his brother, the God-King of Hell's Devil army.

They were the Masters of magic, Guardians of all and the last line of defense for the Light against the Darkness.

Gabriel could already feel the Dark Ones gathering. It usually happened after the birth of a Magi child, when their magic was bound until puberty – not that it was always so. And this time they were in for a bloody great shock.

He growled to himself and wove shields around the other babies and the nurses in the nursery. Only fair that they be kept safe as they were as vulnerable as he would have been born if his had been a normal Magi birth. It was subtle but it meant they would be protected against just about anything that could happen during the coming fight.

The first one came through the door of the nursery, he could feel it: a dark mage on his own, dressed in a ceremonial black robe. He backhanded the nurse who was looking after the babies at that point; she had been cooing over the grimaces and gripes of the children.

That was not a nice thing to do. Gabriel growled to himself again – only it didn't sound like a growl, it was a squeak. A white fireball appeared in his tiny hand and it exploded forward at the dark mage, incinerating him instantly.

A little grin appeared on his face. *Came to take my power, did you, wretched little toe-rags,* the baby thought. *I'll bloody show you why I was feared by the Dark Lords in my previous life.*

Another of the Dark Ones entered the room, and a lightning bolt shot from the crib and Gabriel's hand. It cannoned through her and impacted on the ceiling. The plaster began to fall, bouncing off the shields of the babies below the impact point onto the floor.

Gabriel tried to roll himself but his little muscles just left him flapping; he was trying to do what he had done in his previous life with his body. *I hate reincarnation bloody already*, he grumbled to himself. *Not even twenty-four bloody hours old and I'm already being attacked.*

A number of Werewolves entered the room with a pair of sorcerers. A phantom hand from the baby grabbed one of the Werewolves, smashing it into another and then another, which cannoned them through the glass viewing window and off the wall. The remaining Werewolves looked around to see where the attack had come from, only to be set on fire by the baby. The sorcerers imploded as he hit them with a Combustionasigation spell.

What has the world come to that I can't be left in peace for the day of my birth and leave the chuffing mundane hospital before they start trying to chuffing kill me? He growled away to himself as he launched a pair of Whitefire balls at a group of warlocks who appeared in the room, before they could get their bearings; they were killed instantly.

The baby mage was struggling to roll himself again but was getting absolutely nowhere, and it was starting to annoy him greatly. The next Dark One who appeared was ripped apart by Gabriel's phantom hands, taking the full brunt of the baby's frustration.

More of the Dark Ones appeared through the corridors, each shielded and ready for a pack or two of the Magi Hunters protecting him. *As there bloody should be.* His father was a Pack Master, commander of the Fifth Circle, the most elite Hunter pack of the entire Cadre. Damn well nearly as powerful as the Huntmaster himself, or the Triumvirate. His son should be protected by the best.

If these bozos are teleporting in here, the bloody Hunters or some bloody Guardians shouldn't have any problems with it. The baby squeaked out loud since he couldn't vocalize his frustration in any other way.

The sorcerers were fighting with each other now to get at him, to tap the power from his tiny little body – a battery they would feed off until he was spent of all that power. Magi children were at their peak of power during the day of their birth, and every five years on that day until their fifteenth birthday, their day of ascension, when they became adults in the minds of the Cadre and they chose their path; for most, the day they were filled with the most power. Many of his kind never reached the day of ascension because of the likes of the men and women trying to take his power from him.

The baby cackled away to himself as he launched white fireball after white fireball into the hallway, making sure that he instigated a full-on brawl between the different factions, and keeping his tiny little backside alive.

He was sure some of them weren't there to drain his power. Some of them, especially the demon thralls, were probably just there to kill him. The children of the deep, knowing full well who he was and what he was reborn to do.

His coming had been prophesied, by one of his own siblings no less. He really didn't like the fact that he'd got screwed by his own sister. It was one of the side effects of being who he was: he always got screwed by good intentions and bad mistakes.

He could hear the war cries of the Magi as the Hunters finally appeared. The little baby Gabriel giggled to himself in triumph, but it was short-lived. A dozen of the Midnight Heart, a Cabal of dark magic practitioners, entered the nursery filled with their power and surrounded by their own powerful shields.

All around them they felt shields around the babies, each of the shields identical in construction and with the same stamp of the mage who created them.

"The little sod is here somewhere. Just check every one of them for the Mark," the leader, Anastasia Andolfo, ordered her people. She was a most powerful Dark Wizard, apprenticed by the Grand Necromancer himself, Adjustier Namock, Dark Lord of Hell. "Only one with the Mark could weave this many shields at once and hold them. We must find him before the Hunters break free."

"Did our lord give you any idea how to break his shield?" Jared Dalmuir, murderer of Gabriel's parents' firstborn daughter, asked her. "He may be a baby but he's got the power of a Magi Warmaster."

"Ah, but you can see he left his mark. Not too subtle," she said with a snort.

"Since when have the Magi Warrior Caste done anything subtle? They are brute force incarnate. They don't need to be subtle when they have all the power they do," Dalmuir said as he felt his robes catch fire. He hurriedly pulled them off and began stamping on them to extinguish the fire; it wouldn't go out and started to consume his trousers. His eyes went mad with fear. "Damn, it's Whitefire. The child can use Whitefire. Somebody help me."

"No, Dalmuir, I think you can be of use for something else," Anastasia said with a wicked smile as her ceremonial Athame went across his throat and his blood spilled into a bowl. She put more and more ingredients in the bowl and began chanting in Sumerian. The Sumerians had been expert practitioners of magic and those that followed the dark arts were very good. When she was finished, she blew the contents of the bowl out into the air. Locator dust, fueled by death energy – not a good combination. Gabriel shot his little arms into the air, firing brimstone charges everywhere and sending the Cabal flying away from the babies.

Every baby except for Gabriel was crying by this point. That didn't go unnoticed by the locator dust, which coalesced around his shield. *Oh, crap on a crap stick.*

"Thought you were clever, did you?" Anastasia said with an evil grin. "Brimstone charges, very naughty. I thought all you old ones never used such naughty spells."

"We need to begin," Hermandier Wulfen growled to her. "The night is almost up. His power is at its strongest right now, even with all that he's used to repel us."

"There's something different about this one, Anastasia, I think we should leave him be," Gillian McCord told her. The youngest member of the Cabal was actually a Council of Magic plant in Midnight Heart.

"Go watch the door, McCord," Anastasia growled at her, and she did as she was told. The number of their circle was made up to thirteen, and they began their ritual to take down his shield and then his power. The baby Gabriel clenched his little fists almost to the beat of their chant. He was trying to think of a spell to rid himself of all of them, but he was being drained with every chant.

Gabriel started to convulse and foam from his little mouth. Almost drained of the will to maintain his shield, he was suddenly filled with the power of his ancestors: all the Magi of his line who had come before him, first son to first son. His eyes glowing the bluey white of Whitefire, he shot his baby hands out into his shield, which exploded with such force that it literally shattered every bone in the bodies of those that touched it. The Whitefire consumed their bodies, leaving not even ash.

Anastasia & Hermandier had split seconds to realise their folly in following their master's orders. They felt for that instant the pain of being burned alive and having their bones shattered. It was in that final second that the Hunters broke through the lines of the Dark Ones and into his room.

McCord nodded to the first of the Hunters saluting him, before teleporting away with a wink to the baby.

About damn time, you losers, Gabriel thought as he relaxed the shields.

His father stepped into the room, an imposing man towering over his pack mates. He scooped his son under the arms and raised him like a winning captain holding the Scottish Cup.

"Behold, my brothers and sisters: my son is the one who was prophesied in the Pythian Scrolls," the Warrior Caste leader shouted to them. They all dropped to their left knees, right fists on their hearts and left fists planted on the ground, heads bowed.

All Gabriel could do was ineffectually try to kick out his tiny little legs, and think to himself …

Here we go again.

FINISH THE PAGE
BY TRM

It is such an honour to have been chosen amongst all of my brethren, so many of whom are far more accomplished than I.

Ever since I joined the Order as a boy, I have approached my work with humility. Never have I sought pleasure in the anticipation of a great work or in the contemplation of the finished article. Nevertheless, I must confess to feeling some excitement as the Master places in my hands the large brass key for the doors at the bottom of the staircase leading to the Upper Scriptorium, where only the elect are permitted to work. He tells me to proceed alone, without a word to any of my brothers in the Lower Hall, and to toil as the work requires, in utmost solitude and complete silence.

The great doors yield to the key and I climb the foot-smoothed stone steps in darkness, with only the occasional flash of daylight from a slit in the spiraling walls to remind me that I am still of this world. I emerge into the Scriptorium and marvel at how vast and bright it is. The fan-vaulted ceiling leaps skywards with the grace of a cathedral's nave and the eternal delicacy of a forest's splayed boughs. To my right is an entire wall of mullioned windows, dressed in clear glass! The brightness of the storm-swept November day beyond almost blinds my eyes, accustomed as they are to darkened halls and lightless cells.

259

Amidst all this glory, there is but one steeply angled desk in the vast space, adorned with a most extraordinary riot of colour. Beside it, the tables and cabinets for the preparations are as grey as the rest of this secluded chamber. That sheet of vellum left by my predecessor draws me as a moth would be drawn to a flame.

It is so ornate, its illuminations so wild and shocking and yet so intricate and beautiful, that my head spins and I must steady myself on the lectern. These images are so unworldly, so enticing and yet so perverse! The text leaps out to me. Words toll a warning and yet dare me to read on. The Master told me not to read but only to copy the text from the fragile old scroll beside the illuminated page. I was told to let my hands glide and only depict my feelings as I stand in this chamber.

And so I proceed.

However, I am struck by the realisation that the page on the lectern is unfinished. The inks on the narrow shelf beneath it are still wet and the last corner of vellum has not lost its softness. Before I work on the page allocated to me, I must complete what has been left so agonisingly close to perfection. It is a matter only of a few moments, and I can fill this corner of parchment with hope, pride and expectation, love and praise for the Highest, and dissipate a little the pain, fear and destruction that shrieked from the previous hand's illuminations.

Once I set the completed page aside to dry, alongside the masterworks of previous artists, I may tend to the tasks I truly love: selecting the colours and grinding the ingredients to make my inks, using the rarest of spices and the most precious of stones to give birth to colours that will shine for all eternity. The stock of vellum has been expertly prepared and left tensioned on frames, but I still search through the cabinets for a perfect fragment of pumice and I mix my favoured formula of lime and chalk to scour – no, caress – the surface of the parchment, until it is as soft and as smooth and as welcoming as the most forbidden of dreams.

Finally, I can truly begin, having brought closer and lit the candelabra I shall need when the short autumnal day expires.

As soon as my brush touches the vellum, I am lost in my work. It seems mere moments pass between the first stroke and the last, to transcribe the arcane words onto the page. I shudder, realising that the chamber has been enfolded by sepulchral darkness in the meantime, but even that is nowhere near as deep as the darkness that has flowed onto the page. The glow of the candles isolates me in a bubble of light within an eternity of shadow, alone with my work and the feelings in my heart. The words writhe on the page, enticing and yet horrific, and my heart responds, brimming with passions I have never before experienced.

Once again my brushes and my pens fly over the vellum, casting more colours onto this page than all the sunrises and sunsets I have ever witnessed, laying down gold leaf with more devotion than I have expressed in a lifetime. And yet, for all the transports I feel, for all the giddy joy of creation, terror creeps into my work almost unseen and then reveals itself in every minute detail.

My icy breath catches in my throat and my back hunches in anticipation of a fatal blow, for I now realise – as did each of my predecessors, and as each expressed in the dismay woven into their art – that I am not alone in the shadows of the Upper Scriptorium. There is something else here, peering over my shoulder, whispering suggestions into my willing ears, guiding my treacherous hands. They move as if of their own volition and create visions of infernal horror that I can only denounce as I would the blasphemies of a complete stranger.

An unexpected instinct begs me to finish, pleads with the forces guiding my limbs and aching digits to hurry and dispatch this wicked task, for the tantalising goal becomes clearer with every stroke of brush and swoop of pen. I now know for sure that my only hope of leaving the Scriptorium alive, if not sane, is for me to finish the –

THE ARTIST
BY SOPHIE E TALLIS

She squeezed the cadmium in a bright yellow streak across the palette.

She had painted in every medium, every material possible, but she still loved the richness of oils – that wonderful buttery smear of vivid colour, the smell of the linseed, the texture of the paint as it glided across the canvas.

All of it seemed more real to her than anything else. A life of its own, raw, visceral.

She dipped the sable brush in her own concoction of white spirit and linseed, to thin the paint whilst keeping the gloss. Too much white spirit would dull the verdant hues; too little would make them too sticky, too slick.

Her movements were erratic, not the usual smooth motions of wandering mind and sparkling imagination. She'd often complete a commission in a daze, almost unaware of where she was or what she was doing. Her conscious self, the side of her that was always acutely cautious, would be suppressed, allowing her hands to take over, her fingers to find the form she wanted.

That was where the magic lay … not in the end result, but in its creation.

Today was different.

Today, she was painting for her life.

The music swelled in crescendo, pushing her adrenaline forward, hurrying her hand. The mottled texture of the canvas swirled before her eyes, a flamenco dance of colours.

Titanium white, a flash of cerulean, a dab of burnt umber – and then the thinning haze of vermillion, red as flesh, peering out at her, reminding her of her slowing heart, the constrictions of her arteries. The pulsating electricity through her veins, which told her she was running out of time.

She worked fast now, pounding the canvas until the wooden stretcher creaked beneath the pressure.

The outside noises had faded away. No traffic, no loud Saturday night voices and wailing sirens. It was silent everywhere but inside her head.

Mixing now, hurried new hues emerging from the clogged-up mess. Phaltho blue enriching the green she had created, a hint of lemon, a sparkle of ultramarine.

Throat dry now. Hands shaking, fingers slipping on the brush shaft.

She *had* to finish this.

Shadows clouded her vision. The music soared as eyes emerged from the canvas, eyes she knew so well. Eyes staring into her soul, accusing her, condemning her, gloating at her demise.

"I won't give in, I won't!" she muttered feverishly.

Mars black, thick and glossy, impenetrable, unfathomable … she was losing the fight.

"Why did you leave me?"

Amber liquid pooled in the crevices, little streaks finding a route through the strokes, dripping in splashes at her feet.

She was always fighting gravity, as most women do. Always fighting, yes, her whole life she had been fighting.

Through the gloom, the full image stared back at her.

"So, you finally painted me? Finally … it only took you fifty years," it sneered.

"I … I couldn't do it before. I couldn't see you," she stuttered.

The painting smiled at her. "Are you pleased with yourself?"

"No … no … I just had to see you. I had to say sorry."

"But it's too late for that now, isn't it?"

She dropped to her knees. Her chest compressed in on itself, pain shooting through her shoulder, her arm, down her right side. She knew what this was.

"I need you to … forgive me." She panted, fighting to breathe. The puddles of paint on the floor soaked into her jeans, seeping slowly through the fibres to her bruised knees beneath.

"PLEASE!"

The painting watched as she slumped forward, struggling to keep conscious, fighting as she had done her whole existence. Fighting to try and hold onto something … love.

"Please …" Her voice was raspy, desperate, forcing itself through closing valves, through density of flesh, through spasms of life.

The painting stared down at her as the music floundered.

Thump, thump, thump …

"You don't deserve forgiveness," it whispered to her coolly. "You know what you deserve."

Thump, thump …

"Pleeease! Pleeease!"

"You let her die, didn't you? What did you do to save her?"

"I tried … I …"

The painting took pity on the thing before it, crumpled like an old newspaper, suddenly a child itself. Curling up like an infant – as her infant had been curled up when she found it, smashed by the roadside, barely recognisable. Her baby, her life, gone. Snuffed out in a moment of stupidity and violence.

It had been her fault – she was late. She should have been there as she had promised. Instead her daughter had taken a ride with a friend, a drunken friend. What was left behind didn't even resemble a car any more.

It had been her fault.

"Pleeease Pleeease …" she drooled, words slurred, barely audible.

The painting sighed. Better to quicken her misery than give her hope. "No."

Thump … thump …

Thump.

TROLL
BY K A SMITH

Winter was the hard time, the killing time. For the last two years he had been lucky, finding a place in a shelter over the hardest months, but this year the only places were miles away. The Olympics were coming, and it wasn't acceptable to be homeless anywhere near.

There were rumours, too, about 'disappearances'. Some said the Games organisers were prepared to go to any lengths to keep the street people out of sight. Perhaps some even believed it. That sort of thing might be policy in the Philippines, but even the Iron Lady of bitter memory wouldn't have done something like that … surely not. What was certain was that, for one reason or another, there were fewer and fewer of them on the streets. Some knew of Mad George getting hospitalised; some refused to believe, preferring to hew to their own skewed construction of the world in which he had been taken home by aliens, or sold on the organ black market, or whatever it might be. It would have to be a very black market indeed to find a place for any of George's organs.

Anyway, George was gone. His pitch was still there, though, and nobody had moved in on it, which was odd. A good bridge like that kept the worst of the weather off, and brought a trickle of coins from the passers-by. Why had nobody laid their hat there? Bod had decided to take it on, if nobody could give him a good reason not to. There weren't many pedestrian bridges as nice as that one; the ornate ironwork hadn't been allowed to rust into ruination, and although it

267

had spent a few decades as a bridge to nowhere, the last fifteen years had seen it come back into its own as part of a corridor of cycle-paths and footpaths linking Stratford and Bow, then on to the City one way and out towards Colchester the other. It was never going to be a place for easy pickings, but it was dry, sheltered from the worst of the wind, and there was always someone about.

He turned down behind the rank of pale brick Sixties-built shops to check the bins.

"Here, just don't tell. Okay?" The young girl from the bakery thrust a plastic bag into his hands, the vapour of her breath rising from raspberry-tinted lips to a sky that threatened snow. Her hands shook.

Bod smiled and nodded. She smiled back – as thin and fleeting as a smile could be while still being a smile, but it warmed him long after she had ducked through the back door amongst the ovens and the racks of cooling loaves. He looked in the bag when he reached the subway. There was treasure in there: half a dozen filled rolls and three square slabs of doughy pizza, substantial in a way that most pizza was not, and still warm. He hurried through the underpass, eating in furtive bites.

Why did she give me so much food? She never gave me anything before. Oh ... Christmas. Goodwill to all men, and all that. There they were, the fat men in red; the tableaux of the oddly extended family with one child, three parents and several 'uncles' who had left their sheep outside, not to mention the hangers-on with their perfume and their jewellery. Kings? Really?

It was so easy to forget the festive season, when it started so far ahead of time and had so little to do with you. The first decorations must have been up just after Halloween, so by the time Christmas came the glitter and the gauds were all but invisible. Now, for a few days, people would go around being nice to each other in an embarrassed sort of way, while others holed up, barricading against the false bonhomie.

That's what I used to do. I never had time for Christmas. I'm grateful for any sign or show of friendship now, however it may come.

The old corrugated sheet was flapping slightly in the wind. Pulling it back, he eased under the wooden rail and was gone from the barren street. The smell of wet iron and the tang of snow on the wind brought a skein of red memory to mind. It wasn't the scent of blood, not quite, though perhaps it was the scent of the promise of blood.

Don't be so damn fanciful.

The Portland stone of the Old Kowloon and Calcutta Mercantile Bank had taken more knocking down than most of the buildings on this block. The offices at the back of the bank were almost intact, the strongroom having brought the demolition crew up short, dismayed at the six inches of iron under the reinforced engineering-brick wall. Flurries of sleet dappled the stone pale, then dark, as the big plates of welded flakes thawed. Bod rested his hand on the comforting heft of cut stone. If only the new banks had proven as hard to topple, perhaps there would be fewer people on the streets.

"Hello, Bod."

He nodded at Magua, then at the others, and sidled to the brazier. "Here – girl at Bunce's …" He held up the bag.

"Cor, what?" Otis swiped the bag from Bod, who let him take a slice of pizza, then took the bag back.

"Told you she'd taken a shine to you." Mikey winked as he extracted a floured bap filled with bacon and egg. "What, no brown sauce?"

"What can I say? Can't get the staff these days." Bod gave the bag to Magua to pass around – he didn't want to stray from the warmth – watching as the bag made the rounds until it was empty. "I was wondering why nobody had taken over George's pitch …"

There was a long silence, in which a few significant looks were exchanged.

Bod shifted from foot to foot. *What did I say?*

Ade looked up, his tight curls of white peeking out from under his battered trilby, eyes wide and unblinking. "Well, George was a tough man, hard as nails. Not everybody would want to step into his shoes."

"But ..."

"That's an old bridge, and the one that was there before was ancient. Older than Queen Matilda's, you know what I mean?"

"Uh ... well ..."

"But maybe you will be okay." Ade tipped his head forward and vanished into the gloomy corner, his dark clothes and ebony skin seeming to sink back into the dark wooden panelling.

Bod wanted a second opinion, but nobody would meet his eyes apart from Magua. She shrugged. "What do I know?"

He shook his head. "It's just a bridge."

"That's what Varus said."

Bod found Magua hard to understand sometimes; her English was very good, but the things she said didn't always mean anything, at least to him. He nodded his head. "Well, I don't ..."

"Look at this, look at this!" American Pete, who was from Lincolnshire, was brandishing a bottle of schnapps in each hand. Magua made a beeline for the booze: it was the one thing that Bod didn't like about her, and for him it was a big thing. He leaned back into the comforting solidity of the wall and closed his eyes; he didn't want to recognise himself in these people, but couldn't tear himself away. He'd have to make a decision about the bridge on his own. He didn't expect to get much sense out of anyone else for a while.

Bod didn't find out that Ade had been set on fire until the morning of the funeral. He wanted to go, but didn't want to embarrass any family of Ade's that might be there. In the end he settled for turning up and waiting outside the little crematorium-cum-chapel, so that he was there, but not in anybody's way. He watched the doors as people turned up for the next service, milling outside, voices hushed, occasionally glancing his way, trying to place his angry, puzzled face. Bod evaded everyone's eyes, offended by the haste with which the dead are despatched from this world to the void.

Three people left the chapel. The little crowd outside milled around, unable to believe there were no more. Bod was not surprised to see Magua was one of them; he didn't understand her, but he knew enough to recognise her fierce loyalty and her commitment to anyone she respected. She glanced in his direction, then walked slowly on with the two older men. Bod ducked back as he realised they were police officers who had moved him on more than once – now on the receiving end of one of Magua's harangues, by the look of it.

He didn't know why he had expected some sort of burial, but it didn't happen. The fact that it was happening at a crematorium should have given him a clue. There was no graveside to stand by, no flock of mourners to avoid. Just some ashes, somewhere. *Is that it? No family? Two coppers, one crazy homeless foreigner who sounds like she's walked out of that Joseph Conrad book, and one young fool lurking on the threshold. Not much of a turnout to recognise a life, is it?* Bod felt a lone tear trickle down his cheek, the bitter wind chilling it to a standstill. He wasn't sure he would receive any better a send-off than Ade, and he wasn't at all sure he wanted one. He wondered how Ade would have felt. Would he have been bothered if he had known?

Close-clipped grass carpeted the maze between the monuments. Bod threaded his way through, avoiding the roads and paths. If I die – or when, I guess – I don't really care what they do with me. It's not as if it will make much difference. But then, we don't do these things for the dead, do we? We do them for ourselves. So why did I come? I guess because I liked Ade, but mostly because I thought Magua would give me a hard time if I didn't. So, because I'm a coward, then. Same reason as pretty much everybody else has when they come to these places, I guess. Except the living scare me and the dead don't. Curls of his breath danced on the air, needle-sharp with cold. He closed his chapped and cracking lips, begrudging every iota of warmth stolen by the pillaging wind.

''Hello, stranger, were you avoiding me?''

Bod jumped at the touch of Magua's hand. "No! I ..." He could feel his raw skin turning red, the flaying knives of winter as nothing beside the cuts of embarrassment. He had to do something about that – blushing like a girl. He had to be harder, tougher.

"I shouldn't tease. You are so serious."

Bod took a step back, jaw clacking shut on a mouthful of cold air. *Magua thinks I'm serious?* Magua seemed like a revolutionary throwback, a firebrand anarchist intellectual from the 1840s, and she was calling Bod serious? "Um ..."

"I was glad to see you here. Ade was a good man."

Bod nodded. Ade had been a father figure to all of them. He wondered how much things would change now he was dead. "What happened?"

"Three bastards set him on fire, after they had given him a kicking. The police are saying it was an accident."

"What? How ... I saw you talking to those two ..."

"Dupont and Dupond? Useless." A feral glint of teeth betrayed a silent snarl. Magua shook her head. "It's not their fault. They have been told that they are not interested. I don't think I have ever seen them so angry."

Bod looked at the grey stone monument ahead, the stone figure atop gazing dismissively through him. "I was surprised to see them." *I didn't realise she knew their names, or was that some kind of joke?* "I didn't think they liked Ade."

"Are you joking? A homeless black guy? Of course they didn't like him."

"So why ..."

"It was their case."

"Oh."

"And they aren't at all happy at the thought of three civilians getting away with murder."

I know I should say something, but whatever I do … I know it will be wrong. Bod tried to look understanding, until he realised he had no idea what that involved, so he closed his eyes, squeezing another tear out onto his cold cheek.

It was a fine bridge, there was no doubt about that. Stone piers, fancy ironwork, nothing cheap or shoddy about it. The doubts Bod had were all about whether it was the bridge for him. Ten weeks of hollow disappointment were hardly remarkable, following the last three years of disappointing hollowness, but this emptiness had a focus: the space under the bridge.

It was never as good as it ought to be. The wind would find just the right angle to send showers of water down the back of his neck, or the people crossing the bridge would be too drunk, or too uptight, or just too poor, to want to give. Bod had a stubborn streak to him, though, and was not going to give up the pitch – at least, not this side of the Olympics. Nobody was going to make him move. He was starting to get twitchy when people approached. It wasn't that he believed the rumours about people disappearing; he just didn't want to be shifted elsewhere so a bunch of politicians could pretend he didn't exist.

It was a long way from the bridge to the Old Bank, and the short cold days meant that he wasn't seeing much of the old crew. It just wasn't the same since Ade had been killed, anyway. Magua had come to see him a couple of times, but she had behaved really oddly, looking at him in a strange way, and always seeming as though she was about to say something but never quite getting around to it. He found it frustrating, not least because he liked her and wanted to get to know her better. Much better, if only he knew how. After her second visit had found him tongue-tied and left him resentful, he'd stopped going over to the Old Bank unless the weather was particularly foul, or he had enjoyed unusual generosity and had something to share. When he did go over there, he wondered if they were taking drugs of some kind; they were all jabbering away nineteen to the dozen, jerky as kittens on catnip. The weirdness made him edgy. He had never seen them take anything but booze, and he knew he didn't want to be around if anything else was going on. Booze was bad enough.

Pavement trembled under Bod's feet where tons of water crashed over the subterranean weir on their way to join the Lea at Bow Backs. People had travelled on that water before ever they had made roads. Light reflected from frozen puddles that mirrored the course of the covered river, long entombed in grey concrete. Bod blinked, then raised his hand to shade his eyes. *Morning? Where did the night go?* Thin sunlight struggled with the moist and grubby air, clawing at his eyes, driving him into the stone shadow of the bridge.

Ouch! What's wrong with me? I feel like I've got the mother of all hangovers, but I haven't had a drink in three years.

"Bloody hell, mate! You need help, what's the matter?"

Bod turned, stiff, clumsy with cold. "Who ..."

"Shit! Look at his face! Don't go near him, Henry."

"He might need help."

"Whatever he's got, I don't want you to catch it. You're not sharing my bed if you get any closer."

"But ..."

What is she talking about? There's nothing wrong with my face. Bod peered down at the black ice, the scuffed surface of the puddle giving back a countenance of grey blotches. He looked up again; the couple had gone, and the sun had managed to find its way to the other horizon. *I'm not well. The sun shouldn't do that. Maybe there is something wrong with my face. Or what's behind it.*

"Magua said you were here."

Bod nodded, ducking the brim of his tatty hat. "Pete." The clouds flared red; it wouldn't be long before the first stars were showing.

"She's worried about you. She says you're losing it." Pete held out a bottle, then grinned wryly as Bod ignored it.

"Uh." *Why is he so jittery?*

"You never drink, do you?"

Bod shook his head; his neck grated stiffly. "No."

"It might do you some good to loosen up."

"I don't … I can't, not any more." Bod hung his head. They all knew he didn't want to talk about it.

"Some dark secret, no doubt." Pete looked at the bottle. "It does no good to bury yourself out here, though. People need people."

Bod nodded.

"You're talking awful slow, you know? And your voice, it sounds like you hardly use it. There are plenty of better places than this, places with a bit of company. You need to keep yourself human. Magua would like to see more of you."

Really? She could tell me herself, then. Bod felt an uncommonly strong urge to wrest the bottle from Pete, but he didn't know if it was to smash it, smash Pete with it, or get smashed with it. He sat on his hands, keeping them from movement, feeling the slow pulse of the stone work up through his arms.

"I mean, what did you do today?"

"I was thinking."

"Really? What about?" Pete started to twitch as the silence grew.

"Goats. I don't know why."

"Goats? You know, half the time I can't tell if you are kidding me or not." Pete took a long pull on his bottle. "You're a bright kid yourself, not a burnt-out old drunkard like me or a bloody saint like Magua. Why are you even here? It wouldn't take too much to get you sorted. You know … job … flat … And don't try and tell me you like this life. When was the last time you laughed?"

Bod couldn't remember. "How is Magua?" *And why did he call her a saint?*

Pete shrugged, took a swig, played with the loose flap of sole on his left shoe. "Same as ever."

The stretch of old industrial land had lain unloved since the Iron Lady had decided she would have her revenge on the miners regardless of the collateral damage, until a spate of advanced skulduggery had brought the Olympics back to London. South London was, well, South of the River, so that was out. Everywhere west of Tower Hamlets was far too expensive. It didn't take a genius to work out what was left. Bod wondered if the twisty toe-rags who had brought the Olympics to London had done so with an eye to picking up some cheap real estate; after all, the cost of staging the Olympics in Athens had brought the Greek economy to its figurative knees. Who would benefit from London being sold off at Pound Shop prices? Not that it wasn't all for sale or sold already; Maggie had set the country on that course and no politician since had had the balls to say enough was enough.

Bod mourned the passing of visible history, cloaked now in anodyne surfaces, where before he had been able to see the fingerprints of time in the rubble of worked stone, aborted roads and broken lamp-posts. Visitors to the Olympics would not be allowed to see that London had a past. It was moot which was the greater palimpsest, the ever-rewritten thanato-erotic warrior-fest of the Games or the usurer's topos-mythos that was London – playthings of the rulers, both having recently been opened up to barrow-boys, who had been handily suborned.

The tower of the Bow Quarter twinkled in the distance, matches and phossy jaw now relegated to Yule-tide nostalgia by the wealth that fenced itself about with other people's poverty. The Bryant and May match girls had helped bring the Rights of Man to women, and now the people who lived in the old match factory were disenfranchising their neighbours, the gated community closing off an honourable history of social engagement with electric gates and night-sticks.

Was that why Bod had become homeless? To keep people at bay? To build his own wall, his own fence? A barrier composed of other people's ideas, perceptions, aversions. He could have a wall, and those around him did all the work to build it and maintain it, and all he needed was no property and no money. It was hard to open a gate in it, though, and even harder to close it.

Of course, there were plenty of countries where that sort of tactic earned you a pit, not a fence.

Gates and fences.

Fences and gates.

And goats. But mostly gates and fences. *Goats?*

Bod considered the ratios: how much was in, how much was out, and how long it would be until the proportions were reversed. Again. How brief a span of freedom there had been, when trespass was a myth and the Rights of Man upheld. What had happened? Had Hippy pushed it just a step too far? Had the fall of the Berlin Wall convinced the Rich that there was no credible opposition after all? Retrench and reclaim. With an ever more sophisticated array of instruments, power and land remained in the hands that clutched hardest, snatched fastest, clawed deepest. Why did so few have the wit to see or the memory to recall? Why were so many willing to sell their birthright for a mess of pottage? Divide and rule. Give enough economic power to the pushiest of the poor and they will be your watchdogs.

Judas goats.

And it wasn't envy, it was anger.

Many might look at the homeless and feel fear, or pity, or loathing. Bod had looked and seen a freedom. A freedom not from want, but from wanting. From all the chattels that trammel and control; all the small things that would only ever become less, no

277

matter how many you had. He still didn't know what he wanted, but knew all too well what he didn't want. He didn't want things. He was angry that people sold their time, their lives, for things: baubles, gewgaws, pretties. A world of Gollums, too focused on their precious to realise it was all illusion. It made him angry.

He knew illusion too. Knew it all too painfully and too well. One reason he could not drink, could not allow himself the separation from the real that it brought, was the veil of illusion alcohol imparted: he would think he understood. His righteous rage would tower, believing he knew what he wanted, and what he wanted was destruction. That was not him, it was the booze, and he was never going to let that happen. Not again.

He slapped the wall behind him, enjoying the solidity, the truth of the stone, cold in the late-February dusk. Why must we flee from what is? Why do we need to create so much fear and pain in order to lift ourselves above the herd?

"I don't know."

"Magua?" Bod felt something inside soften. He turned towards the voice, a smile slowly crystallising on his abraded lips.

"Talking to yourself now, are you?"

Bod dipped his head. "I always did."

His fingers ran over a slab of Purbeck marble. Traces of Roman workmanship could be seen in this oddity, in the rump of eighteenth-century wall now relegated to a landscape feature in a strip of green that had no purpose other than to be green. The hewn and polished intent overwritten by a larger hand that found no place for the personal.

"I would like it if you would talk to me."

Bod heaved a slow shoulder. "You know where to find me."

"And you me."

"True." And it doesn't have to be her that accedes. I should know my stubbornness by now. I'm not a rock that I can't move, and I should no more be trapped by myself than by anything else.

"What are you rebelling against?"

"What?" The conjunction between the question and the thought was enough to make Bod wonder if he had spoken out loud again.

Magua looked towards the City, the skyline punctuated by vast black shapes holding myriad small lights. "The young always rebel, and always believe it is the only true rebellion."

"I'm not sure I'm young."

Magua glanced towards him, then away. "You're as young as you'll ever be."

"Thanks."

"Are you hungry? Are you well? Your throat sounds as if you've been gargling with aggregate."

"I'm fine."

"Are you eating well? Pete was concerned. We ... I ... well, I asked him to see how you were."

I haven't felt hungry for weeks, but I can't think what I've been eating. As if there is sustenance in the air. "Thank you."

"There is a place for you at the Old Bank, if you want it. There always was. It has got to be better than here."

"But Otis ..."

"So Browning doesn't like you. He doesn't like anybody. He'll get used to you. In fact, he was talking about you last week – it sounded as if he missed you."

Bod cocked his head.

"He did, really. Here, let me look at you." Magua stepped in close and peered under the brim of Bod's hat. She gasped. "Come back to us, please. For me, if not for you."

"I don't know." Bod raised an expressive shoulder. "Buildings."

Magua looked into his eyes. She nodded. "Try."

She turned too quickly, and walked away too quickly.

Buildings. That was the nub of it. He felt enclosed now; even standing outside a house or a shop was enough to make him uneasy. And he was getting accustomed to his own company. People were so twitchy, so flighty, like sparrows. Magua had flitted into his presence and flitted out again. It wasn't surprising, really, given the twaddle that babbled through his mind. So many thoughts, and why? What good did they do? Mental eructations, as pregnant with meaning as a sunspot, as a wind on the moon; as solid as suspicion and as transient as joy. There – gone. Like the sun, these days.

He hardly seemed to see the sun at all. But he hadn't missed it. In fact, the thought of sunlight made him as uneasy as he felt in the presence of strangers. The darkness was a comfort, familiar as the back of his head, welcome. He relaxed into the darkness, into the city that pulsed slow as a hangover alongside the flash and the whiz, the money and the technology, the trains and the planes.

The thrum of footsteps spanned the iron chord, whispering through the stone. Bod eased himself deeper into the shadows under the bridge. It had been weeks since he'd sought contact with passers-by; his diffidence was now an aversion. His need for solitude, challenged by the visit from Magua, was on him like a monkey on his back. He stilled, nestling into the stone. *Pass me by.*

Sound splintered, brittle as the shattered bottle that ended its arc in a firmament of glass. Laughter followed, dull yet whiny, tarnished by the pall of alcohol, stark against the distant murmur of traffic and the hushed rumble of the hidden river, a staccato counterpoint to the stumbling steps.

Pass me by.

"That was crap."

"Sod you. You didn't do so much."

"Whose fault was that?"

"Yours, you prannet."

The footsteps were descending now, the voices getting louder. Bod hardly noticed them.

"Mine?"

"Yours. You were scared."

"I'm not scared of no-one."

"Double negative."

"Ah! Suck this."

"I know what I wanna suck."

"Here! Look, look!"

"What is it now?"

"You remember that old piss-head we torched? Here's another one."

"Are you crazy?"

"What? It's not like we got into trouble or anything."

"You two have got to be off your rocker. You wanna risk doing time for that?"

"Who's scared now?"

"I'm not scared, I'm just not as pissed as you two farts. Oh, shit! You'll only end up in chokey if I leave you to it."

"Jeez, has he got a wooden leg? I think I broke my toe."

"Shit! It's not one of those poxy sculptures, is it?"

"I don't know, but I just broke a brick on his head. Got a light?"

"Here, I reckon this hat would suit you."

"Are you acting the goat?"

Bod reached up to scratch where his hat had been, scalp gritty with brick rubble under his stubby fingers.

"What in Hell is *that*?"

"It ain't no sculpture."

"Lord love a duck …"

Bod uncurled from the shadows, his laughter falling like gravel on a coffin.

Illustration by Sophie E Tallis

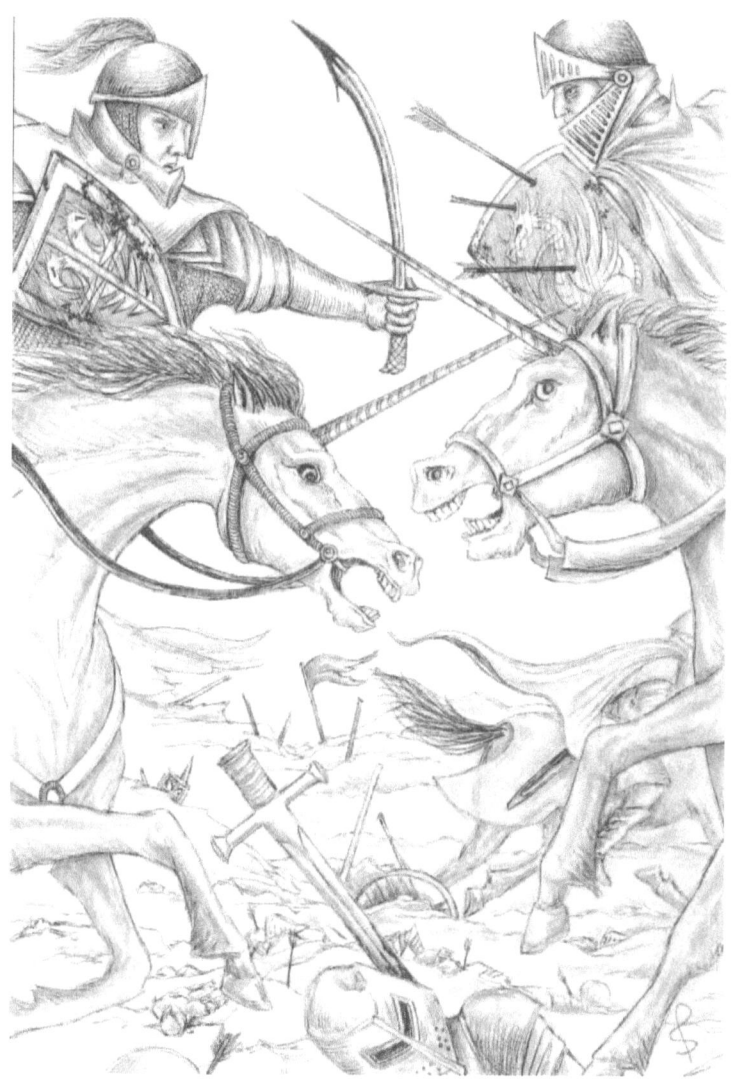

THE BAR
BY WILL MACMILLAN JONES

It started in a bar, as do so many things. A dim-lit cellar bar, where the smoky jazz played by the house band drifted like the haze rising from the myriad of cigarettes. He had been coming to the bar for a couple of weeks, but had not made acquaintances there, not yet. Twice, now, he had seen *her* across the room, her flowing blonde hair shimmering whilst the beguiling music played and the deep-voiced girl with the microphone sang slowly of love and loss, heartache and regret, and – yes – occasionally of passion and joy.

Suddenly, as the music swirled sensually around, she was beside him at the bar. Their eyes met and held in a long, long look before he turned away to order another drink. Disturbed, shaken by the casual intensity of her gaze, he trembled as she lightly placed her hand over his.

"You seem to be alone," she murmured in a velvet voice. He nodded. "So am I, tonight," she said softly, then kissed him and took his hand in hers. Looking into her eyes, he forgot the drink on the bar as she pulled, with such tempting pressure, on his arm. Responding, he moved closer to her, smelt the subtle perfumes, felt entranced. As they moved away from the bar, the bartender swept away the drink with a wry smile.

The music filled the room now, building in intensity, reflecting the emotions sweeping through his mind at the promise implicit in

285

her smile. With a gesture so elegant he caught his breath, she beckoned him to follow her from the bar through a door marked 'Strictly Private'. Her radiance filled his eyes, and he slipped through the door behind her, turning, focused on her face – so filled with love and desire – whilst the door swung slowly closed behind them.

But the near trance was broken as rough hands seized him and with quick movements gagged his mouth, bound his arms and legs. He felt himself swung upside down, and his tied ankles were lifted over a hook that dangled from a beam for that purpose. Wildly he looked around and froze: hanging from a second hook just a few feet away was another bound victim, with a tap thrust through the large vein in his neck. Smiling, the bartender was decanting a large glass for a ready customer.

His vision blurred, and footsteps rang on the cobbled floor of the cellar. He looked back to see *her* approaching him – with a look that blended love, desire, and infinite compassion; and a tap in her hand.

SNIFFERS
BY LINDSEY J PARSONS

It was freezing. Cara's legs would've been numb from the cold if they hadn't gone to sleep hours ago. She wriggled her frozen fingers before wrapping them back around her bow. There would be no hope of getting relieved before sunrise; there just weren't enough of them.

The sound of someone shuffling around in the tunnel to her left made Cara swear under her breath. Peter was making far too much noise – he was going to give them away. Rubbing her sleeve across her eyes, Cara forced them to stay open. She needed to keep watching the mouth of the cave.

Five days of walking were taking their toll and the group were all suffering – their numbers had dwindled from twelve down to eight. The sniffers were always close behind, but their eyes being too sensitive to see in daylight meant they only came at night. If Cara's group could just get far enough away from the city and out into the wilderness ... if they could just survive the nights ...

The invaders were only interested in the cities, in harvesting the buildings. Their enormous ships had descended from the skies, oblivious to man's futile attempts to stop them. They'd hovered over any major cities they came across, destroying every structure with laser blasts. Next came the bulldozer ships: massive, empty cargo ships, shovelling the rubble into their holds. Nothing was sacred. Nothing escaped.

No one had seen an invader, but there were plenty of rumours about what they looked like: little green men, four-eyed six-foot monsters or even the predator from the film of the same name. The sniffers were different, though. Every survivor had seen enough of them, and for most it was the last thing they did see. Named because of the noise they made, sniffers resembled ten-foot-high ants. They were almost impossible to kill due to their impenetrable exoskeletons; only armoured warheads seemed to have any effect, but as the armed forces had been almost completely decimated, there was very little to stop them. The invaders had released the sniffers to wipe out any life-form that got in the way of their harvesting of Earth's building materials.

It was believed that the sniffers stayed close to the bulldozer ships, so it made sense to head for the wilderness – to keep as far away from any man-made structures as you possibly could. To that end, Cara had joined a group of survivors who were heading north to the Green Wood National Park. Hundreds of thousands of acres of wilderness with very few buildings of any description, it was also home to Cara's parents – her dad being a park ranger.

Cara wriggled her fingers again; she needed to keep the circulation going. Her only hope if a sniffer found them would come at the last moment, as it opened its two pincers to grab her. Its most vulnerable spot was the roof of its mouth. If you could pierce straight up through the soft fleshy skin then you had direct access to its brain, causing instant death. A well-placed arrow or spear would do the trick. The downside was, you had to wait till it reared up in front of you with its mouth open.

A snuffling sound outside the cave successfully drove any tiredness from Cara's eyes. Her heart started racing, pumping adrenalin through her body, and clammy sweat ran down her back and across her palms. A sweet, sticky scent drifted back down the cave, making her want to gag, as a dark shadow passed across the entrance. Holding her breath, she tried to steady her trembling hands.

The shadow passed away to the left. *Peter*, Cara thought. *Peter, please don't make a sound.* Peter was guarding the cave entrance to her left, but he wasn't holding up well. Living as they were had shattered his nerves; training as a computer analyst hadn't prepared him for a life on the run.

Cara heard Peter gasp and shuffle backwards towards the cavern behind them. The snuffling noise grew louder as the sniffer entered his cave, and Cara turned to listen. She could hear Peter scrabbling frantically into the cavern with the sniffer following.

A torch and a box of matches lay at her side. Grabbing the matches, she wasted two before her trembling fingers managed to strike one. The torch flared to life, filling the cave with soft orange light. Peter's only hope would be if she managed to momentarily blind the sniffer with the light. Up ahead, she could see Peter backed up against the cavern wall.

"Peter! Over here, quick!" But it was too late – the sniffer was on him already. Cara looked away as Peter's scream cut through the damp cave air.

The return of the snuffling sound made Cara look back. The sniffer was turning around in the cramped space of the cavern, Peter's blood dripping from its pincers. Four large, shiny black discs on its head section fixed on Cara as it started heading towards her. Cara slowly lowered the torch to the ground and drew her bow, an arrow already fixed in place. She took a deep breath, releasing it slowly, forcing herself to stay calm. The sniffer filled the cave, its back pressing against the ceiling. It hesitated, shaking its head at the light from the torch, but already the light was dimming. As it continued forwards with its pincers wide open, Cara could just make out the red flesh of the inside of its mouth.

Not too soon, she thought, taking aim. The rank smell of its breath made her stomach heave. Just as its pincers passed either side of her body, she loosed her arrow. With a loud groan the sniffer plunged forward, knocking Cara skidding backwards across the damp stone floor towards the cave entrance. She lay still, listening for sounds that would tell her the sniffer was still alive, but the sounds never came.

Then, slowly, creeping in from the cave mouth, came long tendrils of sunlight. Dawn had arrived. She had survived another night.

DANTE'S
BY EMILY MCKEON

The polished bar distorted his reflection. He sat there looking at it while the brownish liquor swished around in his glass. There was little more than a sip left. Tilting his head back, he poured the rest of it down his throat. It burnt as it travelled to his stomach, and he let out a satisfied sigh when it hit its destination.

Placing the glass back on the counter, he glanced at the mirror behind the bar. His hair turned gray long ago, yet he still had it all. Laugh lines and wrinkles etched his face. He was clean shaven, with a strong jaw and bright blue eyes that even now twinkled mischievously. Age had been kind to him, and he could still make the ladies stop and stare when he entered a room.

"You still got it, Vic," he muttered to himself.

Dan, the fat, little old bartender, stepped between the mirror and Vic. He refilled Vic's glass and then went back to polishing the glasses behind the bar. Vic watched him for a while. The bartender took each glass off the shelf, rubbed it with an overused rag, put it back on the shelf, then moved on to the next one. He did this until every glass had received treatment before starting the whole process over again.

Vic let out a chuckle and shook his head as he watched Dan perform this ritual. He picked up his glass in time to see the woman walk in.

She was tall with long, untamed auburn hair. Her blue eyes scanned the empty room and landed on him. Without a moment's hesitation, she headed straight for him. Her midriff was bare and as she moved he caught a glint of something on her stomach. When she drew nearer, he saw her navel was pierced. The glint was a ring shaped like a coiled serpent. She brushed past him and sat at a booth in the corner, her back to him. Intrigued, he stood and approached the woman, taking his drink with him.

"Is this seat taken?" he asked, indicating the one across from her.

"No."

"Do you mind if I join you?"

"Not at all." Her voice was soft and low. He sat facing her, his drink between them. Her eyes drifted to his drink, then snapped up to his face.

"Ah, could I get you a drink?"

"That would be great." She gave him a small smile. She smelled like strawberries, and he thought of the summer days and the cool summer nights now occupying the town.

"What do you want?"

"Whatever you're having will be fine."

"Are you sure?" She nodded. "Dan, a drink for the lady. One Phone Call to God."

But Dan had already heard. He brought a second glass of the brown liquid and placed it in front of her. The woman flinched slightly, but quickly returned to her expressionless mask.

"Enjoy," Dan muttered before he turned back to his glasses. She picked it up and took a sip.

"Not bad."

"I'm surprised. Most women I know don't like strong drinks."

"I'm not most women," she purred over her glass rim.

"I can see that. My name's Vic, but most people around here call me Boss. Ain't that right, Dan?" he asked, turning to the bartender. Dan glanced up, gave him a weak smile and returned to his work. Vic turned his attention back at the girl. "What's your name?"

The girl leaned one elbow on the counter and studied him with hooded eyes. Dark pink shadow covered her lids and most of the surrounding area, getting lighter as it got further from her eyes.

"Why do they call you Boss?"

Vic shrugged his shoulders. "Because I run most of the businesses in town. Over half the people around here work for me. Jesus, about the only thing I don't own is the church."

"Pity," she mumbled into her drink. She looked back at Vic. "You're a good businessman, are you? Nice guy to work for?"

"You bet I am. Ask Dan here. I own this bar too, you know." Another weak smile was the only response from Dan.

"Like the feeling of power, huh?" She still hadn't taken her eyes off him.

"Hell, yeah. I mean, who doesn't? Sex, power and money. All the things a guy needs to be happy." Vic stared off, lost in his thoughts for a minute. He took a sip of his drink and refocused on the woman across from him.

"Hey, you still haven't told me your name," he accused her. He leaned on one elbow so he could look into her eyes when they talked. She laughed, her soft pink lips curling up like a fresh watermelon slice.

"I make it a habit not to tell people my name until I know them better."

"How well do you have to know them?" Vic asked, moving closer to her, his face inches from hers. She laughed and sat back.

"Not that well."

Vic smiled, never taking his eyes off the girl. "You don't have anything against getting to know someone that well, do you?"

"Believe me, you don't want to get to know me that well." The smile left her face, and her voice lost all its playfulness. She stared hard at Vic. "Tell me, have you ever been married?"

Now it was Vic's turn to sit back and become serious. "Yes, a long time ago."

"What happened?"

"The bitch divorced me and tried to take everything I owned. She would have, too, if I hadn't been so friendly with her lawyer – if you know what I mean." He gave the girl a wink.

"Why'd she divorce you?" The girl leaned forward, entranced by his story.

"Said I was cheating on her. That I had never been faithful to her."

"Were you?" The girl looked at him with a wide-eyed, innocent stare.

"Of course I was cheating on her. How the bitch ever found out, I don't know. I think it was the girl I was sleeping with's boyfriend. The bastard walked in on us one day. That son-of-a-bitch never liked me, and I think he wanted my wife, but couldn't have her because she wouldn't cheat on me to sleep with him. Now he can have her all he wants. She wasn't very good, anyways."

Vic drank more from his glass and banged the empty on the table.

"You're not from around here, are you? I don't remember seeing you before. I know most of the young ladies here in town, and I would have remembered seeing you." The girl shook her head. "Where're you from?"

"I don't really come from anywhere. I travel to different places all the time, without a place to really call home."

"Job?" Vic inquired.

"I guess you could say that."

"You know, I could get you a job here in town. Then you wouldn't have to travel so much."

She shook her head. "I could never get a job like the one I have now. Besides, I like to travel. The freedom, the adventure. The unknown." She whispered the last part and Vic felt a chill run up his spine. "I do a little bit of everything. But mainly, I undo everything that others have worked so hard to build."

Vic sat back as she finished speaking and looked her in the face. "What?" He squinted, trying to make sense of what she'd said. Was it possible she had been drinking before she entered the bar? Maybe she couldn't handle the liquor she was drinking now.

He watched as she stood and moved around the table to sit down next to him. She leaned toward him and whispered in his ear. "Have you ever been afraid of the unknown?"

Vic jumped back, nearly falling off the bench. She threw her head back and laughed a low, musical laugh.

"Look, miss, I think you've had a little too much to drink tonight. Why don't I call a cab for you, so you can sleep it off?" Vic pushed her out of the way and headed for the phone behind the bar. As his fingers brushed it, the phone rang. Trying not to drop it in surprise, he managed to get it to his ear.

"Dante's, how may I help you?" The other end was just static. "Hello?" A click was the only reply.

"What's the matter? Dead end?" the girl laughed as she approached the bar and sat on the stool next to Vic.

Things felt wrong. Vic couldn't put his finger on it, but this girl was wrong. The conversation had been wrong. The whole night had been wrong. He needed to get the girl out of there and fast. He hung up the phone and dialled the cab company. While he waited, he turned back to the girl.

"Where are you staying?"

"Nowhere." The girl's eyes had become a hard, icy blue. "I'm not staying at a hotel."

"If you don't have money for a hotel, I'll be more than happy to pay for it. I don't want you spending the night on the street."

"What, you don't want to bring me home with you tonight?"

"No, I don't want to take you home. Not now, anyways," he muttered.

"I'm not staying in a hotel," she repeated.

"With family, then?"

"I have no family."

"Well, you have to stay somewhere."

"Hello?" A gravelly voice came on the other end of the phone.

"Yes, this is Vic. I'm at the bar and need a cab."

"Vic? Vic who? What bar?"

"Dante's Bar. C'mon, Gary. I really need a cab."

"I'm sorry, but I don't know nothing 'bout no cabs."

"Gary, this isn't funny. I have a young woman here who's been drinking too much. Now, please, send a cab over."

"I think you're the one who's had one too many, buddy."

"Please, Gary ..." *Click.* The line went dead. A low laugh made Vic turn around. She was sitting, elbows on the bar, sun-browned face resting in her hand, watching him.

"It's hard being powerless, isn't it?" She grinned at him.

"You need to go." Vic was shaking slightly. Something about her was starting to unnerve him.

"Come on, Vic. I just want to talk." She gave him a fake pout that he would have laughed at under different conditions. Now it made him want to scream.

"It's time for you to go home now."

"I don't have a home to go to. Besides, I like it here."

"You can't stay here. Dan …" He turned for assistance from his bartender, only to realize that he hadn't seen or heard him in the last ten minutes.

"Oh, I'm sure he had better things to do. Tell me more about the women in your life. About how you gained power by stepping on all your friends."

Vic couldn't think straight. He had to get that girl out of there, fast. He rushed to her and grabbed her spaghetti strap-clad shoulders. The sickeningly sweet smell of strawberries overpowered him.

"Funny how your perspective on things can change so quick, isn't it?" she asked. Vic spun her around on the stool, pulling her off at the same time. As her feet hit the floor, she stumbled. Vic put his hands up to break her fall, accidentally brushing her bare stomach with his left hand.

"Ow!"

"What's the matter?" she laughed.

"Your ring cut my hand." Vic saw blood dripping to the floor, he quickly put his hand in his mouth and sucked at the wound. When he took it out, he could see two distinct stab marks on his hand. The girl laughed again. Vic looked up and her ring caught his eye, startling him. He thought it had been shaped as a coiled serpent, but now it was poised as if striking. Was his imagination playing tricks on him or was he losing his mind?

He looked at her face and could see the laughter in those hooded eyes.

"Out! Get out now!" Vic pushed her to the exit, terrified of what was happening.

"I was just leaving. No need to push. But don't worry, I'll come back." Her voice had returned to the soft purr she had used when their conversation had been normal. She walked towards the exit, long hair swaying to her rhythmic walk. A sudden urge overtook him.

"Wait! I still don't know your name."

A light, tinkling laugh answered him. He could picture her lips curled back in that soft smile.

"You'll learn my name soon enough." Without turning to look back, she walked out the door, the red exit sign flickering in time with the swinging of her hair.

When the door closed behind her, Vic felt the memories of childhood surge forth. Baseball games, walks in the park and idyllic summer afternoons flooded his mind and then vanished, shut away from him by the slamming of the door. He collapsed onto his stool. Movement behind the bar startled him. He turned to see Dan polishing the glasses as if nothing ever happened.

"Where were you?" Vic demanded. Dan gave him a puzzled look and indicated the swinging door leading into the back room.

"Lot of good you were. Didn't you hear me calling you? I said, didn't you hear me calling you? Dan?"

Dan didn't answer. He had stopped polishing the current glass mid-wipe and was staring intently at something on the floor. Vic turned to look. It glittered from the neon lights that abounded in the windows. Vic went over and picked it up. A tiny golden snake coiled around a ruby apple sat in the palm of his hand. The snake's fangs were sunk into the apple, as if trying to drain it.

Vic shuddered and tossed the trinket onto the bar. Dan glanced at it and recoiled in fear.

"Are you all right, Dan?"

Dan closed his eyes, crossing himself and mouthing silent prayers. Laughter filled the room, low and musical and without a source.

"You're mine," it purred in Vic's head. Suddenly, he knew her name.

INFECTION
BY LUCAS HARGIS

Leto shuffled down the busy sidewalk, hunching over her cane. Periodically, she stopped to adjust the scarf securing her gray wig, secretly eyeing the surveillance cameras. Though her disguise faked her appearance, her Infection was real.

Every face that passed wore a prevention mask. Since the virus arrived, no one was safe from Infection. The elderly. Children. Women. Even the men. None were immune. Leto's worthless mask served one purpose: camouflage.

She avoided the eyes of heavily armed Doctors as she left the sidewalk and mounted the steps to the ten-story before her. Like all the others, the corporate building had been converted into housing for the soaring population that resulted from the Infection.

The woman in Suite 940 was her last hope. While most slurred her as a *Witch*, she called herself Ilithyia. Leto's friend—one she almost trusted—had passed on the information: Ilithyia possessed the ability to help the Infected through the final stages. It was risky. It could be a trap. But Leto's Infection was full-blown. Her pain was increasing. Her breaths came and went too quickly.

Fear swirled in her gut as she approached the GeneTag Scanner. ID cards, fingerprints and retina scans were obsolete. This new technology, constantly upgraded, now guarded entry to any building. Leto found it odd, suspicious. With the airborne virus so contagious, why had the idiots in the skyscrapers designed an ID system that required removal of the masks?

She slid hers off and stuck out her tongue. A couple exited the building, swinging wide around her. The needle emerged from the wall—shiny and sharp, and Leto closed her eyes to brace against the coming pain. With a *pop* she couldn't get used to, the needle plunged into her tongue. Hot fluid injected, then the syringe sucked it back out.

Sirens blared. Strobes flashed. Upgrades.

Infection detection. Infection detection. Infection detection.

Leto, panicking, whirled around. The sidewalk cleared as screaming pedestrians scattered from the threat. Only two figures remained: a pair of Doctors cocking their weapons. Out of nowhere, a guy in a trench coat ran up behind them, shooting both the Doctors in the backs of their heads. He leapt over their bodies and bolted to Leto.

He ripped off his prevention mask, and the pair stood there, breathing one another's breath.

"Come on, granny!" he yelled above the sirens. "You've got to move as quick as you can. More Doctors will be here soon."

"I'm not old," Leto yelled back.

She tossed down her cane and stood upright, exposing the round swell of her Infected belly.

"Follow me. Quick!" He handed her a gun. "There's a safehouse on Delos Street."

Leto's face contorted into a grimace. Pressure wrenched at her gut. She doubled over, panting, and fell into the guy, who braced her until the pain subsided. When she looked up, he saw it in her eyes. She didn't trust him.

With a flourish, he whipped open his coat, revealing the round belly of his own so-called infection of spontaneous pregnancy. "I'm Infected, too."

WORLDBUILDERS, INC.
BY A. F. E. SMITH

When the phone rang, I didn't race to pick it up. I was in the middle of gluing an impassable mountain range across the middle of the Type One world I was working on (quasi-medieval, prophecy-driven, resident Dark Lord), and those damn cloud-wreathed peaks are always fiddly to get right.

"Can someone take that?" I called over my shoulder, then swore. One little jolt of the wrist, and my carefully regular mountains had crumbled into the kind of jumbled rocky wilderness you only get after serious tectonic action.

Oh well. It would just have to double up as the monument to a long-ago magical battle that had wreaked havoc across the continent. Yeah, blame the Dark Lord – that's always a good fallback in a Type One. In fact, a bit more devastation wouldn't go amiss …

"Len? Sandra?" The phone was still ringing. "Can one of you please … oh, never mind."

Abandoning my now severely ominous mountains, I lunged for the handset, in the process ruining the middle of the plains with an elbow-shaped dent. Or perhaps a sinister mist-wreathed swamp.

"Worldbuilders, Inc.," I said into the phone, rather crossly. "How can I help you?"

"Er, hi." The voice on the other end was cautious, as if not quite sure what it was doing there. "I'm ringing to enquire about a commission."

I took a quick glance at the caller display, but it simply read EARTH. That made sense. It's where many of our clients come from: authors of what they call fantasy, taking our work and turning it into little hand-drawn maps and pretending they invented it. I don't have a problem with that. They buy it, and it's up to them what they do with it. We're only the architects.

"That's fine," I said. "Have you used our service before?"

"No. I heard about it from a – a friend."

I appreciated the discretion. The Earth people who know about us tend to keep it very quiet, to avoid giving away their advantage; if someone had told my mystery caller about us then it stood to reason they wouldn't want their name to be revealed.

"Right. I'll just create you a file." I stepped across to the tall grey cabinet by the wall and began flicking through the existing files, each marked with the client's initials: TP, JRRT, JKR, GRRM. "What is your name, please?"

I could almost hear the sound of shuffling feet coming down the phone line. "You can, er … you can call me Smith."

I'll file you with the other hundred-plus Smiths, shall I? I restrained the sarcasm, making my tone as colourless as possible. "We do need unique initials for our files –" Sir? Madam? I realised I couldn't actually tell, and so finished swiftly, "if you don't mind."

"A.F.E," the anonymous voice said. "A.F.E Smith."

"Great." Phone wedged between shoulder and ear, I grabbed a blank file and labelled it AFES. I like it when they have four initials – it makes duplicates less likely. I'm told that's how JRRT and GRRM got their extra Rs. "So what sort of world were you looking to commission from us?"

"It's not actually a new commission I'm interested in," the voice said. "You see, I'm stuck on this short story, and … anyway, I want to use an existing world. One you made for someone else."

"Fine." Again, in itself that wasn't unusual: it's a lot cheaper to reuse a world than to create one from scratch, so some clients take an old one and change the names and leave it at that. I crossed to the second filing cabinet, where we keep the details of all the worlds we've ever built. "Do you have the catalogue number?"

"Yes, I do." A moment's hesitation. "It's 0-0-0-0-0-0-1."

Our new worlds are up in the seven digits by now; even when it comes to reuses, we don't get people asking for much lower than ten thousand or so.

"Are you sure?" I asked. "You want to use the first world we ever made? You wouldn't prefer something a bit more … modern?"

"No, I don't think so."

Wow. This guy – girl – whatever – must really want to cut costs. "Hold on one moment, please."

I put the phone down, then pulled the lower drawer of the cabinet right out and rummaged around at the back of it until I found a dusty file labelled '1'. Presumably we hadn't foreseen the need for a seven-digit system in those days. I flipped it open, stifled a sneeze, and scanned the contents.

World #1: Worldbuilders, Inc. Type Zero world (only one of its kind). Specialist source world or meta-world. Exists solely for the purpose of creating other worlds …

File hanging loosely from the fingers of one hand, I picked up the phone once more.

"This world you want," I said into it. My voice sounded unnatural in my own ears. "This 0-0-0-0-0-0-1 … it's ours. It's this one."

"Yes. Yours is the one I want to use in my story." The unknown author was vaguely apologetic. "Is that OK?"

"But – but it's in our files. Surely we didn't create our own world?"

An audible shrug. "Why not? Someone must have."

"But you don't understand!" I wailed. "All the worlds we build are fictional! They don't really exist! So where does that leave me?"

"Well, I suppose there are two possibilities," A.F.E Smith said diffidently. "One is that every world that ever gets invented becomes real, somewhere, somehow. And the other ... well, the other is that you're just a character in a work of fiction." Long pause. "If I were you, I'd pick whichever you feel most comfortable with. Anyway, thanks very much for your help."

"You're going?" I tried to make sense of everything that had happened. "But what about your story?"

"Oh, it's fine," the voice at the other end of the line said. "I've just finished it."

Author Bios

Illustration by Hazel Butler

ANDREA BAKER

Andrea Baker was born and raised in the beautiful English county of Warwickshire, where she lived with her parents and older sister. She left home to study at the University of Wales, Aberystwyth, from where she graduated with a Bachelor of Science, with honours, in 1992. She now works as an independent management consultant, and lives less than five miles from the town and castle of Kenilworth, in Warwickshire, with her husband and their daughter.

Website	www.AndreaBakerAuthor.com
Blog	www.rosewallauthor.wordpress.com
Twitter	@rosewall15
Goodreads	www.goodreads.com/author/show/6557194
Facebook	https://en-gb.facebook.com/rose.wall.15
Email	rosewall15@sky.com

SAM DOGRA

Sam Dogra is a junior doctor working in the NHS in the UK, and is currently training to become a General Practitioner. Between reviewing drug charts and X-rays, taking blood, saving lives and getting grilled by consultants, she also writes fantasy fiction and is a fantasy artist. She has published her two novels, The Binding and The Parting, with a third sequel in progress, and has co-written 'Fated: A Timeless Series Companion Novel' with author Lisa Wiedmeier.

She's widely traveled, and has enjoyed her visits to France, Germany, Norway, Greece, Egypt, Israel, Rhodes, Turkey, Cyprus, Lesvos, India, Dubai, Australia, South Africa, Canada, Sri Lanka, and Idaho, Seattle, Las Vegas, New York, and Alaska.

Her other main interest is fantasy art and photomanipulation.

In what little spare time she has, Sam also enjoys reading, baking, shopping, watching movies and anime, astrology, video games, collecting cuddly toy animals, and photography.

Website   http://maddoctorartist.blogspot.co.uk/

Facebook   www.facebook.com/pages/The-Chronicles-of-
Azaria-Series/229718793739428

Goodreads
       www.goodreads.com/author/show/6623621.Sam_Dogra

Twitter   @MadDoctorArtist

Pinterest   https://www.pinterest.com/Sam241/

Fanfiction   https://www.fanfiction.net/~maddoctorartist

E. R. ENOKSEN

E.R. Enoksen lives in Norway with her husband and children. She's a Norwegian but she has also got roots in New Zealand, and comes from a long line of writers and artists. She has a great love of fantasy and science fiction and grew up watching Star Trek and reading Asimov, and it is clear to see how her past has influenced her present and will continue to do in the future. Enoksen says there are few things more fun in life than being able to create.

Facebook   https://www.facebook.com/enoksen.art

LUCAS HARGIS

Lucas Hargis writes everything from short form stories to novels, usually with a touch of weirdness. His novel-y bits are represented by literary agent Louise Fury. His ideas often materialize while pimping his other roles as artist, spreadsheet guru, tarot reader, antiques dealer, and tattoo collector.

Website	http://lucashargis.com/
Twitter	@LucasMight

WILL MACMILLAN JONES

Will Macmillan Jones lives in Wales, a lovely green, verdant land with a rich cultural heritage. He does his best to support this heritage by drinking the local beer and shouting loud encouragement whenever International Rugby is on the TV. A fifty something lover of blues, rock and jazz he has just fulfilled a lifetime ambition by filling an entire wall of his home office with (full) bookcases. When not writing, he is usually lost with the help of a satnav on top of a large hill in the middle of nowhere.

His major comic fantasy series, released by Red Kite Publishing, can be found at: www.thebannedunderground.com

And information on his other work and stuff in general at:

www.willmacmillanjones.com

There's a blog. There's always a blog, isn't there?

www.willmacmillanjones.wordpress.com

KAY KAUFFMAN

As a girl, Kay dreamed of being swept off her feet by her one true love. At the age of 24, it finally happened...and he's never let her forget it. A mild-mannered secretary by day and a determined word-wrangler by night, she battles the twin evils of distraction and procrastination in order to write fantastical tales of wuv...twue wuv...with a few bad haiku thrown in for good measure.

She is currently hard at work on the first book in a fantasy trilogy. Kay resides in the midst of an Iowa corn field with her devoted husband and his mighty red pen; four crazy, cute kids; and an assortment of adorably small, furry animals.

Care to save her from the chaos? You can find Kay in the all the usual places:

At her blog, where she shares random pictures and silly poems; on Facebook, where she shares things about cats and books; on Twitter, where she shares whatever pops into her head; on Pinterest, where she shares delicious recipes and images from her fantasy world; on Instagram, where she shares pictures of pretty sunsets; and on Tumblr, where she shares all of the above.

You can also find her poetry collections on Amazon, Goodreads, and Smashwords.

Blog	http://suddenlytheyalldied.com/
Twitter	@kaysiewrites
Facebook	https://www.facebook.com/authorkaykauffman
Amazon	http://www.amazon.com/Kay-Kauffman/e/B007M4DZKE
Pinterest	https://www.pinterest.com/kaylkauffman/
Instagram	https://instagram.com/kaysiewrites/
Tumblr	http://kaysiewrites.tumblr.com/
Smashwords	http://www.smashwords.com/profile/view/kaysielynn

EMILY MCKEON

C.W. Farley is the pen name of Emily McKeon. She resides in the tiny state of Rhode Island with her husband and two children. When not writing, she enjoys playing clarinet. A graduate of Rhode Island College with a B.A. in theater and writing, she spun around and landed on the random career of bookkeeper before returning to her love of writing. She has a children's book out, WHO WILL DANCE WITH ME? and is featured in Pen & Muse's THE DARK CARNIVAL Anthology, both under Emily McKeon.

Blog	http://theabsenteeblogger.blogspot.com/
Twitter	@ERMcKeon

DAVID JM MUIR

Born in Early1983, David JM Muir, that oh so crazy Scotsman, lives in the quiet (and can never write that without sniggering) town of Cumbernauld in the hallowed land of the Gaels and the Picts. His life has been filled with many adventures (meaning his job record is like a book itself) and is currently in his 3rd year of a Bsc in Computer Networking, and writing and perfecting a Military Science Fiction Novel called Warrior Rising, the tales of Captain Caleb O'Hearn, a character who has morphed in so many ways over the years, it's time he finally graced the printed page, which his creator hopes to have happen in the early half of 2016.

An avid reader from an early age, his eclectic taste ranges from Biographies (That means people like Harry Patch and Winston Churchill, not Katie Price and David Beckham), the works of philosophers like Joseph Campbell, computing technical books (sado) historical fiction, Fantasy and Science fiction and everything in-between. He also possesses an eclectic taste in music ranging from Classical to Death Metal (No J-Lo, Britney or their ilk though, each to their own but he thinks they suck).

In addition to Military Science Fiction, he writes in a number of other Genres and sub-genres of fiction, and bashes his head against the wall repeatedly when his brain doesn't connect with the keyboard or the pen and paper, but it eventually gets there.

You can see some of his work or even some of his drunken ramblings, his obsession with Wargaming and his sometimes coherent thoughts on life and MMA on occassion at gabrielofalbaandhismerryfriends.blogspot.co.uk.

Blog   http://gabrielofalbaandhismerryfriends.blogspot.co.uk/

TRM

TRM is a very serious person doing very serious work for very serious people. He started being serious far too young, accumulating law degrees in England and France, and taking part in mock arbitrations between fictional countries presided over by sitting judges of the US Supreme Court. As that was not serious enough, he took a Phd in the laws governing genetically modified food. Still craving more seriousness, he is now a specialist in pensions law based in Newcastle upon Tyne. He is (nominally) the owner of Midnight the Bunny of Doom, but disclaims all liability in relation to her production of cake. In order to remain sane, he is engaged in writing one of the greatest libraries of unfinished fantasy works the world has ever known, when not polishing his collection of grindstones with his nose. His loving family is entirely normal, if slightly exasperated.

Amazon   http://www.amazon.co.uk/TRM/e/B007FHC4FK/

LINDSEY J PARSONS

Lindsey J Parsons was born in Stratford upon Avon, UK, and grew up in nearby Solihull. She lived in a crumbly old farm house in a small village in Warwickshire with her three children and an assortment of animal friends. She enjoyed reading, writing, horseback riding and looking after the numerous animals that lived with her.

Lindsey was also a very talented long-bow archer, competing and winning medals in many professional archery competitions.

Lindsey started her writing career in 2009, and published her first novel, a wonderful paranormal fantasy, Vortex and the first book in her Return of The Effra trilogy in June 2012. Her sequel, Wicked Game, was published in August 2013, by the successful publishing business she set up, AFS Publishing.

Lindsey joined The Alliance of Worldbuilders (AWB) on the HarperCollins writing site, Authonomy, in 2010 where she made fast and firm friends with all of her fellow fantasy writers and soon became the heart of The Alliance. Known for her love of dragons, cowboy boots and for her kindness, Lindsey was also a very talented author.

In her own words:

"My head has always been crammed full of horses, dragons, magic, and adventure, sword fights, castles, and impossible quests. Stories materialise when I least expect them to and take over my mind, desperate to get out. Finally a few years ago I decided to immortalize them in ink and so I write fantasy, because for me, fantasy is the ultimate escape."

Lindsey died suddenly of a brain aneurism on 5th January 2014. She was a wonderful writer and a wonderful friend and will be missed forever.

Amazon   http://www.amazon.com/Lindsey-J-Parsons/e/B008D7RXQ6

JEREMY RODDEN

Jeremy Rodden considers himself a dad first and an author second. He is the author of the middle grade/young adult Toonopolis series of books that takes place in his cartoon universe. He also edited, contributed to, and published The Myth of Mr. Mom, a non-fiction series of essays by stay-at-home dads. He can be found at his author/cartoon review blog (www.toonopolis.com) or on Twitter @toonopolis.

Blog   http://www.toonopolis.com/

Twitter   @toonopolis

List of works:

Toonopolis: Gemini (Toonopolis Files, #1)

Anchihiiroo - Origin of an Antihero (Toonopolis Shorts, #1)

The Myth of Mr. Mom - Real Stories by Real Stay-At-Home Dads

J. C. RUTLEDGE

Jonathan Rutledge lives somewhere in Ontario, Canada, where he was born and raised on books. He soon took a liking to the fantasy genre, which he began reading almost exclusively. It was only a matter of time before he had to start writing his own tales. He now spends his days writing, with his wife Colleen lending her imagination to him whenever his runs dry, and making chainmaille jewelry and armor for their business (www.ringcrafts.com). If you're interested in some of his inane ramblings, they can be found at jcrutledge.blogspot.ca .

Website   http://www.ringcrafts.com/

Blog   http://jcrutledge.blogspot.ca/

Twitter   @JC_Rutledge

A. F. E. SMITH

A.F.E. Smith has been building worlds since she was six, though some of the early ones were a bit wonky. In the world we call real she is an editor, a mother of two young children and an insatiable eater of snacks. Her debut novel, Darkhaven, will be released by HarperVoyager in the summer of 2015.

Website   http://www.afesmith.com/

K A SMITH

Keith Smith is a witty, urbane character of many parts, many of which are in perfect working order. He describes his writing as 'Unpublished, marginally readable and incongruously unrepentant.' There's always one, isn't there?

In the past, he has been a Membership Advisor for the Sunday Times Enterprise network, a commercial brewer, and a landscape painter, presumably painting pictures of the fields rather than spraying the grass itself...

SOPHIE E TALLIS

Sophie E Tallis was born in Bristol, UK, but grew up in a sleepy village just north of it, dreaming of dragons and wild adventures. She lives in the Cotswolds with her family, two enormous white wolves and two even bigger Alaskan Malamutes. Sophie primarily writes epic fantasy and is a full member of The Society of Authors. She has been a full-time teacher for the past 16 years, is a talented writer, poet, painter, artist and illustrator, with a BA (Hons) Degree in Fine Art and a Post-Grad in Education, and now works as a librarian, a dream job being surrounded by books all day!

Website Books	http://thedarklingchronicles.weebly.com/
Website Art	http://sophieetallisillustrations.weebly.com/
Blog	https://sophieetallis.wordpress.com/
Twitter	@SophieETallis
GoodReads	www.goodreads.com/author/show/6442208.Sophie_E_Tallis
Facebook	https://www.facebook.com/sophie.e.tallis
Facebook Book	https://www.facebook.com/FantasyEpic
Amazon	www.amazon.co.uk/Sophie-E.-Tallis/e/B008IVBYEO/
ReadWave	http://www.readwave.com/sophie.e.tallis
LinkedIn	www.linkedin.com/pub/sophie-e-tallis/3a/413/870
Hive	www.hive.co.uk/book/white-mountain/19699148/
UK Arts	http://ukartsdirectory.com/sophie-e-tallis/

Society of Authors: www.societyofauthors.org/node/56641

DeviantArt	http://tollam.deviantart.com/

VALERIE WILLIS

Valerie Willis is a 30-year-old creative mind that pours her imagination into several platforms, whether in the form of sketches, writing, or even developing video games. As far back as Fifth Grade, she would fill composition books full of adventures. As time passed, she found both her poetry and short stories winning awards at her schools as well as being added to Anthologies. When she isn't studying for her courses you can usually find her digging through her books regarding mythology and the medieval times as well as scouring the internet for more resources. Occasionally the boys call her out for a round or two of video games whether it's Halo on the XBOX 360 or supporting her team on League of Legends online.

Website	http://willisartist.wix.com/author
Blog	http://valeriewillis.blogspot.com/
Twitter	@Valerie_Willis
Facebook	https://www.facebook.com/ValerieWillisAuthor
Amazon	www.amazon.com/Valerie-Willis/e/B00FQMV8SU
ReadWave	http://www.readwave.com/valerie_willis/
DeviantArt	http://nitatsu7.deviantart.com/